"Move over Stephanie Plum, there is a sassy, sexy sleuth in town! If you enjoy your cozy mysteries with a good shot of romance, and a love triangle with a sexy bad boy and a Southern gentleman in the mix, then you will love this. Very reminiscent of the Stephanie Plum books, but the laughs are louder, the romance is sexier and there is a great murder mystery to top it off."

—Bella McGuire, **Cozy Mystery Book Reviews**

"...a frothy girl drink of houses, hunks and whodunit narrated in a breezy first person."

—Lyda Phillips, **The Nashville Scene**

"VERDICT: The hilarious dialog and the tension between Savannah and Rafe will delight fans of chick-lit mysteries and romantic suspense."

—Jo Ann Vicarel, **Library Journal**

"... equal parts charming and sexy, with a side of suspense. Hero and heroine, Savannah Martin and Rafe Collier, are a pairing of perfection."

—Paige Crutcher, **examiner.com**

"...hooks you in the first page and doesn't let go until the last!"

—Lynda Coker, **Between the Pages**

"With a dose of southern charm and a bad boy you won't want to forget, **A Cutthroat Business** has enough wit and sexual chemistry to rival Janet Evanovich."

—Tasha Alexander, New York Times bestselling author
of **Murder in the Floating City**

"A delicious and dazzling romantic thriller ... equal parts wit and suspense, distilled with a Southern flavor as authentic as a mint julep."

—Kelli Stanley, bestselling author and Bruce Alexander award winner,
Nox Dormienda

Also in this series:

Savannah Martin has always been a good girl, doing what was expected and fully expecting life to fall into place in its turn. But when her perfect husband turns out to be a lying, cheating slimeball—and bad in bed to boot—Savannah kicks the jerk to the curb and embarks on life on her own terms. With a new apartment, a new career, and a brand new outlook on life, she's all set to take the world by storm. If only the world would stop throwing her curveballs...

Silver bells, silver bells...

It's Christmas time in Nashville, and all Savannah wants to unwrap on Christmas morning is Rafe Collier. Unfortunately, things don't look so good. He's back in town, but not alone: on his arm is a stunning brunette, just the kind of woman Savannah always suspected was his type.

When sixteen-year-old Alexandra Puckett—the daughter of Savannah's late colleague Brenda Puckett—asks her help in figuring out a way to stop Maybelle Driscoll from marrying Alex's father Steven, Savannah jumps on the chance. It'll give her something to think about other than Rafe and the mysterious Carmen, and anyway, she doesn't like Maybelle much herself.

Between investigating Maybelle's past, helping her clients Aislynn and Kylie buy a house, and stalking Carmen and Rafe, she soon has her hands full. And that's before someone starts gunning for her. Suddenly it's not a question of unwrapping anything on Christmas morning anymore; it's a question of whether she'll even survive to see another Christmas.

A DONE DEAL

Jenna Bennett

A DONE DEAL
SAVANNAH MARTIN MYSTERY #5

Interior design: April Martinez, GraphicFantastic.com

ISBN: 978-0-9899434-2-0

MAGPIE INK

One

"It's nice to see you looking more like yourself again, Savannah," Todd said and smiled at me across his Veal Parmesan and my Chicken Marsala.

We were sitting at a table in Todd's favorite restaurant, Fidelio's in Nashville. It was a week or so before Christmas, and Todd had driven up from Sweetwater, Tennessee, a small town some forty five minutes south, to take me to dinner.

He's my brother Dix's best friend. We dated his last year of high school, while Dix went out with my best friend Charlotte. It seemed ordained, somehow. Mother and dad adored Todd, Pauline and Bob Satterfield liked me, and Todd and I got along reasonably well. I never imagined myself in love with him, but I liked him well enough. I thought he felt the same, and it came as quite a shock to realize, just a few months ago, that he liked me a lot more than I liked him.

Mother wanted me to marry him. He's everything I've been brought up to look for in a mate: healthy, wealthy, and white, with a good job, antecedents that go back to the War Between the States—the

Civil War to you Yankees—and enough money to provide for me in the manner to which I have been accustomed. I just didn't feel for him those special feelings a woman should feel for the man she plans to spend the rest of her life with. He was too much like my ex-husband for comfort. And besides, as the romance novels say, my heart belonged to someone else.

That someone was Rafael Collier, and he was pretty much my mother's worst nightmare. If she could pick the last man on earth she'd want me to get involved with, I'm pretty sure Rafe would top the list. Todd, of course, agreed.

Rafe also hailed from Sweetwater. But while Dix and I and our sister Catherine grew up on what's left of the Martin Plantation, in an 1839 antebellum brick home on the north side of town, and the Satterfields owned a big turn-of-the-last-century house near the town square, Rafe spent his formative years in the Bog, the trailer park on the south side. In the parlance of the Old South, the Colliers were white trash, and then LaDonna compounded the offense by getting herself in the family way at fourteen. By a colored boy. The result is that Rafe has more strikes against him than Derek Jeter, and that was before the couple of years he spent in prison and the fact that he knocked me up.

Yes, I'd fallen into temptation and slept with him. And I'd gotten pregnant. And then I'd lost the baby. And because I hadn't told him what was going on, and because of a long line of other misunderstandings, I'd lost Rafe too. He'd left Nashville a few weeks ago, and I hadn't heard from him since. And on top of that I'd gotten shot. And that's what Todd was referring to when he told me he was glad I looked better.

"Thank you, Todd." I smiled back, although a big part of me wanted to bristle at the patronizing tone of his voice.

I didn't let it show. Todd means well. He's been brought up to be a proper Southern gentleman, and it isn't his fault that I've outgrown being a proper Southern Belle.

"Are you back to work yet?"

After divorcing Bradley Ferguson two years ago, I stayed in Nashville and did my best to get my feet under me. Eventually I got my real estate license. It's not like I'm setting the world on fire or anything, but I've managed to nail down a couple of closings in the five or six months since I started. I'm not getting rich, and the bottom of the savings account is still visible, but I'm staying afloat. And in all fairness, the fact that I keep getting dragged into police investigations hasn't helped. It's hard to concentrate on showing houses and negotiating deals while people drop dead all around you.

But with Rafe out of my life, things had settled down considerably. I nodded. "I'm helping two girlfriends look for a house. Aislynn and Kylie."

"Your girlfriends?"

"Each other's girlfriends," I said. I like them well enough, but ours is a business relationship.

"And they want to buy a house together?" Todd frowned, no doubt pondering the legal ramifications. "What if they have a falling-out? Both wanting the same man, or something?"

In Todd's world, every girl wants a man. A man like him.

"I don't think you have to worry about that," I said. "When I said they were each other's girlfriends, I meant they were a couple."

"A couple of girls?"

"Lesbians," I said, eschewing subtlety. "They're together. Romantically. A couple."

Todd looked shocked. I don't know why, because although Sweetwater is small and backwards and planted firmly in the middle of the Bible belt, there are gay people in town. I'd never met any, true, but there had to be some. There are gay people everywhere. And Todd had spent years and years in Atlanta. Atlanta is full of alternative lifestyles. So is Nashville. He shouldn't be shocked at the news.

"Are you sure you should be helping them, Savannah?"

I wanted to ask him why not. Their money is just as good as anyone else's, and I have to pay my bills. How anyone else chooses to live their lives is none of my business. And besides, I like them.

But it wouldn't do any good to get into a theological discussion with Todd—never argue with a trial lawyer, it's a waste of breath—so I said simply, "Someone has to. And they're nice girls."

"If you say so," Todd said. He looked worried. Maybe he was afraid I'd come out of the deal wearing fatigues and a crew cut, and he'd lose all chance of convincing me to marry him.

He didn't have to worry about that. I'm one hundred percent heterosexual. I just don't want to marry Todd.

Don't get me wrong: he's a nice guy. We have a lot in common, and as long as I squash my baser instincts, we get along just fine. He has a lot going for him, and I don't mean to sound mercenary, but I was brought up to look at the bottom line. We Southern Belles may appear fluttery and feminine, but we have calculators under the big hair. Todd would provide for me, love me, and cherish me... but unfortunately he'd also wrap me in cotton wool and put me on a shelf and never, ever let me do anything, because he'd be so afraid something would happen to me.

A year ago, I would have been fine with that. A year ago, I'd have married him, grateful that he was rescuing me from a fate worse than death. Singlehood.

Now I wanted more.

And 'more' didn't mean Rafe. That was over and done with. He'd left me in the hospital to deal with a miscarriage on my own, and I hadn't heard from him since. Not even when I was shot. If I'd needed a clear signal that he didn't care about me, either of those would have done it.

But the little bit of time I'd spent with him, just a few hours here and there over the past three or four months, had taught me that there are men out there who'll let their female counterparts get off the shelf occasionally. There are even a few who won't bother to wrap them up in the first place. Rafe hadn't just let me do things, he'd actively encouraged me. When I needed help, he'd been there to provide it, but only after I asked. He'd made me feel like an equal in ways Todd never had, and I was comfortable with him in a way I'd never been with anyone else. Todd expected me to be proper and ladylike and demure. Rafe had no expectations. In fact, the further I got from the properly brought up Southern Belle I was supposed to be, the better he seemed to like it.

There was probably some food for thought in that. Some big revelation about our now-defunct relationship. But it was something I'd have to think about some other time. At the moment Todd was sitting across from me, sharing this really excellent meal he was paying for, and if I couldn't love him and agree to marry him, I could at least be polite and charming while I ate on his dime. So I put a smile on my face and changed the subject. "Have you finished your Christmas shopping yet?"

Todd smiled back, relieved. "Not quite. It's hard to know what to do for Dix this year."

And just like that, the light atmosphere was gone, almost before it returned.

My brother Dixon, two years older than me, lost his wife last month. It was during that debacle and the aftermath that I got shot. And now my brother was a widower at thirty. A widower with two small children. I didn't know what to get him for Christmas either. I'd loaded up on distractions for the girls—dolls in sparkly dresses, soft stuffed animals, tiaras and magic wands—but all the rhinestones in the world weren't going to make Dix feel better. The girls were five and three; too young to really understand what had happened. They were taking comfort in the fact that mommy was in heaven with the angels, and they could be diverted with paper dolls and glittery glue. But Dix was facing his first Christmas without Sheila, and I had no idea what to do for him. Obviously neither did Todd.

"I think we just have to wait," I said. "And give him time to grieve. It isn't easy, getting over something like that."

Todd nodded. "Will you be at your mother's for Christmas this year?"

Mother has a shindig every Christmas Eve, for family and friends. It brings her children together under one roof, and since the mansion is almost 5,000 square feet, there's plenty of room for all of us. Dix has two children, and my sister Catherine and her husband have three. The whole family comes, including my Aunt Regina—my dad's sister—and her husband, and my mother's best friend Audrey. Various townsfolk come and go throughout the evening, paying their respects to the lady of the manor. The others don't spend the night, of course, since they live in Sweetwater. I do, rather than driving back to Nashville in the middle of the night.

"I always am," I said.

The festivities continue the next day, with Christmas Breakfast and then Christmas Day dinner at one of my siblings' houses. This year it would be at Catherine's, since Dix wouldn't want to, or know how to, cook Christmas dinner for ten or twelve.

Todd nodded. "I'll look forward to seeing you there, then."

Gah.

I don't know why I was surprised. Mother has been carrying on with Todd's dad for a while now. Pauline died years ago, just like my dad, and mother and Bob have always gotten on well. I only learned about the relationship a month or two back, but the others had known for longer. That's what comes from living an hour away.

Anyway, it wasn't strange that she'd want Bob there on Christmas, now that the union was out in the open and everyone knew what was going on. And I suppose she had to invite Todd. He's divorced and an only child, so it's not like he has anywhere else to go for Christmas. Dix has been his best friend since childhood. And in spite of the miscarriage and the knowledge that I'd been involved with someone else, mother hasn't given up on the idea that we'll end up together.

Todd looked coy. "What would you like Santa to bring you, Savannah?"

Rafe, I though, and immediately chastised myself. He was gone, he wasn't coming back, he didn't want me. I smiled. "Nothing. I have everything I need."

"Diamonds?" Todd suggested.

"God, no." That brought to mind engagement rings, and I couldn't imagine anything worse than having to turn down another proposal in front of my entire family on Christmas Eve.

"A puppy?"

From his expression, it was almost as if he thought a puppy would make up for the baby I'd lost. My baby had been barely bigger than a blueberry when I miscarried, but after all the agonizing I'd done over whether or not to keep it, it had become very real to me. And as much as I like puppies, it wasn't the same.

"I live in an apartment," I said. "With a no-pets policy."

"I guess a kitten is out of the question too, then."

"You could get me a goldfish. I'm allowed to have those."

Todd's expression lightened. "Do you want a goldfish?"

"Not really," I said apologetically. "I was joking. I don't really need a Christmas present." There was nothing anyone could give me that I wanted. Especially Todd.

I wondered if I ought to ask him what he wanted for Christmas, but I was afraid of what the answer would be. And I'd bought him a sweater in any case.

I speared a mushroom with my fork and lifted it to my mouth.

"Isn't that Collier?" Todd said, looking over my shoulder.

For a second, my heart skipped a beat and I almost choked. Then I realized two things: 1) he'd probably only said it to get a reaction from me—Todd was suspicious of my feelings for Rafe long before there were any feelings to speak of—and 2) there was no way he could be right.

I swallowed the mushroom and made sure my voice was steady. "I doubt it. If he were back in town, I'm sure someone would have told me."

And it probably wouldn't have been Rafe himself. If he hadn't stuck around when I lost the baby, and he didn't get in touch after I was shot, he wouldn't bother to call to tell me he was back in Nashville, either.

I had, however, become friendly with Tamara Grimaldi, homicide detective with the Nashville PD, and she knew Rafe too, and kept tabs on him through her contact in the Tennessee Bureau of Investigations. I trusted her to let me know if anything important happened. Like, if he died. Or if he'd been shot or hospitalized.

Or if he'd come back to Nashville.

Todd nodded, reassured by my lack of interest, and forked up another piece of veal.

I continued my internal monologue while I chased mushrooms around my plate. Even if Rafe was back in town and nobody had bothered to tell me, he wouldn't be here at Fidelio's. He despises the place. I've had dinner with him here twice, and both times he treated the fancy cuisine and snobbish waiters with irreverent amusement. He wouldn't choose to come here unless it was with me. And since we were over and done, he had no business being here. It was probably just someone with a passing resemblance to Rafe. Todd was a little bit paranoid on the subject; he was probably just seeing things.

"Are you sure he's not back in Nashville?" Todd said. "Because that really looks like him. Just the kind of woman I'd expect him to be with, too."

Woman?

I twisted on my chair. "Where? I really don't think..."

And then my breath went when I saw that yes, it was indeed Rafael Collier on the other side of the restaurant, just sitting down at a romantic table for two. A table I had once shared with him, as it happened. Behind a pygmy date palm. And the woman he was with was exactly the kind of woman I would expect him to be with, too.

A woman very much not like me, I might add.

Like Rafe, she looked like she might be of mixed race. Long, dark hair fell straight like a waterfall down her back, and she had exotic almond-shaped eyes in a stunning face with flawless caramel skin and red lacquered lips. She was shorter than me, and even in four inch heels she barely came up to his shoulder. Granted, he's tall—six three, give or take—but she was still on the petite side. And she was poured into a short, tight, Christmas-red dress that clung to every curve she had, and his hand was right there, on the exposed skin of her back. That, more than anything else, hurt. He was touching her. In a sort of intimate way. Skin to skin. The same way he'd touched me.

I own a red dress too. I'd bought it to coax a proposal from Todd, back when I thought being engaged to Todd would make me less likely to indulge in my feelings for Rafe. Instead, it had been Rafe who peeled it off me at the end of the night.

My dress isn't as short or as tight—hers looked like lycra; mine's satin—but it's also backless, and I could remember disconcertingly well the feeling of his hands on my back, warm and hard and a little rough. I could remember what happened afterwards too, and the thought that they'd be leaving Fidelio's and going home to make love in his bed— the bed where he'd made love to me—was enough to turn the Chicken Marsala to sawdust in my mouth.

She'd sat down with her back to me, which left him facing our table. If he looked up to scan the restaurant, he'd see us. See *me*. I had to get out of here before that happened. But first I had to tear my gaze away from the expression on his face, and it wasn't easy.

Rafe is a good-looking man, if you happen to like the type. Tall, dark, and dangerous, like the heroes of Barbara Botticelli's bodice rippers.

Lately, he's been growing his hair longer than usual, and while the perfectly styled espresso waves are attractive, I kind of miss his short crop. He has brown eyes, as dark and melting as those on a Jersey cow, surrounded by long, thick lashes, and whenever he looks at me—unless we're in bed together, and sometimes even then—they always hold a hint of amusement. Warm amusement, like he's enjoying the company; not like he's secretly laughing at me.

And tonight he was looking at her that way. Like he enjoyed her company. Like being with her made him happy. Like she was interesting and beautiful and special.

The bastard.

"Dessert?" Todd said.

He always asked. Mother brought me up to eat like a bird whenever I go on a date—we wouldn't want a potential husband to think I don't care about my waistline—so I've never in my life ordered dessert when eating with a man. Todd still asked every single time he took me out. Sometimes I'm tempted to say yes just because I really like cheesecake, but the habit is too deeply ingrained. I shook my head with a smile at the waiter, who was hovering beside the table. "Just coffee. Black."

The waiter nodded—it was more like a bow, really—and clicked his heels. Todd ordered the cheesecake. For himself. I wanted to scream at him that we had to leave, that every fiber of my being objected to sitting here demurely while a few yards away, the man I loved was wining and dining someone else, but I didn't. I folded my hands in my lap, dug my fingernails into my palms deeply enough to leave dents, and prepared to wait it out. All the while sending prayers heavenward that Rafe wouldn't look up and notice us. That was all I needed, for him to stop by our table to introduce his new girlfriend, the love of his life.

It seemed like an eternity before the coffee came, along with Todd's cheesecake. And then another eternity passed while he took his time devouring it, rolling each bite around in his mouth before swallowing. If I hadn't been so worried about what was going on behind my back, I would have resented the fact that he got to sit there, savoring raspberry chocolate cheesecake while I had to be satisfied with black coffee, but for once I didn't even think about it. All my attention was focused on the table behind the pygmy date palm and what was happening there.

I didn't turn around to look, not after the first time, but every second I expected to hear his voice. "*Evening, darlin.' Didn't expect to see you here.*"

It didn't come, but eventually the check did. Another thousand years passed while the waiter accepted Todd's credit card and took it into the bowels of Fidelio's to settle the bill. Then, finally, we could leave. Todd got to his feet first and came around the table to pull my chair out. He lifted my wool coat and held it for me. I slipped first one arm and then the other into the sleeves, and risked a glance over my shoulder.

Neither of them were looking at us. Their food had arrived, and they were busy eating. Rafe had ordered Chicken Marsala, the same thing he had when he was here with me, but instead of the plebeian bottle of beer that always gave the waiter conniptions, he was sipping red wine from a stemmed glass. Guess he was trying to impress her.

He'd never bothered to impress me.

"Ready?" Todd said.

I nodded and headed toward the front of the restaurant and the exit.

Just before we got there, I looked back one more time.

Dammit, I'd already known it was over—his actions in the hospital and his silence afterwards couldn't have made it any clearer—but it still hurt to see him with someone else. I guess I just wanted one more look. And maybe a part of me wished, now that I was leaving, that he'd look up and notice me. That he'd acknowledge me, one last time.

But he didn't. All his attention was focused on the woman on the other side of the table. As I watched, he laughed at something she said, then lifted his glass to her. She lifted her own, and they touched them together before drinking. I turned on my heel and walked out.

Two

Fidelio's is off Murphy Road, on the west side of town. I live on the east side, on the edge of one of the historic districts. To get there, we drove down Charlotte Avenue and through downtown, where someone had put nets with small yellow lights on all the trees lining the streets, to celebrate the upcoming holiday.

Nashville's downtown is quite small for a town with a million inhabitants. Most of Music City is suburban, while the downtown financial district is a pretty compact place. Until just a few years ago, nobody lived down there, although that's changed in the past five or six years. Now there are expensive lofts all over the place. Most of the buildings are fairly short: the tallest building in downtown, the Batman Building—so called because of the two pointy towers that look like ears—is under thirty stories tall.

Before the Batman Building came along, the Tennessee Tower was the tallest. It sits on Charlotte Avenue just across from the State Capitol and the War Memorial building, and it has no distinguishing architectural features whatsoever. What it does have, is a nice flat surface for writing things. At the moment, the lighted windows spelled the words SANTA STOP HERE with an arrow pointing to the roof.

From downtown, James Robertson Parkway takes you across the Cumberland River and into East Nashville. I live about a mile from downtown, in an apartment and condo complex on the corner of North 5th Street and East Main. It's gated, quite safe, and in a burgeoning urban neighborhood—and Todd asks me how safe it is every single time he drops me off after dinner. Tonight was no exception.

"I've lived here for almost two years," I said, as I punched my pass code into the keypad next to the gate. It opened slowly. I slipped through, followed by Todd, and headed across the courtyard. "In all that time, nothing's happened to me."

I stopped in front of the door to my building and pulled my keys out of my bag.

"How about that break-in you had back in September?" Todd wanted to know. "That wasn't nothing."

He had a point. However, the break-in—during which the burglar had slashed my favorite nightgown to ribbons and written a bad word on my bedroom wall with blood red lipstick—had been targeted at me specifically, and had nothing to do with either the location of the apartment or the security of the building. It could have happened anywhere. And would have happened wherever I'd lived at the time.

"That was personal," I said and pushed the door open. "Nothing to do with anything."

I walked into the stairwell, again followed by Todd. The outside door closed behind him with a reassuring thud. The stairwell was freshly painted and carpeted, with adequate lighting and nowhere for anyone to hide.

"It had to do with Collier," Todd said, as he followed me up the stairs.

"It's hardly his fault that some old girlfriend of his went off the deep end and started murdering people. He hadn't seen her for twelve years."

I stopped outside the door to my apartment and sorted through the keys on my chain. There's the outside key, the inside key, the key to the office, the key to my car, and the key to mother's house in Sweetwater... there was even a key to Rafe's grandmother's house on Potsdam Street that I'd picked up when I spent a couple of nights with her once, and that I'd never returned.

"That was a pretty girl he was with earlier," Todd said, obviously sticking his toe into the water to gauge the temperature. I made sure my back was turned when I answered.

"Very. Just the kind of girl you'd expect him to be with, too."

My voice was steady, I'm happy to report. And my hands didn't shake at all as I put my coat on a hanger and hung it in the tiny coat closet inside the door. I turned to Todd, a bright smile on my face. "Would you like a glass of wine before you drive home? Or a cup of coffee?"

Todd looked dissatisfied, somehow. I'd have thought my lack of reaction at seeing Rafe with another woman would have made him happy, but he seemed almost let down. He opened his mouth once, then seemed to think better of it and closed it again. "A cup of coffee would be nice."

Of course. He couldn't just get out of my way and let me kick, scream, and cry in peace.

"Just a moment." I gave him another sunny smile and a wave toward the sofa. "Have a seat. I'll be right back."

Todd headed for the living room. I ducked into the kitchen and started the coffee. After putting together a tray with two cups on saucers, two spoons, two napkins, a pitcher of milk and a dish of sugar, I placed both hands flat against the counter and watched the coffee drip from the coffee maker into the pot one drop at a time, cursing Todd and Rafe and the new girlfriend and most of all myself, for having done what I swore I'd never do, namely falling in love with him.

By the time I carried the tray into the living room, I had myself under control again. I was able to put it down on the coffee table and bestow another smile on Todd. "Sugar? Milk?"

"Just black," Todd said, watching me. "Are you all right, Savannah?"

"Of course I'm all right," I said, and gave him his cup with a steady hand. "Why do you ask?"

"I thought you might be upset about Collier," Todd said, stating the obvious. He was leaning back, his suit jacket neatly draped over the arm of the sofa and one leg folded over the other, holding the cup and saucer on his knee and watching my face.

I sat down across from him and crossed my own legs. "It was a bit of a shock at first. I didn't expect to see him. I had no idea he was back in town. I thought someone would have told me."

Todd nodded, sipping his coffee.

"But I wouldn't say I'm upset." Upset wasn't near strong enough for what I was feeling. Hollow, maybe. A bit devastated. Holding it together by a thread. However... "I always suspected there were other women. He never struck me as the faithful kind."

It was true. And since our relationship had consisted of exactly two sexual encounters a couple of months apart, plus a handful of kisses and the fact that he'd saved my life once, it wasn't like I had a right to expect fidelity, anyway. There'd been nothing in writing, nothing verbal, no actual reference to any kind of understanding between us. I'd been a willing participant when he wanted company, that was all.

Hell—excuse me—I'd pretty much thrown myself at him, at least the first time. Showing up at his house late at night, wearing a dress that practically begged to be ripped off, telling him that Todd had proposed and I had said no because I'd spent two years faking orgasms for my ex-husband and I didn't want to spend the rest of my life doing it.

Poor man, it wasn't like I'd given him a choice, was it? Maybe he really hadn't wanted to sleep with me. Maybe he'd felt trapped and like he had to give me what I wanted so I'd leave.

Squirming with a mixture of guilt and memory, my cheeks flushed. I added, "He made it pretty clear that he didn't care in the hospital last month, when he walked out and left me there."

Granted, he'd left me in the loving arms of my family and friends, after mother looked at him down the length of her nose, but I'd sent my sister Catherine after him to explain, and he still hadn't come back inside. And he hadn't written and he hadn't called, not even to let me know he was back in Nashville. Instead he'd just shown up with another woman. A woman he looked at the same way he used to look at me.

"I'm glad you can be so reasonable about it, Savannah," Todd said with approval.

I didn't feel reasonable. I wanted to scratch her eyes out and tear that pretty dark hair right off her lovely head. Barring that, I wanted him dead.

Or perhaps a case of genital warts would be sufficient. A severe case.

Todd placed his cup in the saucer with a click, and then placed the cup and saucer on the coffee table. "I should be going. It's getting late."

He wouldn't get back to Sweetwater until after eleven, and although it rarely gets very cold in Middle Tennessee, the temperatures do drop below freezing this time of year, especially at night. The roads might get icy.

For just a moment I toyed with the idea of asking him to stay. Spending the night with Todd would go a long way toward sticking it to Rafe *in absentia*. Pardon my French. But he'd never know, and it was likely he wouldn't care anyway, and I didn't really want to sleep with Todd. If I did, I'd have to marry him, since I wasn't brought up to sleep around and Todd knows it. The only reason no one expected me to marry Rafe after sleeping with him, was that no one in the family wanted me to marry someone like that.

And since he didn't want to marry me in any case, since he'd already replaced me with someone else, the point was moot.

I got to my feet and smoothed down my skirt. "I'll walk you out."

Todd nodded, shrugging on his suit jacket. "Thank you for another wonderful evening, Savannah."

"Likewise," I said. At least it had been pretty good until that moment in the restaurant when Rafe walked in.

"Would you like to go out again next weekend?"

"That would be lovely," I said demurely. Mother has always said to play hard to get, but I think I'm giving Todd enough of that with the marriage proposals; I don't have to refuse to have dinner with him, too. And free food is always nice. Especially free food the way Fidelio's makes it.

"I'll pick you up at seven," Todd said. He leaned in for a kiss. Usually—at least lately—I've turned my cheek. This time I didn't. There was a moment's hesitation when his lips found mine, almost like he hadn't expected it, and then he deepened the kiss.

I let him. I even responded in kind. It wasn't because I felt anything; just because I knew I was supposed to. I didn't feel anything beyond the guilt. Why couldn't I love Todd? He was loveable. Nice, caring, considerate and pleasant. And he loved me. It didn't seem fair that I couldn't love him back.

Maybe I could fake it. I'd faked it with Bradley for a few years, without even really realizing I was doing it. It hadn't been too bad. Unsatisfying, but hardly painful. There were benefits. The money. The status. The fact that I wouldn't be alone.

I could marry Todd and go back to Sweetwater with him. And settle into the life my mother had always wanted for me. Her life.

There was only one problem. Back when I married Bradley, I hadn't known what it meant to really love someone.

Now I did. For all the good it did me.

But it did mean I couldn't settle for less again.

Todd let me go and stepped back. I smiled. "Good night, Todd."

"Good night, Savannah," Todd said. He walked through the door and into the hallway. I waited until he'd started down the stairs before I closed and locked the door and let the mask slip.

I WON'T DETAIL HOW I SPENT the next few hours. It involved comfortable clothes, mocha fudge ice cream straight out of the container, and a sappy movie on cable, that let me shed copious tears over something that didn't directly relate to my own situation. It also involved a phone call close to midnight, at a time when I was pretty well cried out and practically catatonic, my eyes so puffy they were almost swollen shut and my stomach upset by all the ice cream.

My heart literally jumped when the phone rang. For a second I considered ignoring it, but that proved to be impossible. The Hallelujah-chorus rang like a siren song, and I dragged myself off the sofa and padded barefoot across the room and into the kitchen, over to the counter, where the phone was plugged in to charge.

Trying hard to get my vision to cooperate, I squinted at the display. The number belonged to a girl I'd made friends with a few months ago: my late colleague Brenda Puckett's daughter Alexandra. We'd met at Brenda's funeral back in August, and over the next couple of weeks had become unlikely friends. She was a little young for me—sixteen to my twenty seven—but she seemed to like my company, and to be honest, I don't have a lot of female friends. It's one of the side-effects of being a Southern Belle. We tend to look at all other women suspiciously. Life is very much a contest when you're a Magnolia. But because Alexandra was so much younger, and because we weren't competing in the same category, I was able to move past those feelings and enjoy her company.

I still considered letting voicemail pick up. It was late, way outside the proper limits for calling someone. But she'd once before called me late like this because she'd gotten in trouble and needed a ride home, and just in case something was going on and she needed help, I thought I'd better answer.

"Hello?"

My voice was thick, and I had to clear my throat.

"Savannah?" Alexandra said. "This is Alex. Did I wake you?"

I thought about lying. It would make a handy excuse for the froggy voice. But just because I felt bad, there was no need to make her feel guilty, too. "No, you didn't. I've just got a stuffy nose."

"Oh. A cold, huh?" She didn't wait for me to confirm or deny, just continued. "Can we get together?"

"Now?" A glance at the oven clock showed me it was a few minutes past twelve. She really ought to be in bed. I should be there myself.

Alexandra giggled. "Of course not now. Unless you want to?"

"No," I said, "I'd rather not."

"Tomorrow?"

"That would be fine. I'll have to spend the morning in the office. I always do floor duty on Saturday mornings. But I'll be done by noon. We could meet somewhere at twelve thirty or one. Maybe grab some lunch?"

"Can't," Alexandra said with disgust lacing her voice. "Maybelle has plans."

Maybelle always had plans. And not just for Saturday afternoons.

Maybelle Driscoll lived across the street from the Puckett family on Winding Way, in a very nice neighborhood not too far from my own. Brush Hill, with big properties with lots of trees, close to the river.

Sometime over the past couple of years, since Mr. Driscoll died, Maybelle had started an affair with Steven Puckett, Brenda's husband. Or Brenda's widower, now. Back in August, when Brenda was murdered, I had seriously wondered whether Maybelle, or Steven, or both of them together, had killed her. Steven didn't seem the type, but Maybelle would have slit Brenda's throat without a second thought and then square-danced on the remains. She showed up to Brenda's funeral in a bright blue dress, and got herself engaged to Steven less than a week later. Ever since then, she's done her best to replace Brenda in the Puckett family dynamic. But where Steven seemed happy about it, and Austin—the boy—was non-committal, Alexandra had been actively resisting. She didn't like Maybelle, and she didn't want another mother.

"Sunday, then?" I had to sit an open house for a colleague in the afternoon, but other than that, my time was my own.

"Can't," Alexandra said again. "Maybelle..."

—had plans. Right.

"I'll stop by your office in the morning and talk to you," Alexandra decided. "That OK?"

"Of course. You know where...?" I cut myself off. Of course she knew where it was. Her mother had worked there for years.

"I'll be there by nine or so," Alexandra said. "Bye." She hung up. Without letting me answer. I didn't take it personally, since it wasn't the first time it had happened. Maybe someone had come into the room to see who she was talking to on the phone so late, or maybe she just had no manners. Brenda had been lacking in that department, too.

Leaving the phone on the counter to continue charging, I headed back to the living room, dragging my feet. If I looked anywhere near as bad as I felt, I must be a horrible sight. I should probably chop up a cucumber to take some of the swelling down around my eyes, or steep a couple of teabags or something, but I lacked the energy. All I wanted to do was go to bed and forget this night ever happened, but I figured I didn't stand a chance of actually falling asleep. My body was dragging, but my head was still buzzing. Instead of sleeping, I'd probably lie there, tossing and turning, thoughts spinning, until daybreak. And then I'd look even worse than I did now.

Maybe a shower would do me good. Or better yet, a bath. With lots of warm water and bubbles. Candles. Soft music. Something soothing, to calm my jangling nerves and help me relax.

I padded into the single bathroom and started the water running into the tub, adding bath salts and sweet-smelling bubble mix. And then, when the tub was full, I stripped down to my skin, piled my hair on top of my head—I'd washed it in the afternoon, in preparation for my date with Todd, and I didn't have the inclination to blow it dry a second time today—and sank down into the bubbles.

By the time I got out and dried off, I was feeling a lot more mellow. I'd finished rinsing with cold water, so the face that stared back at me from the mirror above the sink didn't look as awful as I'd feared. My eyes were still bloodshot and a little puffy from all the crying, but other than that, I'd looked worse. Recently, too. The first few weeks after I lost the baby had been pretty bad.

It was my second miscarriage. Losing Bradley's baby three years ago had been disappointing as well as physically exhausting, but it hadn't been devastating. Losing's Rafe's baby—and then on the heels of it losing Rafe himself, too—let's just say I'd had a rough few weeks.

I looked better now than I did just after it happened. Tired, sure. Like I'd spent the night crying. But there was color in my cheeks and light in my eyes; I didn't look like I was near death.

Abandoning the bathroom mirror, I wrapped a robe around myself and headed out of the bathroom. It was almost one o'clock. Definitely time to go to bed. I'd have to be in the office by eight the next morning to answer the phones on the receptionist's morning off—floor duty, in RealtorSpeak—and at this rate, I'd be dragging myself out of bed right about the time I should be unlocking the door over there, bright and chipper.

The lights were still on in the living room, and I headed that way to turn them of before crawling under the covers. Only to stop in the doorway when I saw that I had company.

Three

"Evening, darlin'," Rafe said.

He was lounging in the sofa where Todd had sat earlier, and when I walked into the room, he'd turned his head to greet me.

I regret to say I had no response. Nothing witty or even halfway clever. I couldn't even manage coherent. I had thought the apartment was secure. I'd locked and bolted the door when Todd left, and a quick look in that direction assured me that the deadbolt was indeed still turned and the security chain was hooked across the jamb.

I knew Rafe could work wonders with a lock pick—or for that matter with a couple of bobby pins. I wasn't surprised that he'd gotten past my deadbolt. But surely that security chain must have given him a little trouble?

And entirely aside from that, what was he doing here? Hadn't he done enough damage to my psyche?

"Cat got your tongue, darlin'?"

I took a breath, and then another. When I thought I could trust that my voice wouldn't break, I said, "I didn't expect to see you."

He nodded but didn't speak. As I walked around the sofa over to the chair where I'd sat earlier, he watched me.

"What are you doing here?" I added, tucking the robe around my legs, suddenly very aware of the fact that I was naked underneath.

And speaking of nakedness, I was also barefoot and totally without makeup and my eyes were red and puffy from crying. Talk about being emotionally stripped.

"Saw you at the restaurant," Rafe said. "Figured I'd clear the air."

He must have come directly from what's-her-name, because he was still wearing what he'd worn at Fidelio's. And they were clothes I'd never seen him in before. Usually it's jeans and a T-shirt; occasionally slacks and a button-down. Tonight it was a suit, beautifully cut, something Bradley or Todd might wear, over a starched white shirt and conservative tie. He had loosened the tie already, and had removed both that and the jacket. It was tossed negligently over the back of one of the dining room chairs with the tie peeking out of the pocket, and he was in the process of rolling up the sleeves of the shirt.

His hands and forearms are just as nice as the rest of him, and I averted my eyes. "I didn't see you. You should have stopped by to say hello." My voice was remarkably steady as I spouted these lies.

"You and Satterfield looked pretty chummy," Rafe said. "I didn't wanna interrupt."

Right.

"I'm surprised you were there in the first place. At Fidelio's. Not really your kind of place, is it?"

"Business dinner," Rafe said.

Hah, I thought. She'd been much too pretty and flirtatious for that. And he'd looked much too appreciative.

But since I'd told him I hadn't noticed them, I couldn't really say anything about it. I chewed on my tongue, frustrated.

He leaned back and stretched his arms out along the back of the sofa. I could see the outline of his viper tattoo like a dark smudge through the left sleeve. And the posture—wide open—didn't fool me for a second. There was nothing open about Rafe. There never had been. Posture or no, he was as closed off as ever. He'd show me only what he wanted me to see and no more. "Satterfield propose again?" he inquired, with a quirked brow.

"Not tonight." Not for a few weeks, actually. I'd been pretty fragile after the miscarriage and everything else that had happened, and he'd given me some peace. I wasn't about to tell Rafe that, though. "Something I can do for you?" I added.

For a second he just looked at me. Then— "I hear you got shot."

He'd come here to talk about that?

"In the shoulder." The same place he'd been shot two months earlier. We'd have matching scars. I didn't say that, either. "It wasn't a big deal. Hurt a lot, but it's better now." And I wasn't about to slip the robe off my shoulder to show him the wound. If things had been different I would have, but not now.

He nodded, and we sat in silence again. It was awkward, different from all the other times we'd been together. I'd never had a problem talking to him. Most of the time I talked too much, telling him things I shouldn't. But now it seemed we both had a problem finding words.

"So you're back in Nashville," I said.

He shifted his weight on the sofa. It squeaked. "Drove in yesterday."

And he was already dating. That must mean he'd known her from before. He must have known her while he was sleeping with me. Maybe he'd been sleeping with both of us at the same time. I was aware of a bad taste in my mouth, and because I wasn't thinking straight, I blurted out something that would probably have been better left unsaid.

"Were you planning to let me know? If we hadn't both been at Fidelio's tonight?"

I would have taken the words back if I could, but it was too late. All I could do was wait for his answer, holding my breath and worrying about what it would be.

"Eventually," he said. Eventually. I wasn't sure whether that was better or worse than a straight yes or no. A yes would have made me feel better, like there might be hope. A no would have made me feel worse, but would have settled things once and for all. But 'eventually'... what did that mean? That if his fling with tonight's girlfriend didn't work out as planned, I might make an acceptable substitute for a quick roll in the hay?

"And if I happen to see you again? Out and about? Are you Rafe Collier these days? Or Jorge Pena? Or someone else?"

"If you happen to see me," Rafe said, "you don't know me."

Wonderful. "That can be arranged. I ignored you tonight; I can ignore you next time."

"Good," Rafe said and got to his feet.

I stayed where I was, in the chair, staring at him. That was it? He was just going to walk away? Again?

It looked like he was. He grabbed the suit jacket from the chair and slipped it on. It fit him beautifully—with a physique like his, everything fits beautifully—but I preferred him in jeans and a T-shirt. Or in nothing at all.

"Are you putting yourself in danger again?" fell out of my mouth.

He glanced at me, in the process of making sure the conservative tie was still safely tucked in the pocket. "No more than usual."

And with that he walked to the door, undid the deadbolt and chain, and walked out, closing the door gently behind him. By the time I got there and looked out into the hallway, he was gone. Without a goodbye, without a kiss, without flirting or even smiling at me. And without bringing up the pregnancy or miscarriage. No word at all about what had happened last time we'd seen each other. No anger, no accusations—from either of us—and no resolutions. It was like it never happened.

I was more confused than ever when I went to bed.

THE REAL ESTATE COMPANY I work for started life as Walker Lamont Realty. When Walker went to prison for murder, Timothy Briggs became broker, and the name was changed to Lamont, Briggs and Associates. After a few months, Tim—in an effort to remove the stigma of Walker's name—shortened it to LB&A.

The office is located just a mile or two down the road from where I live, and I made it there a little after eight the next morning, after taking the time to put on nice clothes and to slap rather a lot of makeup on my face to hide the circles under my eyes. Just because I felt like crap, didn't mean I could show the world an unfinished face.

Alexandra showed up just before nine. By then the phone hadn't rung and nobody else had stopped by. I had done what little bit of work I could dream up, I had checked the new property listings and organized Brittany's pencil tray by length and color, and I had given up and was flipping through one of Brittany's fashion magazines while I waited for it to be noon so I could leave.

Back in the old days I used to bring romance novels to the office for something to do during the downtimes. Then I'd learned that my favorite romance author, Barbara Botticelli, was actually a woman named Elspeth Caulfield, who lived in a little town named Damascus about twenty minutes from Sweetwater. We'd gone to high school together. I hadn't noticed her, and I don't think she'd noticed me either, but she had noticed Rafe. In fact, she'd had a bit of an obsession with him. One that didn't go away during the twelve years she didn't see him, between high school and this September.

She spent that time developing a reputation as a bestselling author of bodice rippers. Books where the heroines were always virginal, blonde good girls, and the heroes were always tall, dark, and dangerous bad boys: highwaymen, pirates, Bedouin sheiks and Apache warriors. I saw Rafe in every one of them, even before I knew who Barbara was. And ever since I realized that he not only looked like a Barbara Botticelli hero, but that she'd actively imagined him when she was writing, I haven't been able to read another of her books. Knowing that she'd slept with him in high school and was imagining doing so again was bad enough; reading the sordid details was more than I could stomach. I had tried to find another author to take Barbara's place, but so far no luck. There are entirely too many tall, dark and dangerous bad boy heroes in romance novels, and frankly, I just didn't need the reminder.

As a result, when Alexandra came through the door, I was leafing through the December issue of Cosmo, admiring a rather lovely green velvet dress that would be perfect for Christmas Eve.

"Oh." I looked up when the door opened and put the magazine down. "It's you."

"Hi, Savannah." Alexandra came inside, bringing a blast of frigid air with her, and glanced around the small lobby. "Wow. It looks just like it did when my mom worked here."

I looked around, too. It had always looked like this, as far as I knew. Tasteful and elegant. Walker had lovely, classic taste, and when he furnished something, it stayed furnished. A pity he was a coldblooded murderer, because he was a very nice man apart from that.

Alexandra unwound a long scarf from around her neck and slipped out of a short padded black jacket.

When I first met her, at Brenda's funeral, she'd been dressed in a black cocktail dress that made her look older than she was, with long hair wound into a complicated updo on top of her head. The last time I'd seen her, a month ago, her hair had been shoulder length and choppy, and she'd been wearing jeans and a cropped top showing off her navel ring.

Today the hair was even shorter: a spiky mess with streaks of purple to match the heavy makeup outlining her eyes. She was dressed all in black: boots, jeans, turtleneck and coat. Only the scarf showed a hint of color. Purple, of course.

"Are you going Goth?" I asked, interested.

Alexandra looked down at herself and shook her head. "I just felt like wearing black today."

I'd felt like wearing black too. I frequently do. It's slimming, and I carry a few pounds too many. And besides, it's easy to accessorize. Black goes with everything, and everything goes with black.

My blouse, however, was pink and happy. When I got dressed, I'd thought maybe the bright color might make me feel better. So far it hadn't.

"Are you OK?" Alexandra asked, peering intently at my face from across the desk. "You don't look so good."

Gee, thanks.

"I'm fine, thank you. I didn't sleep well last night." Understatement of the century.

Alexandra nodded sympathetically and dropped into one of the chairs on the other side of the desk. "Bad cold, huh?" She twined one leg around the other.

Not really. But then I remembered telling her I had a stuffy nose when we spoke on the phone last night, and I realized where she'd gotten the idea from. "Something like that. So what's going on?"

"Maybelle," Alexandra said and blew out a breath.

"Did something happen?"

She shook her head. "Nothing new. My dad's marrying her the day before New Year."

That was fast. Brenda died the first weekend in August. So five months, almost to the day, before her husband planned to marry again. That wasn't even the minimum six month's requisite mourning period.

Not that it would have been Steven's idea. Oh, no. He'd been firmly under Brenda's thumb, and now he was just as firmly under Maybelle's. This was her doing.

"I'm sorry," I said.

Alexandra leaned forward, her hands fisted. "I have to stop them, Savannah. I can't have Maybelle for a stepmother."

I wouldn't want Maybelle for a stepmother either, but exactly what did she think she could do about it?

"I'm not sure," she said when I asked. "I thought, since you figured out who killed my mom..." She trailed off.

Figuring out who killed Brenda hardly qualified me to get rid of her replacement. First of all, it had been pure luck, or unluck, that had put me in the path of Brenda's killer. And secondly, what did catching murderers have to do with stopping a wedding?

"I thought you'd ask that," Alexandra said.

"So?"

"What if Maybelle killed her first husband? What if she's planning to kill my dad after they're married?"

I sat up a little straighter. "Do have any reason to think she killed her first husband? Or that she's after your dad?"

Alexandra admitted she didn't. "There's something about her, though, Savannah. I don't like her."

I didn't like her either. But that didn't make her a murderer. "What do you want me to do about it?"

Alexandra dug in her jeans pocket. Then she held her fist above Brittany's desk and opened it. A key dropped in front of me. I looked at it for a second—it was attached to a key chain shaped like a small star—and then back up at her.

"It's Maybelle's spare key," Alexandra said. "I took it from her house."

I blinked. "Don't you think she'll miss it?"

She shook her head. "I borrowed the key she keeps at our house to go across the street to her house to pick up one of the spare keys from over there—she has a couple of them in a junk drawer in the kitchen—and then I took the original key back to our house and put it back. Unless she goes looking for her spare, she won't notice it's gone. And she's hardly ever in her own house anymore. She's moved into ours."

Right. Maybelle must be well-off if she could afford to let her house just sit there gathering dust without anyone living in it. Why didn't she put it on the market and get rid of it?

"What do you want me to do with it?"

Alexandra had folded her hands so hard her knuckles showed white. "I thought maybe you could go over there and have a look around."

Breaking and entering? It wouldn't be the first time, although last time I'd known what I was looking for. And I'd had had company.

"What is it you're hoping to find?" I asked.

"Not sure," Alexandra answered.

"Well, how would I know what to look for?"

"You wouldn't," Alexandra said. "I figured you'd just recognize it when you saw it."

With my vast experience in all matters criminal and murderous, I suppose.

"Hasn't your dad been in Maybelle's house? Wouldn't he have noticed if there was anything criminal sitting around?"

"It wouldn't be just sitting around, Savannah. If it was just sitting around, I'd have seen it this morning. You'll have to search for it."

"But you don't know what it is." And around and around we went.

Alexandra widened her eyes and leaned forward. "Please help me. I can't have Maybelle for a stepmother. I can't. Just go there and look around. Please. Maybe you'll notice something."

I sighed. "Fine. But if I'm going to break and enter, you're going to have to make sure I don't get caught."

"I've got it all figured out," Alexandra said and sat back, in full possession of herself again. "You said you're not doing anything this afternoon, right? You can go over there then. Maybelle and I are going Christmas shopping. Girl time." She grimaced.

"So you'll keep her away from her house?"

"I don't think we're coming back until late," Alexandra confirmed. "Maybelle has her pottery class this morning. When she gets back, we'll get ready to go. She's taking me to lunch first, and then we're going shopping. It'll take hours."

"What about your dad and Austin?" They lived right across the street from Maybelle's house; they might notice me.

"Austin has a basketball game," Alexandra said. "Dad's taking him. They'll be gone most of the afternoon, too."

So the Puckett house would be empty. And Maybelle's cottage would be empty. That left only the other neighbors to worry about. It was broad daylight, after all. They'd be awake, and around.

"I'm not sure about this," I said.

Alexandra widened her eyes again, and I capitulated. "All right, I'll do it. But if I go to jail, you'd better raid your piggy bank to bail me out."

Alexandra held up two fingers in a solemn Girl Scout oath.

Once our business was settled, I expected her to get up and leave, to get ready for her date with Maybelle. She has a habit of being abrupt like that. But instead she settled into the chair for a chat. "How did it go last month with David Flannery?"

I sat back too, in a sort of instinctive rejection of the subject.

Last month, when I'd been helping Dix track down Elspeth Caulfield's heir, I'd used the logo on the boy's shirt, the only clue we had as to where to find him, to trace him to Montgomery Bell Academy, one of Nashville's premier prep schools. As it happens, Austin Puckett attends MBA too, and when the office staff refused to help me, I contacted Alexandra, and through her, her brother. When I showed him the photograph I'd found in Elspeth's bedside drawer, Austin identified the boy in the picture as David Flannery. And Alexandra, once she got a good look at him, identified David's father.

I'm talking about David's biological father, not Sam Flannery, the man who adopted him. Sam and Ginny Flannery have been David's parents for as long as the boy's been alive. But he'd been conceived during a one night stand in Sweetwater almost thirteen years ago, when Rafe had been drunk and Elspeth used it to take advantage of him.

Alexandra Puckett has always had a sort of crush on Rafe. Not seriously, because—as I'd made sure to point out—he was too old for her and not the kind of man a nice girl should get involved with. But she liked him a lot. And because David looks a lot like Rafe, she'd had no problem guessing the relationship.

I should have been prepared for the question this morning. I wasn't.

"It went OK, I guess." Apart from the fact that David had run away when he got the news that the people he thought were his parents weren't really his parents, and Rafe had come back from Atlanta to help look for him, and I hadn't told him I was pregnant, and then I'd had a miscarriage and my life had fallen apart.

Talking about David Flannery opened up wounds I preferred not to have to deal with.

"I'm sorry about Rafe," Alexandra said.

"Me, too." Although at the moment I was more angry than anything else. I'd resisted him as long as I could, and I'd finally given in and slept with him, and I'd gotten pregnant and gone through hell trying to decide whether to keep the baby, only to lose it after all... and during all of that, he'd had another girlfriend? The bastard.

But how did Alexandra know any of that? I hadn't told her.

And then I realized what she was talking about. The last time we'd spoken, I'd told her Rafe was dead.

It's a long story. Back in September, a hired gun named Jorge Pena showed up in Middle Tennessee to kill Rafe. At this point, I still didn't know who had hired him, and I had no idea whether Rafe did. In the process, Rafe got shot and Jorge got dead—along with Elspeth Caulfield—and in the aftermath, the powers that be at the Tennessee Bureau of Investigations dreamed up a rather convoluted plot in which Rafe was declared dead in Jorge's place and then Rafe became Jorge while trying to figure out who had sent Jorge after him. Everyone was told he was dead. I was told he was dead. For eight interminable hours—an eternity—I'd thought he was. Then I'd found out the truth:

that in order to protect his cover and his life, it was important that everyone believed he was dead. So that's what I'd told Alexandra.

By now, my family, along with Todd and Bob Satterfield, had seen him and knew he was alive and well. But I hadn't heard that the investigation was over, so I didn't think I should tell Alexandra the truth. Much as I wanted someone to talk to about what had happened last night.

"I should go," Alexandra said. "Are you OK, Savannah?" She looked at me with concern.

I forced a smile. "I'm fine, thank you. I'll go over to Maybelle's after I leave here at noon. If anything changes between now and then, let me know. You have my number, right?"

Alexandra nodded. "Text me when you're done. That way I know it's safe to come back home."

I said I would and she put on her jacket and wrapped her scarf back around her throat and headed out. I went back to Cosmo while I waited for the phone to ring.

Four

The Pucketts live in a big brick Tudor on a winding suburban road some fifteen minutes from the office. I'd been there twice before. Once for the aftermath of Brenda's funeral—a catered affair where her friends and colleagues gathered to commiserate and celebrate— and once to drop Alexandra off at home that night she'd called me in despair after finding out that her unsuitable boyfriend may have had something to do with her mother's death.

Maybelle's house was across the street from the Pucketts', a much smaller English cottage in gray stone. I'd never been there, other than to get into her car once when it was parked in the driveway. This was while she was still making a pretense of living there, before she'd moved right into Brenda's life—and Brenda's home.

The driveway ran along the right side of the property. Luckily, it curved around to the back, and I was able to pull my Volvo all the way behind the house, so it couldn't be seen from the street. That wouldn't save me from the piercing glances of the neighbors on either side, let alone if Maybelle came home earlier than expected and decided to tuck her Christmas purchases away in her own house for safekeeping, but it was better than nothing.

I got out and slammed the car door behind me, taking a thorough look around as I wandered slowly toward the back door, fumbling in my pocket for the key.

The house on the left was a 1940s brick bungalow: it had the half-timbered Tudor accents on the eaves and porch, but apart from that it had the shape of a story-and-a-half cottage. I couldn't see the house on the other side too well; it was farther away, and there were a few trees and bushes along the property line. Most were bare now in December, but one or two were evergreens, which effectively blocked my view. I could see glimpses of red brick, and I was pretty sure what was over there was a classic mid-century cottage, but I couldn't actually see it, or any sign of life in that direction.

The key Alexandra had given me fit perfectly in lock of the back door. I held my breath as I twisted it and pushed the door open. If Maybelle had an alarm system, and kept it armed, I was in trouble.

She didn't. There was no telltale red or green light blinking, and no threatening wail cutting through the silence. I started breathing again, and stepped over the threshold, closing the door behind me before looking around.

I was in Maybelle's kitchen. White cabinets, many of them with glass fronts. Granite counters. Stainless steel appliances. Tile floor and backsplash.

It was beautiful, and bespoke excellent taste and enough money to indulge it. It wasn't ostentatious, but it was tasteful and costly, and I knew a lot of people who wouldn't be able to afford a kitchen like this. If it came to it, my own kitchen was nowhere near as nice. I didn't own my apartment, and it was fairly basic in design, with maple cabinets and a laminate counter. Nothing wrong with laminate, although granite does look a lot nicer. My appliances weren't stainless steel either, but plain white.

Anyway, Maybelle didn't look like she was hurting for money. She wasn't marrying Steven Puckett for his. Unless she subscribed to that old adage that a woman can never be too rich or too thin.

Leaving the kitchen behind, I wandered into the dining room, taking in the antique table and chairs, gleaming with polish, and the matching sideboard sporting a bowl of fake fruit, a pair of candle sticks in what looked like real silver, and a few photographs in matching frames.

Outside, a car door slammed, and I jumped. After a minute, when nothing had happened—no knock on the door or anything—I slunk over to the window and peered out, while making sure to keep behind Maybelle's sheer curtains.

There was nothing to be seen. No car in the driveway, no sign of life. Shaking off the instant of panic, I went back to the sideboard and picked up one of the pictures.

It was Maybelle, a few years younger than now, standing on what looked like the Great Wall of China. Other than being younger, she looked exactly the same. Fluffy blonde hair, sweet smile, short stature and a little too much junk in the trunk. Maybelle is what's usually called pleasingly plump, and the man who had his arm around her in the picture seemed to be getting in a good squeeze.

It was probably her late husband, whatever his name was. I didn't think I'd ever heard it. Whenever she'd talked about him, Maybelle had just called him her husband. They hadn't had any children, I knew that; that was probably why she was so determined to glom onto Alexandra and Austin.

The other photographs were of Maybelle and Mr. Maybelle, as well. They had traveled extensively, not only to the Far East, but to Egypt and Venice and what looked like Hawaii. There was a volcano in the background of one of the pictures, anyway. He was always keeping an arm around her, and she always had her hands in her pockets or folded across her front, which seemed telling. I had seen a few pictures like that of myself, while I was married to Bradley. He kept a possessive arm around my waist or shoulders, and I smiled at the camera and endured.

Not that I minded Bradley, you understand. I'd married him. He was everything I was brought up to look for in a husband, and we got along reasonably well. Everywhere except in bed, anyway. But because that aspect of our marriage was questionable—with Bradley telling me it was all my fault and me assuming it was just the way sex was supposed to be: bad—I didn't like for him to touch me, and I liked less to touch him, since I was afraid it would lead to more bad sex. Maybe Maybelle and her husband had had a bad sex-life too.

Hopefully hers and Steven's was better.

And then I cut off the train of thought before it could go any further. I had no need to speculate on Steven Puckett's prowess or lack thereof in bed.

I opened the drawers in the sideboard, but there was nothing of interest there, just folded tablecloths and napkins, silverware and the like. I recognized the pattern. *Old Master* by Towle. Introduced in 1942; current value $120 per dinner fork. My ex-mother-in-law, Bradley's mother, had owned a set, jealously guarded. I dare say, if John had threatened to divorce her, she would have let him keep the antebellum mansion and the Cadillac before she would have parted with the *Old Master*.

The two doors on either side of the drawers held flat- and hollow-ware. Genuine Wedgwood, with the traditional blue stripe. Expensive and lovely. Only the best for Maybelle.

The living room was next to the dining room, and was a lovely creation in cream, brown, and more blue. Maybelle had excellent taste. There were a couple more photographs, as well as an almost life-sized oil painting of Maybelle hanging above the marble-trimmed fireplace. She was wearing a dress in what must be her favorite blue—the same blue she'd worn to Brenda's funeral, and the same blue that was in the chair and sofa pillows—and she was smiling serenely out of an ornate gold frame.

I went from the living room down a short hall to the bedrooms. It was a small house, so there were only two. One opposite from the hall bath, outfitted as an office-cum-guestroom, and one at the end of the house. It was large, with a king sized bed—blue bedspread, of course—and a sitting area over by the front bay window. Like everything else in the house it was exquisitely lovely, expensive, and unlived-in.

I checked the drawers in the bedside tables, but there was nothing there worth mentioning. Maybelle didn't read romances; I found a book on do-it-yourself financial planning on one side of the bed and a true crime on the other. Either could have belonged to Maybelle, just like either could have belonged to whoever shared her bed last. Steven or her late husband, or for all I knew, someone else entirely.

There was an attached bath, which held only what you'd expect a bath to hold—including a lot of marble; Maybelle must be a fan— and a huge walk-in closet with a lot of summer clothes, the majority in shades of blue, and a few cardboard boxes and plastic containers. Maybelle must have moved her winter clothes over to Steven's house. I checked a couple of the boxes and found, among other things, a sewing machine, old issues of Southern Living, Christmas and Halloween decorations, and extra linens. It was just over a week until Christmas, and the decorations were still in the box: I assumed Maybelle wouldn't be decorating her home for Christmas this year. She was probably too busy decorating Steven's house.

The last room was the office, and I walked in and stopped in the middle of the floor, hands on my hips, looking around.

It was much smaller than the master bedroom. Must have been intended as a kid bedroom, maybe, when the house was first built. Or perhaps Maybelle and her husband had done renovations to the house at some point and combined two smaller bedrooms into the master. Maybe all the bedrooms had been smaller originally.

There was a futon against one wall: fake suede and stainless steel. A glass-topped desk sat under the window with a container of pens and pencils on one corner and another photograph on the other. There was no paperwork and no computer. If Maybelle owned one, she must have taken it across the street to Steven's house. The picture was a portrait of Maybelle with the ocean in the background. Maybe the husband had taken it.

There were no drawers in the desk, nowhere to hide anything. I looked around.

A filing cabinet stood in the corner, matte black in color. The top drawer yielded to my pull, and turned out to hold the usual kind of domestic paperwork. Bank statements—Maybelle *was* well off, although she wasn't what I'd call filthy rich; her bank balance was in the low six figures. Considerably higher than mine, yes, but hardly anything suspicious. Tax returns, IRA reports, a file for medical information which yielded nothing of interest, mortgage statements, old bills, and so forth. The tax returns from more than three years ago told me that Mr. Maybelle's name had been Harold and that he'd been a CPA. The financial planning book in the bedside table must have been his. Or maybe Maybelle had pretended an interest in her husband's work by reading it.

The bottom drawer was locked, and refused to open when I pulled on the handle. Frustrated, I looked around for the key. There had to be one. And if Maybelle was like most of us, she'd keep it nearby. Even if she kept a key to the filing cabinet on her key ring, and took it with her when she left the house, she'd want a spare just in case the other got lost.

I checked the desk, inside the pencil container and behind the photograph. Along the windowsill. I felt around the edges of the filing cabinet in case it was taped underneath.

Nothing.

Straightening, I scowled at the pristine room. Where else could it be?

Alexandra had mentioned finding the spare house key in the junk drawer in the kitchen. Maybe the file cabinet key was there, too.

Leaving my bag on the floor of the office, I headed back down the hallway to the kitchen. It took a few tries, but eventually I located what Alexandra had called the junk drawer. Like everything else in Maybelle's house, it was organized to within an inch of its life. I have a junk drawer in my kitchen, and it's a jumble of rubber bands, paperclips, screws and nails, a bottle opener, and a collection of Allen wrenches, to name just a few things. Maybelle had all of those things too, but they were sorted into little compartments in a plastic tray, neatly separated by shape and function.

There were a couple of keys nestled together; one I recognized as another spare house key, one as a spare car key, and then there were a few others, which looked like they might go with the couple of padlocks in a separate compartment of the drawer.

I spent a minute or two matching them. After that was done, I ended up with two keys that didn't fit the padlocks, the house, or the car. Those I took back to the office with me to try in the filing cabinet.

By now I'd been in Maybelle's house for thirty minutes or so, and I was starting to get a little more comfortable. I shrugged out of my winter coat and hung it over the back of the desk chair. Maybelle didn't live here, so she kept the thermostat set in the mid-sixties: high enough that the pipes wouldn't freeze and low enough that the bills would be negligible. Too warm for wool. I'd probably start getting chilly in a little bit, but for now, it was easier to be without the coat. That said, I kept my leather gloves on. I had no reason to think that Maybelle would realize I'd been here, or that she'd call the police who would do a sweep and collect fingerprints, but it was just as well to be careful. The Nashville PD had my prints on file from when I found Brenda Puckett's body, and I didn't want to take any chances. The gloves made it a little harder to handle the small keys, but I decided it was worth the hassle.

One of the keys fit the file cabinet drawer and I pulled it open, my heart beating a little faster. If she kept it locked, surely there must be something of interest in there.

At first glance it didn't hold anything of interest. Just more paperwork. A closer look showed me that the information was more personal than in the top drawer. This was birth- and marriage certificates, insurance payouts, and some additional medical information.

Harold Driscoll had died of a heart attack, in his own home, with only his wife in attendance. He was 56, a good bit older than Maybelle, who was 39 at the time, and there was nothing sinister about his death. He'd left a million dollar insurance policy payable to his wife. I hadn't seen a sign of the money in the bank folder in the top drawer, but there was more financial information here, including a few time deposit accounts and mutual funds. Between them, they accounted for the million plus some. Maybelle was *very* well off.

She had been born in Florence, Alabama, forty three years ago. Her maiden name was Maybelle Hicks. She married Harold Driscoll four years before his death, right here in Nashville. But by then her name was Maybelle Rowland.

I sat back on my heels. Was there a second husband, then? Or a first one, more accurately?

Or had something else happened? Like, Maybelle's mother—what was her name? I looked on the birth certificate again—Laura had divorced Bobby Hicks, or maybe Bobby had died, and then Laura had remarried and her new husband, Mr. Rowland, had adopted Maybelle?

No way to know without further research, and there was no other marriage certificate, nor any adoption paperwork, in the drawer. There was, however, a combination printer/scanner/copier on a table next to the desk. I wandered over to it and opened the lid. Might not hurt to make a copy of the birth certificate and the marriage license, just in case.

That done, I put everything back in the drawer and prepared to leave. There was nothing here. No evidence of anything sinister. No proof, or even a suggestion, that Maybelle had murdered Harold. No real reason to think she had.

Sure, the million dollar life insurance policy made for a dandy motive. Maybelle was wealthy. But it wasn't like she'd been suffering before. Harold clearly doted on his wife, as evidenced by the photographs in the dining room. He'd probably given her whatever she wanted. And if bad sex by itself was a motive for murder, Bradley wouldn't have survived the two years we'd been married.

I stuck the papers in my bag and shrugged on my coat. I locked the filing cabinet and turned out the lights and made sure everything looked the way it had when I arrived. I put the keys back in the junk drawer in the kitchen, including the spare key to the back door. If I took it with me, Alexandra would just have to make another trip over here to put it back, and it made more sense to just leave it now. If Maybelle came to check on the place and found the deadbolt unlocked but the key in the drawer where it was supposed to be, she might just conclude she'd been amiss last time she was here and had forgotten to lock up. It seemed the safest, simplest solution.

I hitched my bag securely over my shoulder and opened the back door, making sure I had everything I had come with, and that everything looked the way it had when I arrived. Cold air rushed in. I flipped the switch on the handle behind me and pulled the door shut, waiting for the click that signaled that the lock had caught. And then I turned around preparatory to going back to my car and walked right into someone.

I bounced back, and was grabbed by the elbow and steadied.

"Miz Martin," a voice said, and my heart sank all the way into my boots when I recognized it.

"Officer Spicer." I did my best not to let it show. "What are you doing here?"

Officer Lyle Spicer and his partner, Officer George Truman, were the two cops who had responded to my call back in August when I contacted 911 to report Brenda's murder. I'd seen them quite a few times since then. They were special friends with Tamara Grimaldi, my acquaintance in the Metro police department, and she often sent them on special errands for her. Whenever she wanted to talk to Rafe, which had happened a few times, Spicer and Truman were the ones she charged with bringing him in. As a result, they'd caught the two of us together on more than one occasion, sometimes doing things we shouldn't have been doing, at least according to my mother.

Clearly, this time they'd caught *me* doing something I shouldn't have been doing. And not just in my mother's eyes.

"Gotta call," Spicer said laconically, backing up a step after he'd made sure I was able to balance on my own. "Neighbor-lady called, said something was going on over here."

Damned nosy neighbors. I shot a glare over the bushes lining the driveway to the house beyond and smiled sweetly at Spicer.

"It's just me."

"Right," Spicer said. He removed his uniform cap and scratched the top of his head through the thinning, ginger hair. "Whatcha doin' here, Miz Martin?"

"A favor for a friend," I said firmly.

"You and Miz Driscoll are friends?"

"We're friendly." Sort of. "But I'm talking about Alexandra."

"Alexandra who?" Spicer wanted to know, while Truman just watched and listened. He's no more than twenty two and still blushes when I smile at him. I did it now, just to see if it would work. He blushed.

I turned back to Spicer. "Alexandra Puckett. You know, Brenda's daughter? They live across the street, in the big Tudor. Maybelle's engaged to Steven Puckett."

"The widower?"

I nodded. "Alexandra was supposed to keep an eye on Maybelle's place, but she forgot. And she can't do it right now. So she told me where to find a key and sent me over to do it instead."

"Uh-huh," Spicer said. "Where's the key?"

"I left it inside. In the junk drawer."

He arched his brows and I added, indignantly, "Surely you don't think I picked the lock? Where would I learn how to do that?"

"Couldn't say," Spicer said, and then added, "How's Mr. Collier?"

I swallowed the first and second responses that came to mind. "As far as I know he's fine. I saw him last night. He looked healthy."

"Uh-huh," Spicer said again. "Back in town, is he?"

"So it seems. And he never taught me to pick locks."

Spicer nodded. "So whatcha lookin' for, Miz Martin?"

"I told you," I said, "I'm not looking for anything. I'm just doing a favor for a friend. You can call Alexandra if you want, and ask her. I've got her number right here." I pulled out my phone.

Spicer looked askance at it. And then we both jumped when it signaled. Truman smiled.

"Speak of the devil," I muttered.

"Scuse me?"

I held it up. "It's a text. From Alexandra."

"Lemme see." Spicer took the phone in one beefy hand. I read over his shoulder.

On our way home. Everything go OK @ M's?

"See?" I said.

Spicer sent me a sideways look. "How'd I know it's from her?"

"Do you want to call her? That's her number right there." I pointed. Spicer hesitated.

"Would you like me to do it? She'll tell you she asked me to do this. I swear." I held my breath. I had no doubt that Alexandra would back me up, but I didn't want her to have to do it in front of Maybelle.

"No," Spicer said eventually, "I guess not. If you say you're just helpin' out a friend, I guess that's all you're doin'."

"Thank you."

"But next time you might wanna knock on the door over there and tell'em your here. It's one of these neighborhood watch neighborhoods. People look out for each other around here."

"I'll keep that in mind," I said.

Five

Spicer and Truman backed their cruiser down the driveway and I followed suit. We drove together up the street to the big intersection with Gallatin Road, where they zoomed south towards East Nashville and I turned north toward Briley Parkway because it was in the opposite direction of the one they were going.

That was close.

In fact, if I hadn't been lucky and it had been another pair of cops, I'd probably be on my way to jail right now. Handcuffed in the back seat of the cruiser.

I shuddered, and the Volvo shuddered too, as I turned onto the ramp for Briley Parkway.

I was home twenty minutes later, after making a sort of loop around East Nashville instead of driving straight through. After parking in the garage, I headed up to my apartment and booted up the laptop while I sliced a couple pieces of Brie to put on crackers, and popped the top of a Diet Coke. I'd skipped lunch in my hurry to get to Maybelle's house, and I was starving.

The phone rang while I was slicing, and I put down the knife to answer it, expecting Alexandra. It wasn't.

"Hi, this is Aislynn?" the voice on the other end said.

Of course.

"Hi, Aislynn. How are you? And Kylie?"

"We're fine," Aislynn said, "Hey, d'you have any time tomorrow to show us a couple houses?"

"I'm sitting an open house from two to four," I said, tucking the phone under my cheek to keep slicing while I talked, "but other than that I'm free. Before or after?"

"Um... before?" Aislynn had a tendency to speak in questions, as if she wasn't quite sure she meant what she was saying.

"Ten o'clock? Eleven? Twelve?"

"Um... twelve?"

"That's fine," I said. "Give me the addresses or MLS numbers of the properties you're interested in, and I'll schedule the showings and call you back."

She gave them to me, her voice rising at the end of each one. It gave the impression that she was asking me questions, as if expecting that I'd come up with some reason why she wouldn't be allowed to see the houses.

"I'll call you back in a little bit to confirm," I promised, and abandoned the Brie to get on the computer and schedule showing appointments for the next afternoon. That done, I gave Aislynn a call back to tell her where to meet me. Work accomplished, I returned to the Brie, and then the Brie and I returned to the computer to get some work done.

Not real estate work this time. No, I was looking for information on Maybelle Driscoll, her husband, and her past.

I'll be the first to admit I don't have a whole lot of knowledge when it comes to cyber investigations. Membership in the realtor's association allows me access to some information that the general public can't get—for instance, how much someone owes their mortgage company and whether they're at risk of foreclosure—but it's all real estate related. Property tax records are public in Davidson county. I did check the records for Maybelle's house and saw that she had been added to the deed a month or so after marrying Harold, seven years ago now. Before that, Harold had owned the place by himself for just six or eight months, after a quit claim deed removed someone named Carolyn Driscoll from ownership.

A quit claim deed is something that often happens after a divorce. Whether Maybelle had been married or not before marrying Harold, it looked like Harold may have been married before marrying Maybelle.

The house was paid off by now, I noticed. I guess that's why Maybelle could afford to let it sit empty; she didn't owe anything on it.

Another property search, this time on Carolyn Driscoll's name, turned up a handful of women by that name who owned property in Davidson county. I started to eliminate them, one by one. Three were married to men named Driscoll and so couldn't be Harold's ex-wife. Two had lived in their homes longer than Carolyn and Harold had been divorced. One had bought her house as recently as last year. She was a possibility; Carolyn could have rented for a while before buying another house, although renting for six years seemed a little excessive. Then again, I'd rented for the past few years myself, after getting divorced, so maybe I had no room to talk.

The last Carolyn Driscoll lived in a stone cottage in Madison. Two bedrooms, two baths. The exterior looked very similar to Maybelle's house on Winding Way. The interior layout—which the powers that be had supplied as part of the tax records—was also similar. And the clincher: she had bought it within a month of Harold's marriage to Maybelle.

I wrote down the address and the phone number, not quite sure what I planned to do with it, but at least now I'd have something to share with Alexandra when next we spoke.

Now, for Maybelle and her changing last name.

Her birth certificate said she'd been born in Florence, Alabama. I Googled the town and found their tax records, as well as their demographics and the name of their hometown newspaper, the Times-Daily. It went back a few years, and a search of their archives, on the name Maybelle Hicks, showed me that in the dark ages of the 1980s, Maybelle had been active in high school drama club. There was a grainy picture of her as Sandy in "Grease," younger and thinner than now, in a poodle skirt and yellow blouse, with her hair in a bouncy ponytail.

So she'd been Maybelle Hicks until her teens. That pretty effectively ruled out an adoption by a stepfather. Adoptions don't usually happen once a child is that old.

Marriage was more likely. If she'd married Harold at—I counted on my fingers; forty three minus three minus four more—thirty six, then she'd had eighteen years during which to get married and divorced before marrying him.

I tried the Times-Daily announcements, but without success. If Maybelle had gotten married in Florence, there hadn't been a wedding announcement published.

When I married Bradley, mother announced it everywhere. The Sweetwater Reporter, the Tennessean and the Nashville Banner, the Natchez Sun and Democrat (where Bradley was from), the Savannah Chronicle and Morning News (where mother's family was from), the Charleston Post and Courier, where I'd gone to finishing school... it was a major miracle that she didn't take out ads in the New York and L.A. Times to announce the marriage of her lastborn.

Of course, two years later, when I quietly divorced Bradley, there wasn't an announcement anywhere.

Would she announce my second marriage? *Margaret Anne Martin is pleased to announce the marriage of her daughter, Savannah Jane, to Rafael Collier...*

But no. Mother wouldn't be pleased, and would not announce such an embarrassment publicly. Nor would there be anything to announce, since the groom was busy wining and dining another woman. Bastard.

I abandoned the fantasy and dragged myself back to the case at hand. There was no marriage announcement for Maybelle. No divorce announcement either. But that didn't mean anything. Lots of people get married without announcing it first.

After a moment spent gnawing on my bottom lip, I Googled 'public marriage records' and hit Enter. In just a few seconds, a glut of websites appeared on the screen that promised to give me what I wanted. I played around with them for more than an hour, but eventually I had to admit defeat. I could get the records, but I would have to pay for them, and under the circumstances I wasn't sure I wanted to.

So I did the next best thing and called my brother.

Like my father, my grandfather, and my great-grandfather, not to mention my sister, my brother-in-law, my ex-husband and the man who wants to marry me, my brother's a lawyer. He and Jonathan, Catherine's husband, run Martin and McCall, on the square in Sweetwater. Our great-grandfather started the firm, and Martins have run it ever since. When Catherine married Jonathan, their name was added to the window. I'm the only Martin of my generation who didn't get a law degree. I started, but ended up dropping out to marry Bradley instead. And I don't regret it, but there are times—like now—I wished I had access to the various databases and search engines that lawyers do. And that's when having a big brother comes in handy.

I dialed the number and waited while the phone rang. Once. Twice. Three times.

"This is not a good time," my brother's voice said in my ear.

"Nice to talk to you too," I retorted.

"Yeah, yeah. Can this wait, sis? I'm kind of busy."

I heard noises in the background, and not the kind of noises I expected. It was a Saturday night, going on seven o'clock by now. I figured I'd find him at home, hanging out with Abigail and Hannah. I expected the background noise to be the sound of a Disney movie.

Instead, it sounded like he was out somewhere. There was the low buzz of voices in the background, and the occasional clink of glasses.

"Are you on a date?" I asked suspiciously.

"Of course not," my brother answered.

Good to know. It was less then a month since Sheila had died, and she and Dix had had a good marriage, from all I knew about it; I'd hate to think he was out there searching for her replacement already.

I waited for him to elaborate, since it sounded very much like he was in a restaurant somewhere, even if it wasn't on a date, but when he didn't, I said, "Well, can you do me a favor when you get home?"

There was a moment of silence. "Does this have to do with Rafe Collier?" my brother asked.

I blinked. "No."

"Oh," Dix said, sounding relieved. "Sure. What do you need?"

"You have access to marriage records, right?"

"I do," Dix said.

"Can you look someone up for me?"

"He's never been married," Dix said.

I rolled my eyes. "I know that. Todd looked it up back in August. I told you, this has nothing to do with Rafe. Why do you keep bringing him up?"

"No reason," Dix said and sounded a little guilty. "Whose marriage is it you want me to look up?"

"A woman named Maybelle Hicks." I told him who Maybelle was, and that I wanted to know where the last name Rowland had come from.

"How do you know all this?" Dix wanted to know.

I hesitated, but eventually told him the truth. He was quiet for a few seconds and then he asked, "You broke into her house?"

"Of course I didn't break in. I had a key."

"Right," my brother said, with what I was pretty sure was an eyeroll. "This is Collier's fault, isn't it?"

"It is not!" I was damned if I'd give Rafe that much power over me, even in conversation with my brother. "I did it for Alexandra. She doesn't want Maybelle for a stepmother. I don't blame her. I don't like Maybelle either. So I'm trying to do what I can to help. Now listen: She lived in Florence, Alabama, when she was a child. Now she's in Nashville. She married Harold Driscoll seven years ago. It's the time between I'm interested in."

"Fine," Dix said. "I'll look it up. But it won't be until tomorrow. I'll be home late."

Uh-huh. "Where are you, anyway?"

"Dinner," Dix said.

"Alone?"

He hesitated. "No."

"Who are you with? Todd? Jonathan?"

"No," Dix said.

"Catherine?"

"No."

"Someone else? A woman?"

He didn't answer.

"I thought you said it wasn't a date."

"It isn't a date," Dix said. "It's a business dinner."

"Sure." The same kind of business dinner Rafe had had last night, no doubt.

"Just leave it alone, sis. Everything isn't always what it looks like."

I was aware of that. "Yvonne? Are you on a date with Yvonne?"

"Yvonne who?" He sighed. "I told you, Savannah. It's not a date. But this conversation is making me look stupid, and I don't want to. I'll talk to you tomorrow."

He hung up. I did the same, more slowly.

When the phone rang five minutes later, I figured it was Dix calling back. It wasn't, and for a second my heart stopped when I noted the name on the display. Why was Tamara Grimaldi calling me? It rarely betokened good news, and right now—with everything that had happened over the past twenty four hours—it was more likely than ever to mean something horrible.

"Detective. Is something wrong?"

"You tell me," Tamara Grimaldi said. "What are you doing breaking into Maybelle Driscoll's house?"

My heart stuttered. "How did you... oh."

Spicer and Truman, of course. For a second there I'd had the crazy idea that my brother and Detective Grimaldi were having dinner together. But of course that was insane. "Spicer and Truman told you?"

"Of course they told me," Grimaldi said. "They answered a call about a break-in and found you on the premises. It was an official call, so they had to file an official report, and because they know I know you, they copied me on it."

"Don't you ever stop working?"

"Yes," Grimaldi said, "I do. More to the point, don't you ever stop getting yourself in trouble?"

"I'm not in trouble. Am I?"

"I don't know," Grimaldi said, "are you?"

"Not as far as I know. Although..." I hesitated, but since I had her attention anyway, "did you know that Rafe's back in town?"

"Is he?" Her voice was absolutely neutral.

"I saw him last night," I said. "At Fidelio's restaurant. Having dinner with someone."

"A date," Grimaldi said.

"He said it was a business dinner. I'm not sure I believe him."

"You spoke to him?" She sounded surprised.

"Not then. I pretended I hadn't seen him and made Todd take me home. I didn't think he'd seen me either. But he stopped by later."

Much later. A part of me, the not so nice part I endeavor to keep silent, wondered if he'd rolled out of *her* bed to come talk to me.

"He did?" Grimaldi asked.

"He said he wanted to clear the air."

"And did he?" Her voice was back to neutral again.

That depends on what clearing the air meant. "Not as such," I said. "He said he was back in town, working on something, and that if I saw him again, I should continue to pretend I didn't know him."

"That's probably a good idea," Grimaldi agreed.

"He knew I'd been shot. But he didn't say a word about the baby."

There was a moment of silence. "I'm sorry," Grimaldi said, sounding like she meant it. "Do you want me to talk to him?"

"No." I shook my head. "God, no. If he doesn't care enough to ask, I certainly don't want anyone telling him he should. I just wish he'd stayed away. In Atlanta or wherever it was he went." Dealing with the fact that he didn't want me would be much easier if we were in different states.

"Maybe he'll finish what he's doing and leave again," Grimaldi said. "So tell me what you were doing in Maybelle Driscoll's house this afternoon."

"Didn't Spicer and Truman tell you?" I didn't wait for her answer, just took a breath and launched into the same excuse I'd used with the officers, one hand sneaking up to twist a tendril of hair around my finger. I do that whenever I fib.

"Right," Grimaldi interrupted, before I'd even gotten halfway through the spiel. "That story might work on Spicer and Truman, but I know you better. And between you and me, it didn't work that well on them either. Officer Spicer just happens to like you, and he knew you weren't breaking in to steal anything. But he also knew you weren't there to water the plants."

Great. I had escaped arrest not because of my eloquent lies but because Lyle Spicer had a soft spot for stupid blondes.

"Fine. Alexandra doesn't like Maybelle. She doesn't want Maybelle to marry Steven. She thinks Maybelle killed her first husband."

"Any evidence to indicate that she did?" Grimaldi wanted to know.

"None I could find. But it isn't like she'd keep it sitting around her house, is it?"

Grimaldi conceded the point.

"He had a million dollar life insurance policy with Maybelle as the beneficiary. But she wasn't exactly suffering before he died, either. And it seems he divorced his ex-wife for Maybelle, just a few months before they got married."

I didn't mention the photographs and the conclusion I'd drawn about their marriage from the way he'd held her and the way she'd avoided touching him. It was spurious evidence at best, and said rather a lot about me and my personal life, things I didn't necessarily want the detective to know.

"That doesn't mean anything," Tamara Grimaldi said.

"I'm aware of that. There was one interesting thing, though. When she was born, her name was Maybelle Hicks. When she married Harold Driscoll, it was Maybelle Rowland. But there was no information in her filing cabinet about another marriage. I've asked Dix to look into it. My brother, remember?"

"I remember your brother," Grimaldi said. "How is he?"

"About as well as can be expected, considering that he lost his wife last month. He's hanging on."

"That's good," Grimaldi said. "If he comes up with anything you feel I should know, inform me."

It wasn't a request.

"Can you do anything about it?"

"That depends on what it is," Grimaldi said. "If I have ten free minutes on Monday, I'll pull the files on Harold Driscoll's death. Just to see if there's any reason to suspect foul play."

"I appreciate that."

"Sometimes you have good instincts, Ms. Martin. If you think something might be going on, you may be right. It's worth a second look. And if it can keep you from getting yourself arrested, so much the better. No more breaking and entering, please."

"I didn't technically break in," I said, "I had a key—"

"Of course you did. But did you have the home owner's permission?"

She paused politely as if waiting for me to respond. I didn't, of course, which she had known very well that I wouldn't.

"Don't do it again, Ms. Martin. I don't want to come in to work tomorrow morning and find you in jail. Your mother would have kittens."

I shuddered. Mother wouldn't just have kittens, she'd have a cow. "I'll be good. And I'll let you know if Dix comes up with anything interesting." Or if I did. Because she hadn't forbidden me to drive over to Carolyn Driscoll's house and talk to her. Then again, I hadn't exactly told her my plans, either.

"Do that," Grimaldi said. "Stay away from Maybelle Driscoll's house. And if you see Mr. Collier again, it would probably be best if you took his advice and pretended you didn't know him."

She hung up without saying goodbye. I rolled my eyes. What was with everyone I knew and their lack of manners?

Six

I met Aislynn Turner in November, two days after my sister-in-law Sheila died. When Sheila's body was fished out of the Cumberland River and her last debit card purchase was for lunch at Sara Beth's Café in Brentwood, I went there to see whether anyone knew anything about what she might be doing in Nashville that day. Aislynn was my waitress, and had been Sheila's, as well. At the time she told me that she and her girlfriend were thinking about buying a house, and she called me a few weeks later to talk more about it. So far I'd shown them three properties, none of which had been just right, and now we were going back for two more.

Neither Aislynn nor Kylie—or Kyle, as Aislynn called her—looked anything like Todd's worst nightmare. There wasn't a pair of camouflage pants or a crew cut between them. Aislynn has dreadlocks and piercings and enough eye-makeup to make Cleopatra—and Alexandra Puckett—weep with envy, but Kylie looks a lot like me. Susie Whitebread, with shoulder-length blonde hair with streaks and a bit of wave to it, blue eyes, and no visible body art. She even drives the same kind of car I do: a blue Volvo a couple of shades darker than mine. She's a banker in her daily life, so I guess a certain amount of decorum is to be expected. And the job ensured that they were prequalified for a loan and knew exactly how much they could afford. Thanks mostly to Kylie's job, it was a comfortable amount. I didn't have to search the real estate equivalent of the bargain racks, and it was a good thing too, because they wanted to live on the south side of town, near Brentwood, and that area doesn't come cheap.

Today, we were looking at a mid-century ranch in Crieve Hall, a nice forested neighborhood not too far from the Travelers Rest historic home—quite similar to Maybelle and the Pucketts' neighborhood, Brush Hill, on the north-east side of Nashville. After that we'd be heading over to Nolensville Road and Lenox Village, a recent planned development of townhouses and shops. My money was on the townhouse, since an established neighborhood of ranches and tree-lined streets didn't seem like it would be Aislynn's speed. Her reaction to the Crieve Hall house was about what I expected.

"This is nice, I guess." She looked around at the towering trees, bare of leaves so close to Christmas, and the yard full of hibernating grass and spiky, dead plants.

"It looks a lot more inviting in the summer," I offered. "I've seen pictures. The yard's lovely."

"Big," Aislynn said and measured it with her gaze.

"Half acre. Yards are a good size around here." I smiled.

"Who's gonna cut the grass?" Aislynn wanted to know, turning to Kylie.

"Not me," Kylie said. "We can hire a service."

Aislynn nodded, chewing on her bottom lip. Her lip ring was moving up and down, and I averted my eyes.

"It's a good price for the area. Well within your price range. And an easy commute to work for both of you."

They nodded. "It's just very..." Aislynn hesitated, "woodsy."

Woodsy tends to be a good thing. A lot of people who live in the city want woodsy. Obviously Aislynn wasn't one of them.

"Why don't we take a look inside," I suggested, "and then we'll drive over and check out the townhouse in Lenox Village. That might be more to your taste. Not so much yard, no trees to speak of, and practically no mowing required."

They nodded. I unlocked the door and we headed in.

As soon as the door closed behind us, my phone rang, and I excused myself to take the call while they wandered on their own. Unlike a pair of my previous clients—a young newlywed couple who had spent their time trying out each master bedroom to see which would give them the biggest bang for their buck before deciding which house to buy—I wasn't worried about letting these two explore on their own. They wandered off, and I put the phone to my ear.

"This is Savannah."

"It's Alex," Alexandra Puckett said. "How did it go yesterday?"

"That depends. The neighbor on the left called 911 and the police showed up just as I was leaving."

Alexandra breathed a word of the kind Maybelle—and my mother—would not have approved. "Were you arrested?"

"Luckily, no. I told them that you'd asked me check on the place, and they believed me. Although they did write up a report. So it's on record that I was there."

Alexandra said it again—that same word—and added, "I'm sorry, Savannah."

"It's all right," I said. "Could have been worse. They didn't arrest me."

"So did you find anything?"

I hesitated before saying, again, "That depends. Maybelle's first husband's name was Harold. He died from a heart attack. He had a million dollar life insurance policy and a wife it seems he divorced to marry Maybelle. And I think Maybelle may have been married before, too. A friend of mine is checking to see whether there were any suspicious circumstances around the heart attack, and my brother is trying to find out about the first husband, if there was one."

"I remember Harold," Alexandra said. "I think I even remember the wife he had before Maybelle. What happened to her?"

"I'm trying to find her," I said. "So far, my best bet is an address in Madison."

"When are you going there? Can I come?"

"I don't know yet," I said, in response to the first part of the question. "That depends on when I have time. I'm showing houses right now. Then I have to sit an open house for Tim. Tonight?"

Alexandra thought for a moment. Maybe she had to work around Maybelle's schedule. "What time?"

"The open house is over at four. How about five?" Having her along might not be a bad idea. If she remembered Carolyn Driscoll, Carolyn would probably remember Alexandra as well, and she might sympathize with Alexandra's desire to get rid of Maybelle.

"I'll meet you there," Alexandra said. "What's the address?"

I gave it to her. She hung up without saying goodbye. Again.

"So what do you think?" I asked Aislynn and Kylie when they came back into the living room after their exploration of the house.

Aislynn glanced around the living room. "It's nice, I guess."

There was still a marked lack of enthusiasm in her voice. I turned to Kylie, who shrugged. "I like it. But the neighborhood is maybe a little sedate for Aislynn."

Kylie was my age or just above, pushing thirty. Aislynn was younger; maybe not even twenty five yet. I guess it made sense that she'd want something a little more fun than this conservative, settled neighborhood of older people and families.

"On to Lenox Village, then?"

Kylie nodded. "Let's go," Aislynn said, with more enthusiasm than she'd shown so far.

So we piled into the Volvos—the two of them in Kylie's, I in mine—and drove the fifteen minutes over to Nolensville Road. Where Aislynn took one look at the pristine beauty of the planned neighborhood and rebelled. Her mouth turned down at the corners and her nose turned up.

"We can't live here."

"It's a nice place," I said, looking around at the walking trails running along the gently winding creek, the fenced playground, the ruler-sharp, postage stamp sized front yards, and the doggie stations with free plastic bags in dispensers, and tiny trash cans with tight lids.

"I can't live on Hobbit Lane," Aislynn said. "This place looks like that town in the movie where all the women were robots. Except the eyes."

Stepford. Right.

"Do you at least want to go inside?" I looked from Kylie, who didn't seem to mind the neighborhood, to Aislynn, who looked like I had taken her into the worst of Nashville's ghettos and left her there. She shook her head.

"There's no sense in it. We can't live here."

"Kylie?"

"Whatever Aislynn wants," Kylie said.

I hesitated, looking at the pristine front of the two-story brick townhouse. It was immaculate, but it was, perhaps, a little lacking in personality. "I know the two of you said you would prefer to stay on the south side of town. But have you considered looking in other areas? I can think of a few neighborhoods you might like better than this. You'd have a longer commute to work, but you might enjoy living there more."

The two of them looked at one another. "Kyle?" Aislynn said.

Kylie shrugged. "I'm game. Never hurts to look. Did you have something in mind, Savannah?"

"I'm hosting an open house for my broker this afternoon," I said. "It's in East Nashville, so on the east side of downtown instead of the south. But it's right off Interstate 24, so you'd be in Brentwood in twenty minutes. And it's more of a non-traditional neighborhood."

In fact, when the rejuvenation of East Nashville started some twenty years ago, it was the bachelors who first moved across the river and started renovating the old Victorian houses. And by 'bachelors' I mean the gay men. East Nashville still has a higher population of people living alternative lifestyles than any other part of town. There are restaurants and bars, organic grocery stores and home-made ice cream parlors, coffee shops and scooter stores there, and I thought Aislynn and Kylie would feel at home.

"What kind of house is it?" Kylie wanted to know.

I told her it was a Victorian cottage. "Ten foot ceilings, three fireplaces—including one in the master bedroom—updated kitchen and baths, city lot..."

"What's that?" Aislynn interrupted.

"A city lot? Usually 50 feet by 150. Sometimes 45x150. Grid pattern. Numbered streets running north to south, named streets and avenues running east to west."

"Smaller than that monster yard at the other house?"

I nodded.

"Let's go," Aislynn said.

I glanced at Kylie, who nodded. "We'll follow you, Savannah."

"Sure," I said, and headed for the Volvo. It wasn't until I had my hand on the door handle that I realized I was standing next to Kylie's car and not my own. "Oops."

She smiled. "No worries. Last time we got together, I started for yours before I realized it wasn't mine."

"I'd rather have a different kind of car," I confessed, passing her on my way to my own blue Volvo, "but I can't afford to replace it right now."

"Why did you buy it if you didn't like it?" Aislynn wanted to know, from the other side of the car.

I slowed down to answer. "I didn't. My ex-husband did."

And it wasn't that I didn't like it, exactly. It's a nice car. But looking at it reminded me of Bradley, and I could do without the reminder of my failed marriage.

"Must be a husband-thing," Kylie said, opening her own door. "My ex bought this one, too."

"You've been married?"

I must have sounded as surprised as I felt, because she grinned. "Youthful stupidity. I was twenty three and thought it was what I was supposed to do."

She closed the door and cranked the key in the ignition. I had more questions—how could she have been married? She was gay!—but the conversation was obviously over for now, so I hotfooted it over to my own Volvo and got in. As we rolled sedately out of the subdivision and headed up Nolensville Road towards town, I couldn't help but remember my own reasons for marrying Bradley. Namely, I'd been twenty three and thought it was what I was supposed to do, too.

"I don't mean to pry," I said when we were back in East Nashville, a mile or so from my apartment, standing in front of the Victorian cottage with Tim's LB&A For Sale sign in the yard, "but why would you choose to get married? Didn't you know that you were... um..."

"Gay?" Kylie said. "To be honest, no. I knew I wasn't getting a whole lot out of sex with guys, but I figured that was just because they were the wrong guys, you know?"

I nodded. I hadn't gotten a whole lot out of sex with Bradley, either.

"Once I found my true love and married him, I thought it would be different."

"But it wasn't?"

Kylie shook her head. "I loved him. I really did. But the sex wasn't good and there was just no passion there, you know?"

I nodded. I knew. There hadn't been any passion between me and Bradley, either. And I'd thought I loved him, too.

"There was this girlfriend I had," Kylie said, "that I spent a lot of time with. I'd rather spend time with her than with Damian. I didn't think anything of it, until one day he accused me of liking her better than I liked him. I told him it wasn't true, but..." She shrugged.

But it had been. "And that's when you knew?"

Kylie nodded. "That was the beginning. I thought about it for a while, and I realized he had a point. At first I tried telling myself I just liked her better. Personalities, you know. She never made me feel guilty the way Damian did. She was just easier to be with. But finally I had to admit that there was more to it than that. I felt more..." She hesitated, "alive when I was with her."

It was my turn to nod. I felt more alive when I was with Rafe, too. I felt more of everything, really, even the bad feelings. Like jealousy. Fear. Pain. And while I didn't like the way I was feeling right now, whenever I thought of him and that woman he'd been with on Friday night, I knew I'd rather feel something—anything—than go through life like the sleepwalker I'd been with Bradley.

"So I left him," Kylie said. "It's three years ago now. Last year I met Aislynn." She reached for Aislynn's hand, and the two of them smiled at each other. I smiled, too. It's nice to see people in love.

As long as they weren't Rafe and his new girlfriend, anyway.

"So this is it?" Aislynn said, looking at the house.

I nodded. "This is it." A circa 1900 Folk Victorian cottage, pale ochre with white and navy accents. Transom above the front door, side porch with gingerbread trim, tall, skinny windows with rounded tops.

"I like it," Aislynn said. "Can we go in?"

"Of course." I opened the lockbox and got the key. "Knock yourselves out."

Since I had to set up for the open house anyway, I figured I might as well start. So while they wandered and looked at everything, I started emptying the trunk of cookie trays and napkins and candles and fliers, all the while pondering what we'd just talked about.

Kylie had been married. At twenty three, like me. Because she thought it was expected of her, like me. And it had been bad, like my marriage. So she'd left him, like me. And she'd gone on to shack up with Aislynn.

See, I told myself, there were worse things I could have done than take up with Rafe Collier. I could have left Bradley and decided I was gay.

I tried to picture taking Aislynn home to meet mother, but came up short. There was just no way to imagine the ensuing scene. Perhaps because I couldn't think of Aislynn that way. Or someone else with her internal plumbing.

I tried to picture taking Rafe home to meet mother, and I had no problems. I could see the scene in detail. It involved mother's nostrils quivering as if she'd smelled something rancid, and Rafe being excruciatingly polite, with just a hint of that amusement that showed me he didn't take it seriously, whatever it was.

I pictured taking him upstairs to show him my old room in the mansion after the meeting with mother, and I pictured tumbling onto the bed with him. And then I remembered that the scenario I was imagining would never happen, and I put it out of my mind.

"We like it," Aislynn announced when they came back into the living room.

I looked up from arranging chocolate chip and oatmeal raisin cookies in a pleasing pattern on a round platter. "You do?"

She nodded. "It's great."

"We'd like to have a look at the neighborhood before we make any decisions, though," Kylie added.

"Of course. If you go four blocks in that direction—" I pointed through the wall, towards ten o'clock, "you'll get to Five Points. There are restaurants and bars and an organic grocery store there. And a couple of art galleries and the post office. I live six or seven blocks that way." I pointed at seven o'clock. "Due east is a park, two golf courses, a greenway, and a dog park." Twelve o'clock. "Due west is downtown and the interstate."

They were both looking around, heads swiveling. "Wow," Aislynn said. I shrugged. "So are you going to stay here, Savannah?"

I nodded. "My open house starts in thirty minutes. I'll just get ready and then wait for people to show up."

They exchanged a glance. "Are you expecting a lot of people?" Kylie asked.

I switched two cookies around on the platter. "I'm sure there'll be a few. This is a desirable area, and a nice house. And besides, the weather's good. That always helps. People don't like to go out in bad weather." So yes, to answer the question they hadn't asked, someone might stop by who'd fall in love with the house. If they were serious about it, it would be better not to drag their feet.

They exchanged another glance. "We'll call you," Kylie said, towing Aislynn toward the front door.

"I'll be here." I turned back to the cookies as the door closed behind them.

As expected, I stayed busy after they left. The weather *was* nice, and so was the house. People came and went for two hours, traipsing through the rooms, asking questions about square footage and taxes, and making small-talk. I made everyone sign the visitor registry, both so I could tell Tim on Monday how many people had seen his listing, and because it's sometimes possible to turn some of those visitors into clients. Gary Lee and Charlene Hodges, my first clients, had come from an open house. I'd spend the first part of Monday, after the weekly sales meeting, hand-writing notes to everyone who attended the open house, inviting them to call on me if I could be of further assistance. Email would have been a lot quicker, but mother always told me a hand-written note makes an impression, and I hoped mine would.

At four twenty, I locked the door after the last stragglers—there are always a few—and by four forty, I had packed up all my stuff, made sure all the windows and doors were locked and all the lights were off, and I was in the Volvo on my way to Madison to see Carolyn Driscoll.

Madison is one of the suburban areas that exploded in the 1950s, as people left the inner cities in droves. It's a lovely, shady neighborhood full of winding roads and big properties with low-slung ranches, populated by older people who bought their houses new fifty years ago and younger people who inherited them from their parents. In fact, it looked a whole lot like Crieve Hall, except it's on the north side of town instead of on the south.

It wasn't hard to find the Driscoll house, and not only because I'd seen a picture of it, but because Alexandra's fire engine red Mazda Miata was parked outside. It's an eye-catching car—Alexandra's Sweet Sixteen birthday present from her mother just before Brenda died—and in this sedate neighborhood of well-maintained ranch houses and equally well-maintained Chryslers, it stood out like a beacon. I pulled the Volvo in behind it and got out.

Alexandra didn't, and when I took at closer look at the Miata, I saw that it was empty. She must have gotten here early and knocked on Carolyn's door on her own. Hopefully Carolyn wasn't some rabid axe-murderer who had Alexandra tied to a chair inside at this very moment.

I hesitated for a moment between going to the front door—half a mile away, through the grass—or going up the driveway to the back door, where Carolyn surely did her own entering and exiting. The front door is usually reserved for company, so I should probably use that, but it would mean slogging through the yard in my pumps, and I didn't feel like it. And besides, mother wasn't here and would never know. I went to the back door and knocked.

It took a minute, and then the door opened. I found myself face to face with a woman my mother's age, with cropped gray hair and a handsome, if not precisely pretty, face.

"Yes?"

"I'm Savannah Martin. I'm looking for Alexandra Puckett." I tried a smile.

She stepped back. "Come in."

I moved across the threshold, into a kitchen that was an almost exact replica of the one in the house on Winding Way. White glass fronted cabinets, granite counters, tile floor. In fact, the whole house had a similar look to it. Maybelle's house was older by a few years, a 1940s cottage rather than a 1950s ranch, but Carolyn's home was also built mostly from stone, with a parking area around back and a view of mature trees and a winding road through the front windows. I had assumed Maybelle had decorated the house on Winding Way, and maybe she had put her stamp on some of it, but it seemed the kitchen had been left over from when Carolyn was Harold's wife.

Alexandra was perched on a chair in the dining room, looking out of place in her black clothes with her raccoon makeup. "Hi, Savannah."

"Hi," I said. "I thought you'd wait for me outside."

Alexandra shrugged. "Mrs. Driscoll came out when she saw the car. We got to talking."

"Have a seat," Carolyn said, indicating the chair beside Alexandra. She walked around to the other side of the table while I sat. "Alexandra tells me you're friends."

I glanced at Alexandra, who glanced back. "I guess we are."

"And you're the one who found Brenda."

I nodded and swallowed. The memory of Brenda, lying there on the floor with her throat cut from ear to ear, still had the power to turn my stomach four months later.

"And you want to ask me about Maybelle?" Her voice was calm, perfectly even, giving me no clue as to how she felt about her replacement.

"If you don't mind," I said, trying to feel my way forward.

Carolyn grinned. "I don't mind at all. The little tart stole my husband; I'll tell you everything I know. Where do you want me to start?"

I shot another look at Alexandra, and said, "Why don't you start at the beginning? You were married to Harold Driscoll."

Carolyn nodded. "We married in our mid-twenties. It was just the two of us. We never had children—Harold had lazy swimmers—but we enjoyed being together. We saw the world, traveled a lot, experienced things we wouldn't have been able to see and do if we'd had a couple of kids in tow. We had a good life."

"And then Maybelle showed up?"

"Basically," Carolyn said, her face darkening. "I guess it's eight or nine years ago now. He met her at work. She needed help balancing her checkbook." She snorted.

"Maybelle?" She hadn't struck me as someone who couldn't add and subtract.

"Oh, yes." Carolyn nodded. "I thought Harold was smarter than that, but apparently not. In the end, he told me she was everything I wasn't and he liked that she made him feel like he was in charge."

"I see." And I did. Carolyn came across as a strong woman, someone who knew what she wanted and went after it, no questions asked. She and Harold had probably been equals in the relationship. Maybelle was a strong woman, who knew what she wanted and went after it... but she did it the classically female way. By subterfuge and fluttering eyelashes and a presumption of weakness. She had known exactly how to balance her checkbook, but she'd known that the way to a man's heart isn't through his stomach, it's through the parts further south. His manhood. Appeal to a man's vanity, and you'll get him every time. Make him feel like a stud, and he's yours.

Yes, they teach that in finishing school, too. If not precisely in those terms.

It was the same thing Shelby had done for Bradley, I realized, if in a slightly different way. Bradley's and my sex life had been, for lack of a better word, poor. Bradley had blamed me, but it was certainly possible that he had blamed himself too, without articulating it. If Shelby came along and had multiple orgasms every time they made love, it was no wonder he preferred her to me.

For a second my thoughts slipped sideways to Rafe and the new girlfriend. What did she have that I didn't? I'd certainly never made him feel inadequate in bed.

And then I remembered what I'd done, or at least what he thought I'd done: I had kept it to myself that I was pregnant and he'd believed I didn't want his baby. Talk about making a guy feel emasculated.

But thinking about that right at the moment wasn't helpful to the discussion. I shook off the distraction and focused back on Carolyn. "What did you think of her?"

"What did I think?" She had gray eyes, and they were the color and consistency of rock right at that moment. "I thought my husband was too smart to fall for such a scheming little witch. I thought I didn't have to worry, that he'd see right through her. But in the end, it turned out that he was ruled by his gonads, same as every other man. I wanted to rip her face off."

Naturally. But I was more interested in her impressions beyond the obvious.

"So you thought she was playing him?"

"Hell, yes!" Carolyn said, "Whoever heard of a thirty-three year old woman who couldn't balance a checkbook, for God's sake? Of course she was playing him."

"Why?"

My question brought her up short for a second, and she stopped, almost mid-rant, to stare at me.

"Did he have money? Influence? Something else she wanted?"

Carolyn blinked. "He was a middle-aged accountant with thinning hair and a liking for Indian food. Nothing special."

Except to Carolyn, I assumed. "What about the life insurance policy?"

"What life insurance policy?" Carolyn said.

"The million dollar policy that paid out after he died."

She shook her head. "I don't know anything about that. He had a policy while we were married, just like I did. Two hundred and fifty thousand. But when we split up, I cancelled mine, and obviously he cancelled his too. Or, if you're right, he changed the beneficiary to his new wife and upped the payout to a million dollars."

"He died of a heart attack," I said. "Did he have heart problems?"

"Not that I knew about," Carolyn said. "But he was only 51 when we divorced. Maybe they hadn't developed yet. Or maybe having a much younger wife he had to keep up with brought them on."

Maybe. Alexandra shifted on her chair, and I knew she was thinking the same thing I was. Maybe the heart problems had a been a result of something Maybelle did, and not by being fifteen years younger than her husband.

Carolyn looked from one to the other of us. "What?"

I glanced at Alexandra.

"I think she killed him," Alexandra said.

Carolyn stared at her for a second without speaking. "That's a horrible thing to say."

"I don't want her to marry my dad," Alexandra said, sticking her bottom lip out. "I don't want him to die, too."

Carolyn looked at me. "Is she serious?"

I shrugged. "We're considering it. There's no evidence one way or the other yet."

"And you thought I'd have some?"

"We thought you might have a few thoughts. Maybe some knowledge we don't. Or suspicions."

She shook her head. "I never once considered that she'd killed him. But then I never considered that she'd married him for any other reason than that she wanted him, either."

Because every woman must want a middle-aged CPA with thinning hair who smells of curry.

"There's no reason to think anything happened, other than that he died of a heart attack. But I have a friend in the police department who says she'll pull the file tomorrow, if she has time. She'll let me know if there's anything suspicious."

"And you'll tell me," Carolyn said. It didn't sound like a request.

I smiled sweetly. "Of course."

Seven

We walked out of Carolyn's house a few minutes later. Alexandra stopped next to her car at the end of the driveway and looked at me. "What do you think?"

"Not a whole lot," I admitted, drawing my coat a little closer. It was getting colder at night this late in the year. We'd had no snow yet, and we hadn't really dipped below freezing either, but it was chilly standing outside in the evening. "She didn't know much we didn't already know ourselves."

Carolyn had mentioned the fact that she thought Maybelle had been married before stealing Harold. Apparently, that was how she had explained away the inability to balance the checkbook and the general air of helplessness. Her husband had taken care of everything and had treated her like a queen, and she'd never learned how to do anything for herself. A lot of men seem to like that in a woman. It was what mother had trained me to pretend to be. I'm expected to know how to do it all, but poorly, so as not to make a potential husband feel like I don't need him. It's OK for me to know how to do it, just as long as I let him know that he can do it *better*.

"She said he didn't have heart problems," Alexandra said.

I nodded. "But they may have developed after she divorced him. My dad died of a heart attack in his early fifties. With no warning whatsoever. We had no idea he had problems."

"I'm sorry," Alexandra said.

"Thank you. It's a few years ago now. I've learned to deal with it." Although sometimes I still missed him. "It's possible Harold just died from a heart attack, Alexandra."

Alexandra stuck her lower lip out, petulantly. "What about the life insurance policy?"

The life insurance policy was suggestive. The fact that he'd upped it from $250,000 to a cool million after marrying Maybelle, and then, four years later, he was dead, was interesting. Murder has been committed for a lot less than a million dollars.

"A friend of mine is looking into it," I said. "When I hear from her, I'll let you know what she says."

Alexandra nodded. "I'll be in school tomorrow. You can send me a text. Maybe I can cut out early and we can meet."

"What about after school?" I didn't want to be responsible for her cutting classes. I was corrupting her enough as it was.

"Monday is family movie night," Alexandra said. "We'll probably watch a Disney Princess movie."

"You're kidding."

She grinned. "Yeah. But Maybelle insists on what she calls wholesome family movies. Last week it was something called The Goonies from—like—the nineteen eighties." She rolled her eyes.

"I was born in the 1980s," I said.

Alexandra shrugged. "There was a cute guy in it, at least. Although he's probably old by now."

Probably. Or at least too old for Alexandra. Maybelle's age, maybe. She'd probably grown up seeing The Goonies.

"I'll send you a text if I hear anything tomorrow," I said. "Let me know if anything happens, OK?"

"Like what?" Alexandra said and opened the car door.

"No idea. Just anything." I opened my own and slid behind the wheel.

She followed me through the neighborhood over to Gallatin Road, where we both headed south. Alexandra peeled off first, by the Inglewood library, and I continued on toward home. I was almost there when the phone rang. I put it on speaker to keep my hands free.

"Kylie?"

"We want to make an offer," Kylie said, without so much as a how-do first.

"Excuse me?"

"The house in East Nashville. We want it."

"Really?"

The word just slipped out, I swear. But I'm not used to clients who see a house and decide to buy it right away. I'm not used to going out with clients twice, and finding their dream house. Gary Lee and Charlene had kept me hopping for weeks, if not months, before we managed to find something they liked. I know I shouldn't look a gift horse in the mouth, but this seemed too good to be true, and I've learned to be wary of those.

"Now," Kylie said. 'We want to make an offer now. What do we have to do?"

"Are you sure you don't want to sleep on it, at least?"

"No," Kylie said. "Is there a reason we can't do it now?" A touch of panic crept into her voice. "Did someone else already make an offer? Did someone come to the open house who wanted it?"

I hastened to reassure her. "Not at all. Nobody made an offer at the open house." Honesthery compelled me to add, "Although there were a few people who seemed to like it a lot."

"We need to make an offer *now*," Kylie said. "Can you meet us somewhere?"

"Sure." It wasn't very late, and I had no other plans. All I had to look forward to was a lonely evening at home with an inferior romance novel and a TV dinner. "Where?"

She named a coffee shop on the south side, about halfway between our two locations, and I told her I'd be there in twenty minutes and stepped on it.

The coffee shop was hopping when I got there, and the parking lot was full, but after driving around the building a few times, I managed to find a parking space in the back, out of the way, and tucked the Volvo in beside the dumpsters. Inside, I snagged a table in a semi-quiet corner, and sat down to wait. Aislynn and Kylie walked in a few minutes later, and we got to work crafting an offer I felt comfortable taking to Tim. They gave me their earnest money check—a little extra high to show how deathly serious they were about wanting the house—and we walked out together.

"I'll give Tim a call when I leave here," I told them as we passed into the darkness of the parking lot and headed toward the blue Volvo on the corner of the building. "He'll probably tell me to wait until tomorrow to give him the offer—I'll see him at the sales meeting first thing in the morning—but at least he'll know it's coming."

"You don't think he'll take another offer tonight, do you?" Aislynn said.

"That's why I'm going to call him. So he'll know we have an offer to submit, too. In case someone else does, as well."

She nodded. "Thanks for coming out again tonight, Savannah."

"It's no problem," I said. "It's what I do. And I want you to get the house you want."

The sooner the better, since I could use the income. The commission on this one was a nice, healthy chunk, that would keep me afloat for the first few months of the new year.

"You think this'll work out?" She let go of Kylie's hand and walked around the car to open the passenger side as Kylie undid the car alarm.

"I think you stand a good chance. It's a good offer." I hesitated for a moment before adding, "In case another offer comes in and Tim asks for highest and best... do you have a little flexibility, or is this as high as you can go on the price?"

They exchanged a glance over the roof of the car.

"We can go up a little higher," Kylie said. "Not much, but a little."

I nodded. "It's always good to leave yourselves a little negotiating room. Most offers aren't accepted exactly the way they are, and if you have the opportunity to go up just a bit in a later round, it might make the difference."

Both of them nodded. "Do what you can, Savannah," Kylie said.

I promised I would. "I'll call you as soon as I know something, OK? It'll probably be tomorrow. Most likely in the afternoon." I'd have to give Tim the offer, and he'd have to track down his clients, and they'd have to think about it, and call Tim back, and he'd have to get back to me... tomorrow afternoon was actually pretty optimistic. Tomorrow evening or maybe even Tuesday morning was more realistic.

"We'll look forward to it," Kylie said, and folded her legs into the car. Aislynn followed suit, and they backed out of the parking space and made their slow way to the road while I walked around the building and got into my own car.

The first thing I did—even before turning the car on—was call Tim, to tell him the good news. "I have an offer for you."

"Oh, goody!" Tim said, and I pictured him rubbing his hands together.

"What do you want me to do with it? Drop it off to you? Scan it or fax it?"

There was a short pause while Tim thought it over. "You might as well wait till the morning," he said.

Bingo, I thought. "Are you sure? I don't mind dropping it off. It's practically on my way home." Tim lived in 12 South, the area around 12th Avenue, and although it wasn't exactly on my way, I didn't mind driving a few extra miles, either. I wasn't too far away as it was.

"I wouldn't be able to look at it tonight anyway, darling. I have other things to do. You know how it is." He giggled in my ear. Tim is unapologetically gay, and he enjoys rubbing my nose in his sexual antics. Not literally, of course, but he likes to see my reactions to his often uninhibited statements. Or, in this case, hear my reactions. I wasn't brought up to discuss those kinds of things, especially not with members of the opposite sex. And this time he didn't even have to say anything: I recognized the giggle.

"Will you be at the sales meeting tomorrow morning?" I persisted. "Can I give it to you then?"

"Sure," Tim said.

"If you get another offer, you'll consider ours first, right?"

"Yes, Savannah," Time said, with obvious patience. "Get it to me in the morning, and if I get another, I'll look at yours first. And ask you for a highest and best offer price."

Of course. But I guess I couldn't really fault him for that; his job was to get the best price for his clients, while mine was to get the best price for mine.

"I'll see you tomorrow," I said. "Enjoy your evening."

"Oh, darling," Tim fluted, "I mean to!"

He hung up with another giggle. I winced as I did the same.

I was almost home, off the interstate and on my way up 5th Avenue toward East Main Street, when my phone rang again. It was getting to be a nuisance, especially when I saw who the number belonged to. As a result, my voice was perhaps a little shorter than it should have been.

"Aislynn? What can I do for you?"

"Savannah?" Her voice was choked with tears, and I sat up straighter in my seat. This didn't sound like just another call to ask me a question about the house or the contract or when we'd have an answer back from the sellers. Or—God forbid—to tell me that they'd had a moment of buyer's remorse and wanted to change their minds.

"What's wrong?"

"We had an accident," Aislynn said, between sniffles. "On our way home. Kylie..."

"What about Kylie?" My own voice took on a hint of panic. "She's all right, isn't she?"

"She's in the hospital," Aislynn sniffed.

"Which hospital?"

"Vanderbilt," Aislynn said. "In the ER. I'm scared, Savannah!"

"I'm on my way." I turned the car around in a U-turn, across four lanes and the turning lane in the middle of the street, to head in the opposite direction. About halfway across, I narrowly missed having an accident of my own, when a white Toyota in the lane next to mine didn't slow down and almost broadsided me. I guess the driver wasn't paying attention for that second or two and didn't notice my admittedly kamikaze-like maneuvering.

I MADE IT TO VANDERBILT UNIVERSITY Hospital in record time, and pulled into the parking garage with a squeal of brakes before jumping out of the car and running up to the emergency room. "Kylie Mitchell?"

The desk nurse looked up at me down the length of her nose. "Are you family?"

"Sister," I said. We might look alike enough that she'd believe it.

"She's in the O.R. The doctors are working on her."

"O.R.?"

"Operating room," the nurse said, in a tone of voice that conveyed eloquently her opinion of my intelligence.

"What about her girlfriend?"

The nurses eyes slid sideways to the waiting area. "The state of Tennessee does not recognize common law marriages."

"Excuse me?"

She repeated it.

"She means I have no rights," Aislynn's voice said next to me. "Kylie and I live together, we're buying a house together, and we want to have a baby together, but I don't get to see her in the hospital, because only family is allowed, and I'm not family!"

By the time she got to the end of the statement she was shrieking, and the nurse was wincing.

"Will you tell me when she comes out of surgery?" I asked.

She nodded.

"We'll just wait over here." I grabbed Aislynn by the arm and towed her over to the waiting area. "Listen. That kind of behavior won't get you what you want."

"I know that," Aislynn said, and ran the back of her hand over her face, smearing the wet makeup. "But it's so frustrating. They won't tell me anything!"

"They probably can't. It's the law."

"The law is wrong," Aislynn said, with a sniff. "How come they'll tell you?"

"I lied. I told them I'm Kylie's sister. If they ask, you'll have to back me up."

She managed a watery smile. "Thank you."

"It's no problem." I sank down on one of the padded chairs in the waiting room and pulled her to a seat next to me. "What happened?"

"We were on our way home," Aislynn said, still sniffing, although she had stopped actually crying by now. "Just talking, you know. About the house and the offer and whether they'll take it and what it would be like to live there."

I nodded.

"We were on our way down Edmondson Pike. There's an area there, just below the agricultural center, where the road dips. There's a four way stop at the bottom of the hill, and the entrance to a subdivision. One with big brick gates. Forest Crossing."

I nodded. I was somewhat familiar with it, having sat an open house in that area once for Tim.

"When Kylie stepped on the brakes, they didn't respond. We just kept going. Straight toward the four-way stop. Faster and faster."

She swallowed. "For a second I thought we were going to slam right into another car. But I kept my hand on the horn while Kylie tried to control the car, and everyone got out of the way. All except one car. We were going really fast by then, and when Kylie tried to swerve to avoid it, she lost control of the car. We hit one of the gates instead."

Her bottom lip trembled. I winced. I'd seen those gates, and the memory didn't fill me with a whole lot of confidence. "What happened?"

"I jumped out," Aislynn said. "Opened the door and rolled onto the grass a second before the car hit the brick wall. Kylie tried, but she didn't make it. She couldn't get her seatbelt to open." Her eyes filled with tears again. "I had to reach across her to unhook her seatbelt, and she fell out of the car."

"Unconscious?"

Aislynn nodded, tears trickling down her cheeks again. Black tears.

"That's probably a good thing," I said. "If she's unconscious, she won't feel the pain. That might be the best thing for her right now."

"I guess." Aislynn kept dashing at her cheeks, but the tears kept coming.

"How are you?" I wanted to know. "Has anyone looked at you? If you jumped out of a runaway car, do you maybe need some medical attention too?"

She shook her head. "I'm OK. I just tucked and rolled. I got a little banged up, but it's just bruises. It's Kyle I'm worried about. She didn't wake up, Savannah. Not when I got her out of the car, and not when the paramedics came. Not on the whole way here."

"I'm sure she'll be all right," I said, although truthfully, I had no idea. "They'll be out soon to tell us something."

Aislynn nodded, but she didn't look like she believed it any more than I did. We sat in the waiting room, hand in hand, and waited.

IT WAS TWO HOURS LATER BY the time a tired-looking man in green scrubs with a silly little hat on his head came into the waiting room. "Kylie Mitchell?"

Aislynn jumped up. I followed suit a second later. "That's us."

"Family?" the doctor asked, looking from one to the other of us.

"Sister."

He inspected me for a second, through tired, baggy, still sharp eyes, but I must have passed muster, for he nodded. "She came through the surgery OK. There's a couple of broken ribs, a punctured lung, some internal bleeding, and a lot of bruising from the seatbelt. There's also a concussion and some injuries associated with whiplash. At the moment she's still unconscious. You can see her for a moment if you want, but she won't be awake."

"I want to," Aislynn said, clutching my hand hard enough to hurt.

I nodded. "Please. Just for a minute."

"Follow me." The doctor headed down the hallway. We trotted after, to a room down the hall, dimly lit and with beeping machines.

I let Aislynn duck in first, and turned to the doctor. "How is she, really?"

He swept the cap off the top of his head and rubbed his eyes. "She'll make it. We repaired the lung, but until it gets better able to do the work on its own, we'll keep her on the ventilator. The ribs will hurt for a couple of weeks, but they'll heal. The concussion will get better sooner, and so will the whiplash. We'll keep the neck brace on for the next few days, at least."

"Will her insurance cover this?" Hopefully I hadn't set myself up for extensive medical bills by claiming kinship to Kylie. That was all I needed; Vanderbilt Hospital sending me bills for one of my clients' medical treatment. Bills I couldn't pay.

The doctor nodded. "It should."

"Good. Thank you."

He nodded. "I'm Simon Ramsey, if you have any other questions."

"I appreciate that." I glanced through the door, where Aislynn was standing next to the bed, holding Kylie's flaccid hand and murmuring. I could see the teardrops on her cheek catch the light from above. "I guess I should go in and see her now."

Simon Ramsey nodded. "If all goes well we'll move her out of the ICU tomorrow, and into a regular room. Then anyone who wants to can visit her during visiting hours, not just family."

"She'll appreciate that," I said.

"Tough situation to be in, when you're unmarried, or can't get married, and something happens to your partner, but you're not considered family." He nodded to me and left. I entered the room, softly.

"How is she?"

"Breathing." Aislynn spared me a glance before turning her attention back to Kylie again. "She looks horrible."

"She'll heal." I recapped what Doctor Ramsey had said while standing on the other side of the bed looking down at the unconscious Kylie. "He didn't seem worried about her survival. And really, it could have been a lot worse, I think."

Broken ribs and a punctured lung, a concussion and whiplash, didn't seem too big a price to pay when I remembered those brick gates.

"Sure could," Aislynn said with a sniff and a shudder, while the medical machines continued their steady beep.

"They won't let you stay here tonight. But he said if all goes well, she'll be in a regular room tomorrow, and then it won't matter that you're not a relative."

Aislynn nodded.

"Why don't you say goodnight, and I'll drive you home. You won't do her any good staying here. What she needs is rest. And so do you."

Aislynn nodded and, sniffing, she bent down and kissed Kylie's forehead, the only part of her face she could easily reach. "I'll see you tomorrow, babe." She smoothed a hand over Kylie's blonde hair and stepped back, wiping her cheeks with the back of her hand.

"Do you have a way to get to the hospital in the morning?" I asked twenty minutes later, when we were parked outside the condo complex where the girls' apartment was. We'd driven mostly in silence, at least until we got to the part of Edmondson Pike where the accident had happened. The car was gone now, but the grooves where the tires had ripped through the grass and dirt on the way toward the brick gates was still very much in evidence, and the gate itself was reduced to a pile of rubble. That's when Aislynn's lips had started quivering and the tears began again.

Aislynn nodded. "Scooter." She indicated a cute little Italian-looking one parked a few spaces down.

"The car is shot, I'm sure?"

"Completely," Aislynn said, wiping her eyes. "The police asked where they should have it towed, and I gave them the name of the place where Kylie takes it for maintenance. But I don't think there's anything they can do for it. The front is totally mashed in."

"Did you have insurance?"

"Oh, sure. Kylie is good about that kind of thing." She sniffed and reached for the door handle. "Thank you, Savannah."

"My pleasure," I said, which was a little strange, I suppose, given the circumstances. "Let me know if you need anything."

She nodded. "You'll call me if the hospital calls you, right?"

"Of course. Um..." I shifted from one foot to the other.

"What?" Aislynn said.

"I was just wondering... I know it isn't the right time, and you've got other things to worry about, but... you still want me to submit the offer for the house tomorrow morning, right?"

I held my breath. And yes, I felt guilty asking, but I asked anyway. I have to make a living.

"Kylie loved the house," Aislynn said, as her eyes slowly filled with tears again.

"Kylie still does. She isn't dead."

"Right." Aislynn blinked back the tears. "Yes, please. Submit the offer. Get us the house. It'll make Kylie happy."

Excellent.

"I'll call you tomorrow. Sooner, if they call from the hospital. But definitely once I hear about the house."

"Thank you, Savannah," Aislynn said again. Impulsively, she leaned over and gave me a hug. "Good night."

"Good night." I was wiping mascara stains off my cheek as I drove away.

Eight

The hospital didn't call, and Aislynn didn't either. Nor did anyone else, for that matter. I got up the next morning and got dressed in business attire, since I had to attend the weekly sales meeting at the office. 9 AM Monday morning, like clockwork. For the first time ever, I was almost excited about it, since I actually had some good news to share. It's not much fun sitting there listening to everyone else extol the virtues of their new listings or recounting how many offers they've written the week before. But for once, I had news of my own, so I didn't mind too much.

The meeting went about as expected. I sat through it, delivered my news, received my congratulations, and—after the meeting was over—handed Tim the offer with the following caveat. "The buyers were in a traffic accident last night."

"Oh, dear," Tim said, looking up with a wrinkle between his brows. He's in his mid-thirties, with bleach-blond hair and bright, baby-blue eyes, and a prettier-than-average face. He also has a brassy tenor voice. At one point he thought he'd make it on Broadway, but when that didn't work out, he came back to Nashville and became a realtor instead. He's quite good at it; probably better than he would have been at musical theatre, although I'm quite sure he would have enjoyed the applause.

"One of them is in the hospital, and still unconscious." At least I hadn't heard differently so far this morning. "The other is fine. But I may have a problem getting signatures."

"But they still want the house?"

I nodded. "They definitely still want the house. I made sure of it."

"I'll present the offer to my sellers and let you know what they say," Tim said. "It'll probably be this evening before I get back to you."

I nodded. I'd expected that. "Thanks."

"My pleasure," Tim said with a grin, and I knew he was thinking he'd be able to run circles around me in the negotiations. He probably would, too. Technically, we weren't even supposed to do this. Tim was my broker, the one I was supposed to go to when I had problems; he wasn't supposed to be on the other side of the transaction trying to take my clients for every dime they had.

But oh, well... I'd muddle through somehow. And maybe I'd surprise him.

Since I was there anyway, I spent a little time in my office, a converted coat closet off the reception area, checking the new listings and catching up on paperwork. It was while I was sitting there, scrolling through the morning's new offerings, that my phone rang, showing Dix's number.

"Morning," I told him.

"Same to you," my brother said. "I've got that information you wanted."

"About Maybelle's first husband?" I grabbed a pen from the desk and dragged a piece of paper closer.

"That's it. And you're not going to like it."

"Why not?"

He told me. "The groom's name was Joshua Rowland. The marriage took place in Natchez, Mississippi."

I put the pen down without writing anything. There was no way I'd forget this. "You're kidding."

"I'm afraid not," Dix said.

"My mother-in-law's name was Rowland." Althea Rowland, of the Natchez Rowlands, an old and revered Southern family, same as the Martins.

"Yes," Dix said. "Small world, isn't it?"

Sure is. "Anything else you can tell me?"

"Not much," Dix said. "The marriage took place in Natchez City Hall. Joshua was quite a few years older than Maybelle. Forty eight at the time. She was twenty nine."

"So another May-December romance."

"So it seems," Dix said. "I checked, but I couldn't find another marriage for Joshua. This seems to have been his first."

Confirmed bachelor, maybe. Misogynist won over late in life. Or a geeky romantic who never found the love of his life before Maybelle came along.

Chiding myself for cynicism, I asked, "Anything else?"

"I don't think so. Sorry, sis. There's just not a whole lot of information to be had."

"Did you happen to look for divorce papers? Or are those harder to find?

"They're harder to find," Dix said, "but they're public record. I looked. I couldn't find any."

So Maybelle and Joshua Rowland were either still married, making Maybelle a polygamist, or Joshua was dead. Like Harold.

"I appreciate it. So are you going to tell me what you were doing the other night? And who you were with?"

"No," Dix said, and relented. "Dinner with a friend."

"A female friend?"

Dix hesitated for long enough that I figured the answer had to be yes. "Anyone I know?"

"No," Dix said. "You don't know her at all. Absolutely not."

Huh. I thought he protested too much. "Yvonne McCoy?"

"God, no." He sounded horrified. Yvonne was a woman we'd gone to high school with, who'd had a crush on him back then, and she was about as different from Sheila as it was possible for one woman to be from another. I wasn't surprised that Yvonne didn't appeal to my brother that way; I just couldn't imagine anyone else he might be having dinner with. It wasn't like he had a whole lot of female friends. And Charlotte, his girlfriend from high school, my best friend back then, lived in North Carolina, so it wasn't her.

"Marley Cartwright?" I ventured.

Marley had been a friend of Sheila's, and had gotten acquitted of murder—not Sheila's murder—just a week or two ago. It was during that whole debacle that I'd managed to get myself shot. I supposed it was just possible that she and Dix had gotten together to reminisce about my late sister-in-law.

"Have you lost your mind?" Dix said. "Marley just got reunited with her son. She won't let him out of her sight for a year at least."

"Who, then?"

"I told you," Dix said. "You don't know her."

"How can I not know her? I grew up in Sweetwater." And it wasn't like a whole lot of people had moved there in the past ten or twelve years.

"Maybe she isn't from Sweetwater," Dix said.

Huh. Maybe not. "Columbia? Pulaski? Nashville?"

"Just let it go, sis," Dix said. "There's nothing going on. My wife died less than a month ago. I'm not ready for another relationship. It was dinner with a friend, that's all. I like her, but it's too soon to be anything but friends."

"Sorry."

"No problem," Dix said. "If—or when—I go on a date, I'll let you know, but until then, just leave it alone, if you don't mind."

He was right. I apologized again, and we sat in silence for a moment.

"Have you seen Collier?" Dix asked.

I steeled myself against the reaction I knew was coming. Just the sound of his name brought it on. "Twice. First at Fidelio's on Friday night. I was having dinner with Todd, he was having dinner with someone else."

"Who?"

"No idea," I said. "Pretty woman with long dark hair. Just his type."

"I thought *you* were his type," my brother said.

"Obviously not. Not after he got what he wanted from me."

Another few seconds passed. Then Dix said, "What about the second time?"

"He knocked on my door later that night. Said he'd seen me at the restaurant and wanted to clear the air."

"And did he?"

"No," I said tightly, "he didn't. All he did was tell me he was back in town and working. He didn't say a word about the baby. Not one word."

"Did you?"

"Of course not! If he doesn't care enough to bring it up, I'm certainly not going there!"

"I see," Dix said. "What about the woman? Did he say anything about her?"

"Nothing. Just that she was none of my business." The bastard.

Another silence fell.

"The reason I ask," my brother said.

"Yes?"

"The DNA test came back for David Flannery."

"And?"

"He's the father."

"I see," I said. "Was there ever any doubt?"

Dix admitted there hadn't been. "But it's good to have it confirmed, officially."

"I suppose. I guess I don't have to ask whether Elspeth was the mother?"

"No," Dix said, "you don't. Do you want to tell him? I don't have his number."

"I don't either." And whereas, in the past, I'd always been reasonably certain he'd turn up sooner or later, now I wasn't. "Your best bet is to try to contact him through Detective Grimaldi. Do you still have the number?"

Tamara had investigated Sheila's murder, and she and my brother had met then. After I got shot and—incidentally—caught Sheila's murderer, Dix was the one who had called her to impart the good and bad news.

"I have it. I'll try to get hold of him that way. Thanks, sis."

"You're welcome," I said, and refrained from asking him to relay what, if anything, Rafe happened to say about me if Dix managed to get hold of him. "Thanks for the information about Maybelle and Joshua Rowland."

"You're welcome. You're not going to do anything stupid, are you, Savannah?"

"Like what? I might call Bradley and ask him whether Joshua is a relative, but beyond that, there's not a whole lot I can do. And it's not like you have to worry about Bradley doing anything to me."

"True," Dix admitted. "Just... hang in there, sis. OK?"

"OK," I said, and hung up.

By the time I made it across town to Vanderbilt Hospital, it was almost lunch time. When I walked into Kylie's new room, out of the ICU, she was awake, and Aislynn was sitting by the bed, feeding her bites of chocolate.

"Are you sure she's supposed to have that?" I said, and Aislynn turned to me with a big grin.

"I don't care. Look, Savannah! She's awake!"

"I can see that," I said, wandering over to the bed and looking down. "Hi, Kylie. How do you feel?"

"Crappy," Kylie whispered, her voice hoarse.

I nodded. She looked sort of crappy too, not that I'd tell her so. But at least she was conscious now, and breathing on her own. "I'm so sorry about what happened. But the doctor said you'll be fine." I gave her an encouraging smile.

She nodded. He must have come by to tell her the same thing.

"Any word on the house?" Aislynn wanted to know.

I shook my head. "It's too soon. I gave the offer to Tim a couple hours ago. He'll have to call his clients. Depending on how they want to handle it—over the phone, by email, or in person—he might have to wait until tonight to present the offer. They'll need time to think about it and decide what to do. We might not hear until tomorrow. Or we might hear later tonight. I'll call you the second I know anything."

They both nodded.

"Any idea when you'll be out of here?" I asked Kylie.

She shook her head. "I'm breathing on my own, but it's uncomfortable. A couple of days, maybe."

"Do you have insurance to cover this?"

"Yes, thank God. If it had been Aislynn..."

She glanced at Aislynn, who made a face. "No health insurance at Sara Beth's. And since we're not married, Kyle can't put me on her policy at work."

"I pay for my own," I said. "There are no benefits in my line of work, either. I was on my husband's policy while we were married, but that ended with the divorce."

And that reminded me: I had to call Bradley, to ask him about Joshua Rowland.

I wasn't looking forward to it. That was why I hadn't called earlier, as soon as I got off the phone with Dix.

I hadn't seen Bradley in the more than two years since he divorced me and married Shelby, and although I was over him—completely and utterly—talking to him again might still prove to be awkward. I wouldn't go out of my way to avoid him, he just wasn't important enough for that, but I wouldn't mind continuing not to see him, either.

However, that didn't seem to be a possibility, so when I left Kylie and Aislynn, with another promise to call them the minute I heard anything from Tim, I stopped in the Vanderbilt hospital lobby and pulled out my phone.

Even after such a long time, Bradley's cell phone number rose from the murky depths of my mental filing cabinet with just a little prodding, and I punched the keys on the phone and waited until he picked up and introduced himself.

"Bradley," I said.

There was a beat—and I admit I waited to see whether he'd recognize my voice without any further prompting. Then—"Savannah?"

There seemed to be no point in confirming it. "How are you?"

"Fine," Bradley said cautiously. "You?"

"Also fine, thank you." A little white lie, but I certainly didn't want to tell my ex-husband any of my problems. He and his new wife were pregnant, did I happen to mention that? I'd run into Shelby a few weeks ago, during another open house I'd sat for Tim. It had been during the time when I wasn't sure I had the courage to face down my family and all the good people of Sweetwater over Rafe's baby. And then Shelby had showed up, glowing and delighted about being pregnant, and I'd wanted to kick her. "I saw Shelby recently. Congratulations."

"She didn't mention that," Bradley said, and I pictured the tiny line between his sandy brows I knew would be there.

"I guess she didn't feel the need. It was just for a few minutes. I was hosting an open house in Green Hills and she stopped by with a couple of girlfriends."

"I see," Bradley said. "So you sell real estate now? How is that going?"

"Well, thank you." Again, I wasn't about to tell him that I could barely make ends meet. "What about you? Are you still with Ferncliff and Morton?"

Bradley allowed that he was. And then he must have had enough small talk, because he added, "What can I do for you, Savannah?"

"I wanted to ask you a question," I said. "About someone named Joshua Rowland. From Natchez, Mississippi."

"My uncle?" He sounded surprised, as well he should. "How did you know my Uncle Joshua? He was dead by the time we got married, wasn't he?"

I imagined he would have had to have been. By the time Bradley and I got married, roughly four and a half years ago, Maybelle had moved on to Harold. And anyway, if I'd ever met Joshua, I'm sure I would have remembered.

"His name came up," I said. "A friend of mine is getting a new stepmother. Apparently stepmom used to be married to your Uncle Joshua. Or at least to someone named Joshua Rowland who lived in Natchez."

"Maybelle?" Bradley said. "Are you talking about Maybelle?"

"You remember her?"

"Yes, I remember her!"

And obviously not fondly, judging from his tone of voice. I could hear him take a breath, one of those long ones, through the nose, and then his voice came back on the line, deliberately calm. "I don't think I want to talk about this over the phone. Are you available for dinner?"

"Won't your wife mind?"

"It's Shelby's night with her mom," Bradley said, which didn't really answer the question, but which I took to mean that she'd never know.

"Couldn't I stop by your office sometime this afternoon?" And keep things on something of a professional level?

"I have meetings," Bradley said.

Of course he did. "Fine. Dinner."

"When should I pick you up?"

I was tempted to tell him I'd drive there myself, wherever 'there' was, but I decided against it. If he wanted to pick me up, he could. On his dime. That way he might not realize that I was still driving the car he'd bought for me. It was the one thing I'd salvaged from my marriage, aside from the chunk of change that had all but evaporated out of my savings account by now. Oh, and my dignity.

"Five thirty?" Early, but I didn't want to spend all night with him, after all. Better to get our business done and over with.

"I'll see you then," Bradley said, and hung up. I wondered whether I ought to call him back to tell him where I lived, but then I decided he could figure it out on his own. It would give him something to do. Or rather, his assistant. The one he'd hired to replace Shelby after he married her.

And then—I admit it—since I was on the south side of town anyway, I headed for the Green Hills mall, to see if I couldn't find a new dress. Maybe something I could wear tonight as well as to Christmas dinner at mother's house. I couldn't go out with my ex-husband in a dress he'd bought and paid for, after all.

The Green Hills mall is one of the snobbier shopping experiences in town. I used to buy my clothes there all the time when I lived in Green Hills and had Bradley's money to play with. I even worked there for a while after the divorce, at the makeup counter at Dillard's. Until I left to put my real estate license to good use.

It was sort of nice to be back. A few things had changed—some shops had gone out of business and others had replaced them—but for the most part it was still the same. I avoided Dillard's, and for that matter Macy's and Nordstrom's, and instead wandered the mall itself, looking in the windows of the various small designer shops. And it was there, while I was standing outside The French Shoppe, peering up at a green velvet dress that looked a lot like the one I'd admired in Brittany's issue of Cosmo yesterday, that I caught the reflection of a woman in the window. When I turned, I saw that my eyes had indeed not deceived me. There, on the other side of the aisle, walking briskly toward the exit to the parking garage, was the woman Rafe had had dinner with three days ago.

Nine

All right, so I know it's juvenile and possibly even immature to spy on your ex-boyfriend's new girlfriend.

Not that Rafe was even my boyfriend in the conventional sense of the word. But that aside: teenagers with crushes spy on their ex-boyfriend's new girlfriends. Not grown women with a marriage behind them. It was something I might have done at thirteen, if I'd been aware of Rafe that way back then. But it certainly wasn't something any self-respecting woman my age should be doing.

That knowledge notwithstanding, I forgot all about the green velvet dress and headed for the parking garage too, a couple of yards behind, while I tried to look like I just happened to be going the same way at the exact same time.

The new girlfriend was dressed in jeans and boots: tight jeans that fit her butt like a second skin, and high heels that made that same butt swing tantalizingly left to right. Several men turned to stare on the short walk to the exit doors, and I felt quite sedate in my knee-length coat and knee-high boots. Maybe that was what Rafe liked about her.

She was sexy. I'm a lady.

Figured he'd prefer the tramp.

The Green Hills mall has two levels. The attached parking garage has three: two inside plus the roof. The street level spots tend to get filled first. Since it was the lunch hour and just a week before Christmas, I'd had to drive up to the roof in order to find parking. As I wandered along I wondered what I'd do if Miss Thing had parked on a lower level. I could follow her and see what kind of car she got into, but then I'd have to run up to the roof for my own car, and by the time I got outside, I'd probably have lost her.

Or I could go directly to the roof and get my car, and cruise through the parking garage and hopefully pick up her car on its way out, but what if she wasn't planning to leave? Maybe she just wanted to dump some of the dozen or so bags she was carrying in her trunk before going back into the mall to do more shopping. If so, I'd have given up my parking spot for nothing, and I probably wouldn't find another.

In the end, Miss Thing made it easy. She headed for the stairs and started climbing to the roof herself, so all I had to do was follow. Once up there, I lingered just inside the stairwell and watched as she went straight for a red Mercedes parked a few spaces over from my Volvo. It was a convertible, but the top was up now in the middle of winter. I heard her undo the alarm with a couple of quick beeps, and then the lid of the trunk raised up all on its own. She dumped the shopping bags inside and the lid lowered again, slowly and expensively. I have to slam my own lid, so it's possible I was just a tiny bit envious. Not only did she have Rafe, but she had a better car than I did, too.

She hesitated for a second before getting in, and I held my breath, ready to scurry back down the stairs if she looked like she planned to return to the mall. But she didn't. She just glanced around once—I shrank into the shadows, out of sight—before opening the car door and sliding into the front seat. I watched as she reversed out of the parking space and pointed the nose of the car toward the ramp to the lower levels. And although I was worried about losing her, I made myself wait until she was out of sight before I ran across the concrete to my own car, cranked the key in the ignition, and followed.

I caught up downstairs on street level, and idled behind her as she waited to exit the garage and merge with traffic on Hillsboro Road. I wasn't the only one, so I didn't think she'd necessarily notice that I was following her. There was a Jeep behind me, also signaling to go left toward downtown and the interstate, followed by a small white compact—a Toyota, I thought, although it might have been a Honda or a Nissan—and then some kind of black SUV with tinted windows. Next to us were four cars heading in the opposite direction, south on Hillsboro, toward Forest Hills.

The light down on the corner changed, and Miss Thing zoomed across four lanes of road and made tracks. I gave a quick look left and right and left again and followed. Behind me, the Jeep pulled up to the white line, just as two lines of cars emerged from over the hill. Looked like everyone else would have to wait.

Green Hills noontime traffic is killer, though, and by the time we'd made it up and over the hill, and down the other side to the second set of traffic lights, the Jeep, compact and SUV had caught up. Or maybe they were different cars, not the ones I'd seen. There are thousands of white Toyotas on the road, and black SUVs are also plentiful. This might just be another white compact and another SUV with tinted windows. At any rate, all but the Jeep headed down the entrance ramp onto Interstate 440 and spread out over the three lanes there. I moved one lane over but made sure to stay behind the Mercedes—maybe that way, Miss Thing wouldn't realize I was following her—while the compact stayed behind me and the SUV sped up and merged into the far, fastest, lane.

I-440 happens to be the way back to East Nashville and home, but Miss Thing didn't go that way. Where I would have merged onto I-65

North after a mile or two, the red Mercedes continued straight for a few exits, and then signaled to leave the interstate at Nolensville Road. I did the same, and slid in behind her halfway up the exit ramp, as if I'd just realized I was in the wrong lane for turning right.

And off we went down Nolensville Road. It's one of the more seedy parts of town, with a lot of ethnic grocery stores and storefront churches with lettering in different languages. I counted Spanish, Korean, and what looked like Swahili, but which may only have been some variety of Caribbean. There were lots of people of various ethnicities wandering around: short Hispanic women with children in tow, men in turbans and women in saris, the occasional tall African in a tribal patterned caftan and matching cap.

Just after we passed the Krispy Kreme donut store near the corner of Thompson Lane, the Mercedes signaled a right turn into more of an industrial area. By now, I'd managed to put a few cars between us, and I thought it would be safe to follow, as long as I kept a bit of distance to the Mercedes. It wasn't difficult to do: the red car stood out among the gray road, gray buildings, and gray, leafless trees like a beacon; all I had to do was keep it in sight.

Miss Thing drove for a few blocks, and then turned left into a parking lot beside a big warehouse building. There were a couple of other cars in the lot as well, but no indication what sort of business it was. I drove slowly past, while Miss Thing got out of the Mercedes and undulated her way toward a door on the corner of the building. By the time I had reached the stop sign on the next corner, she'd disappeared inside.

I drove another block and then turned around, trying to decide what to do next.

By now it was going on two o'clock. I had three and a half hours until I'd be picked up for dinner. It wasn't like I planned to make much of an effort for Bradley—he didn't deserve my effort, the jerk—but at the same time, no woman likes to go out looking less than her best.

And no ex-wife likes to look less than stunning when coming face to face with her ex-husband. So I'd definitely have to make sure I looked halfway presentable.

Miss Thing would be back outside sometime. It wasn't like she lived here. It was a warehouse, not a residence. She'd have to go home sometime, and I could follow her and figure out where she lived. Although she might work here, and if so, she'd probably stay until five or even five thirty. And by then, I'd have to be home getting ready for Bradley.

And I didn't even have anything appropriate to wear. In the excitement over seeing her, I'd forgotten all about needing a new dress. My savings account was thanking me, since I didn't really have the money for a new dress, but it made things more difficult. It wasn't like I could show up in something Bradley's money had paid for.

That's as far as I got by the time the phone rang. A quick glance at the display told me the caller was Tamara Grimaldi.

"Detective?"

"Ms. Martin. I have that information you wanted."

I had to think about it before I remembered what kind of information I'd asked her for. "About Mr. Driscoll?"

"That's it. Harold Driscoll died of a heart attack. At home in his own bed in the middle of the night, with no one in attendance except his loving wife. No suspicion of foul play. No autopsy. The wife claimed they'd had wine and sex before going to sleep, and the general consensus was that the effort had been too much for his heart. His wife was considerably younger, so it made sense that he might have had a hard time keeping up."

"I suppose," I said, dissatisfied. "His ex-wife said he didn't have heart problems."

There was a pause.

"Excuse me?" Grimaldi said.

"He was married before Maybelle. And left his wife for her. The first wife said he didn't have a bad heart."

"You talked to her?"

"How else would I know what she'd said? And before you can start yelling at me, I didn't go alone. I took Alexandra Puckett with me. Since they used to be neighbors, I thought it might make her more likely to talk."

"You took a sixteen year old girl with you to interview a witness." It was a statement of fact, uttered in a very calm, non-committal voice. It was, frankly, pretty scary.

"It's not like I went into the ghetto," I said defensively. "Carolyn lives in a nice stone cottage in Madison. Very quiet, settled neighborhood. What Tim likes to call Old Lady Acres. And it wasn't official police business. I'm not meddling in an open investigation. You said it yourself, that Harold died of a heart attack."

"That doesn't mean I want you to go to his ex-wife and give her the idea that it was something more," Grimaldi said. "Especially if it *was* something more. Some people do crazy things when they think you suspect them of murder."

That's certainly true.

"Sorry," I said. "But I don't think Carolyn had anything to do with it."

"Let's hope so," Grimaldi said. "And in the future, I'd appreciate a call if you decide to do something stupid like that. Your mother's a scary woman. I don't want to have to call her to explain that something's happened to you."

"Just call Dix and have him tell her," I said.

"Sure. I'll do that. Or you could just stay home and behave in a way appropriate to your mother's daughter."

There was a pause while I thought it over. When I didn't answer, Grimaldi spoke again. "Did the first Mrs. Driscoll say anything else?"

I thought back. "Not much. Although she did confirm that Maybelle had been married before. Her first husband doted on her, so after he died she needed help balancing her checkbook, and that's how she met Harold Driscoll."

"You're kidding," the detective said.

"Sadly, I'm not. It seems Harold bought it, hook, line and sinker. Carolyn didn't, of course, but there was nothing she could do."

"Right." Grimaldi hesitated, perhaps intrigued despite her better judgment. "Anything else?"

"Not from Carolyn. But Dix called me back with information on Maybelle's previous husband. Joshua Rowland from Natchez, Mississippi. As it happens, my ex-mother-in-law's maiden name was Rowland. And Althea is also from Natchez."

"Small world."

I agreed that it was, for the second time today. "I called Bradley. Turns out Joshua was his uncle. Bradley and I are having dinner tonight to talk about it."

"I thought your ex-husband was remarried," Grimaldi said.

"He is. But she's busy."

"Uh-huh." Her voice was dry. "You're not planning to do anything stupid, are you, Ms. Martin?"

"Like what?" And then I realized what she was getting at. "Oh, gack! No. Not at all. Bradley's a jerk. Shelby's welcome to him. And Rafe isn't important enough for that."

"Glad to hear it," Grimaldi said, although her voice didn't lose that dryness that made it sound like she didn't believe me. "So you're getting together with your ex to discuss his uncle?"

"Apparently Uncle Joshua was married to Maybelle for a few years. He was in his late forties, she was in her twenties when they got married."

"Big difference."

I nodded into the phone. "There was fifteen years between her and Harold, so a little better the second time. As far as Steven Puckett goes, I don't think he's more than a few years older than she is."

"So maybe she's just always liked men in their forties," Grimaldi said. "Long before she was in her forties herself."

"Maybe so. Do you want me to call and tell you what I find out?" If anything at all.

"Tomorrow's sufficient," Grimaldi said. "Big night tonight."

She hung up. I did the same, and went back to waiting and watching.

It was boring, and by three o'clock I was ready to leave. There'd been no activity since Miss Thing went inside the warehouse. No one coming or going, no deliveries or pickups.

Annoyingly, I didn't even know what sort of place it was. It ought to have a sign on it, something other than just the street number on the corner of the building.

On impulse I dialed the number for the office. A moment later, Brittany's perpetually perky voice came on the line. "Thank you for calling LB&A. How may I direct your call?"

"It's Savannah," I said.

"Oh." The perkiness slipped right off. It's reserved for customers. "What do you want?"

"I need you to look something up for me in the tax records."

"Why can't you do it?"

"Because I'm in the car," I said, "and I need the information now, while I'm here. I can't go home and look it up and then drive back across town once I get it. It'll take you thirty seconds. Please."

She huffed. "Fine. What is it?"

"A commercial property. I have the address." I gave it to her. "I need to know what kind of business it is and who owns it."

I could hear the tapping of computer keys through the phone. "Belongs to a corporation called BGH," Brittany said. "There's a mortgage to the tune of two million on the property. The zoning is CR-10."

Restricted commercial. Businesses with CR-10 zoning are away from city center, and they are non-customer related businesses. Warehouses and wholesalers, mostly. Exactly the kind of zoning I'd expect for a warehouse in this depressing part of town.

"Anything else?"

"No," Brittany said, sounding pleased.

"Can you look up BGH? See if they own anything else?"

Brittany huffed but did it. "Another commercial property in the same area." She gave me an address on Nolensville Road, that I scribbled down on the back of an old receipt for coffee I dug out of my purse. "This one has a CPC-10 land use."

Commercial property, subject to certain conditions. In other words, a business where, most likely, ordinary people could come and go. Store, clinic, restaurant, hookah lounge.

"Any idea what kind of business it is?"

Brittany didn't. "Why don't you just drive over there and see? If you're in that area anyway?"

"Maybe I will. Anything else?"

"One more," Brittany said. "Another CR-10 out here in East Nashville. Looks like it might be on the river." She gave me an address I scribbled below the other one on the envelope. "Anything else I can do for you?"

Her tone of voice suggested that the answer had better be no. She was probably overdue for updating her Facebook status.

"No," I said. "Thank you." And then I put the phone away and started the car. There was no sense in sitting here any longer. Rafe's girlfriend was probably hard at work inside the warehouse and wouldn't be out until long after I would have to leave to get ready for dinner with Bradley. I might as well head out and take a look at the other properties BGH owned on my way home.

The address on Nolensville wasn't hard to find. I took a right and drove six or seven blocks, past the entrance to the Nashville Zoo and past Harding Place, into the Tusculum neighborhood. And there it was, on the left side of the street: a long, low building painted black with purple trim, with no windows and a reinforced steel door. On the flat wall next to the door was a mural: a rather uninspired painting of a couple dancing what looked like a tango, with a palm tree and what I thought was supposed to be the ocean in the background. Curving above them were the words *La Havana*.

A nightclub?

At this time of the afternoon, it was deserted. The parking lot was empty and there was no sign of life. I pulled into the lot, contemplated the building for a few seconds, and pulled back out, in the direction of home.

Fifteen minutes later I was back in East Nashville and on my way down South 5th Street in the direction of the Cumberland River. It wasn't the first time I'd driven here, and the closer I got to the address Brittany had given me, the more my sense of déjà vu increased. When I turned a bend in the road and saw my destination up ahead, there was no surprise involved at all. I had once spent a couple hours in my car in the parking lot across the street, watching Melendez Import/Export, hoping to see the boss, Julio Melendez, to determine whether he looked enough like Rafe to be able to pass for him in coveralls and a ski mask.

That's another long story. And after all my efforts, Julio hadn't turned out to be a murderer after all. Someone else had killed my friend Lila. But here I was, back again, and there was a sense of inevitability about it. A feeling of fate, of things coming full circle.

I pulled into the parking lot across the street, the one belonging to a children's charity, where I'd spent the time last time. And then I cut the engine and sat there for a few minutes peering over at the warehouse while the air inside the car got chilly.

The warehouse looked deserted now. Last time I was here, things had been going on over there. A tractor trailer had been backed up to the loading dock on the side of the building, and there'd been cars in the parking lot. Eventually, at the close of business, people had come outside and had gotten into those cars and driven away. All except Julio. I never did see him. Before I got that far something else happened. Namely, I'd sat here a while and then Rafe had shown up and invited himself into my car. We'd spent twenty minutes or so talking, and then MNPD's finest—Spicer and Truman—had come along and rousted us. They were coming to apprehend Julio, and they wanted us—or at least me—out of the way first.

None of that happened this time. Nothing changed across the street, and nobody accosted me. After a few minutes, I turned the car back on again and headed for home, enjoying the blast of hot air from the vents.

It had been a while since I'd thought about Julio Melendez. He was still in jail, or so I assumed. I hadn't heard differently. Tamara Grimaldi had nabbed him along with several of his cronies back in September, and had managed to scrape together enough evidence to prove that they were behind the open house robberies, even if they hadn't been guilty of Lila's death. Rafe had skated through as usual, although he'd been involved in the open house robberies up to his eyebrows. At the time, I'd thought he'd just been lucky. He'd had a lot of that kind of luck over the past ten years.

Now I knew that it wasn't luck so much as design. The TBI needed him on the loose; it was the only way he could keep working for them. So they allowed him to be hauled in for questioning once in a while, and sometimes they even let local law enforcement hang onto him for a few days, but he was always let go again for lack of evidence.

Anyway, it was just a couple of months ago that Julio had been arrested; there was no way he'd have gotten released again so soon. Although I supposed I could call Tamara Grimaldi to check, just to make sure.

I had the phone in my hand and was dialing by the time I realized that it might not be such a good idea to tip the detective off to what I was doing. If I called and asked about Julio Melendez, she'd want to know why, and then I'd have to explain about BGH and the warehouse in South Nashville. I couldn't fib, because the detective is almost as good at smelling a lie as my brother Dix. It probably comes with the territory. I would have to confess to having followed Rafe's new girlfriend from the Green Hills Mall to the warehouse, and that would make me look and feel like an idiot, and the detective wouldn't hold back when she pointed it out—so perhaps it was better if I didn't call. I put the phone back down on the seat next to me.

Julio had had a girlfriend, a professional stager named Heather Price. (A stager is someone who works closely with realtors and people trying to sell their houses. She—sometimes he—helps to decorate, or stage, the home to show to best advantage.) Heather had staged all the houses where things had been stolen, and Tamara Grimaldi had been pretty sure she'd turned Julio on to the valuables. But there had been no evidence of it. Heather had sworn up and down that she'd talked to her boyfriend in good faith, never imagining he'd use the information she shared to rob her clients, and he had sworn up and down she hadn't known what he was doing with the information he got from her. There was nothing Grimaldi could do but to let her go.

Heather and I hadn't been close, but we'd been casual acquaintances. If I gave her a call, she might tell me whether Julio was on the loose.

I picked the phone back up and scrolled through my numbers with one hand while I steered the car with the other. I was pretty sure I'd added her name to my address book back then, since as a realtor, I never knew when a stager might come in handy.

The phone rang a couple of times on the other end, and then the machine picked up. "This is Heather with The Right Price Staging. Please leave your name and number at the sound of the tone, and I'll get back to you. Thanks."

I waited for the beep and gave my name and number, reminding her of who I was. I didn't mention my reason for calling, since I wanted her to call back, and if she knew it was about Julio, she might not. Better to let her think I might be calling about business. No, I'm not above using subterfuge when I have to. Of course I didn't actually say I was calling about business—I don't lie unless it's absolutely necessary, mainly because I'm so bad at it—but I didn't say it wasn't, either.

With that done, and nothing more I could think of to do at the moment, I headed home to prepare for my date with Bradley while I waited for something to happen.

Ten

True to his word, Bradley rang the buzzer at five thirty sharp. By then I was dressed and made up, in the red dress I'd bought for Todd's proposal and strappy silver sandals. My hair was piled on top of my head with tendrils floating down, and I looked, if I do say so myself, good. Bradley's reaction when he saw me reinforced the impression. And although I didn't really care, deep down it gave me a certain level of satisfaction to see his eyes widen and his jaw drop for a second before he pulled himself together. "Savannah. You look lovely." He bowed over my hand.

"Thank you, Bradley," I said demurely, reverting back to the proper Southern Belle I was supposed to be.

He took my elbow and guided me toward the car. It was a BMW, idling at the curb; new since we'd gotten divorced. "I hope you don't mind. I made reservations at Fidelio's."

Fidelio's again. And yes, I did mind. I was sick of the place. If I never saw the inside of Fidelio's again for as long as I lived, it wouldn't be too soon. But of course I didn't say so.

"Wonderful," I said instead and let him hand me into the passenger seat and close the door behind me. He has beautiful manners. Mother had always liked that about him. I had, too. Right up until he slept with Shelby.

We spent the drive mostly in silence. Bradley was battling rush hour traffic through downtown, and had to keep his concentration on the road. And I enjoyed the smooth ride and the smell of the new leather interior, and figured I'd just wait until we were at the restaurant to tackle the question of Uncle Joshua and his wife.

Of course, there was the small talk to get through first. "So how have you been, Savannah?" Bradley asked as soon as we were seated.

"Good," I said. "You?"

He leaned back and sort of expanded. "Very well, thank you. You said you've seen Shelby, so you know we're expecting."

I nodded. "I'm very happy for you." And happier for Shelby, since—when I'd been married to him and expecting his baby—he hadn't seemed to care much. The fact that he was excited now boded well, I thought.

Bradley thanked me, without making reference to the fact that he and I had once been pregnant too. "So what have you been doing with yourself lately? I haven't seen you around."

That was because we'd stopped traveling in the same circles once we got divorced.

"I worked at the mall for a while," I said, "right after we separated."

Bradley nodded. "I was honestly surprised that you didn't move back to Sweetwater."

"I guess I wanted to prove that I could survive on my own, without help." And by then I'd started to question my long-held belief that mother always knew best. If she did, shouldn't my life have turned out differently?

"And the real estate?" Bradley asked.

"That came later." A year and a half later, specifically. I'd gotten tired of the makeup counter by then, and worried that if I stayed there, it was all I'd ever do. Plus, mother was pushing me to go back to school and finish my law degree, and I couldn't imagine anything I wanted less. Unless it was getting remarried. But I did agree that it was time to do *something*. I'd always enjoyed architecture, and spent most of my Sunday afternoons, when I wasn't working, visiting open houses in the neighborhood. That's where I'd met Walker Lamont, my first broker, who had noticed me coming and going weekend after weekend. At first he thought I'd been looking for a house to buy, but I wasn't in a financial position to be able to do that. I'd told him I just liked looking. He'd told me I should become a realtor. I'd thought about it and decided he had a point. So I'd gone to night school to get my real estate license, and then I'd sought out Walker and asked if I could work for him. And the rest, as they say, is history. All the way up until I accused him of murder and he went off to prison.

"And is it working out well for you?" Bradley asked.

I smiled. "I can't complain." Mostly because I didn't want Bradley to think I wasn't excelling on my own. The truth was, I could certainly be doing better. But I was keeping my head above water, and that's all he needed to know.

"Wonderful," Bradley said and showed all his teeth in a blinding smile.

He's a good-looking guy, if you like the type. Tall, cool, and blond in a business suit and tie, with gray eyes and a very slightly pointy nose. He looked affluent, well-educated, and a little self-satisfied. Marriage to Shelby seemed to agree with him, because I estimated that he'd gained fifteen or twenty pounds since we'd gotten divorced, and he was looking just a little thick around the middle. His forehead might be just a touch higher too, but that could have been wishful thinking on my part.

Since by this point my idea of male beauty was Rafe—who looks like he's stepped off the cover of a romance novel about Navy SEALs—Bradley left me indifferent. A good thing too, since he was married to someone else by now and I shouldn't be thinking about him in those terms.

I had thought I might, to be honest. Or I'd been worried I would. We'd been married for two years, and had dated for a year or two before that. We'd had good times during those years. We'd been reasonably close and physically intimate. I'd wondered whether, seeing him again, it might be awkward, whether some of those old feelings might come back, just out of habit.

They hadn't. I looked at him and felt very little of anything. Being here wasn't awkward, but it wasn't particularly comfortable, either. I wasn't happy to see him, but on the other hand, I wasn't unhappy. He was just there, something I had to deal with. I guess it's true what they say: the opposite of love isn't hatred, it's indifference.

"Tell me about your Uncle Joshua."

"Right," Bradley said. "Uncle Josh. What's going on?"

I thought I'd already given him this information, but I went over it again. "A couple of months ago, a colleague of mine named Brenda Puckett was murdered. You probably saw it on the news. There was a lot of media interest. I happened to find her body."

"I remember that," Bradley said, diverted. "How horrible for you, Savannah."

"It was pretty unpleasant. Anyway, Maybelle Driscoll got herself engaged to Steven Puckett, Brenda's husband, less than a week after the funeral. Turns out they'd been sleeping together for a while already."

And come to think of it, Maybelle had used the same sort of ruse on Steven as she had on Harold seven years earlier. Her husband was dead and she was all alone, a poor, defenseless, helpless widow in need of a big, strong man. And Steven, who'd lived his life firmly under Brenda's thumb, had taken one look at Maybelle—so different from the strident, bossy shrew he'd married—and fallen like an overripe pear.

Bradley looked a little uncomfortable at the mention of the adultery, which hadn't been my intention. The fact that we'd divorced because he'd cheated on me hadn't even crossed my mind, to be honest. Not that I minded giving him that quick jab. It was nice that he cared enough to feel guilty. He'd never evinced much guilt when we went through our divorce.

But that was neither here nor there at the moment. "They've set a wedding day just before New Year. And Brenda's daughter is unhappy. She doesn't want Maybelle for a stepmother."

"No one in their right mind would want Maybelle for a stepmother," Bradley muttered. "She's the type of woman who'd eat her young. And probably her husband too, after coitus."

Interesting observation. "What makes you say that?"

Bradley opened his mouth, but just then the waiter reappeared with the drinks we'd ordered—white wine for me, red for Bradley; I should have known when we had different tastes in wine that it would never last—and lingered to take our food order. I ordered what I always ordered at Fidelio's: the Chicken Marsala. Bradley asked for good old-fashioned Chicken Fettuccine Alfredo, and threw in some steamed broccoli, perhaps to help him feel virtuous. The waiter retreated.

"Eat her young?" I prompted.

Bradley shook his head. "I probably shouldn't have said that. I can't prove anything."

"This is off the record," I said. "Nobody's going to hold you to anything. I'm just trying to gather some information for Alexandra."

Bradley nodded. He grabbed a piece of still-warm bread out of the basket the waiter had left, plunged it into the fragrant oil beside the basket, and lifted it, dripping, to his mouth. I waited while he chewed, trying to contain my impatience.

"The thing is," Bradley said, around a mouthful of bread—I guess I wasn't important enough to rate a display of proper table manners, "I don't know anything. Not really. Just that I don't like her."

"Why don't you just let me ask you a couple of questions?" I tried not to feel too much like Sally Baxter, girl reporter.

Bradley nodded, his mouth full of bread. "Shoot."

It was clear to see where those extra twenty pounds had come from.

He was happily married, settled in his career, and past thirty... I guessed he'd decided that it wasn't important to keep his boyish figure.

Rafe was past thirty, my treacherous mind reminded me, and he hadn't let himself go. Of course, he wasn't married or settled in his career; maybe that would make a difference.

And then I remembered that I wasn't likely to be around to see whether he went to pot after he settled down, and turned my attention back to Bradley.

"Your uncle was in his late forties when he married Maybelle, right? Had he ever been married before?"

Bradley shook his head, chewing.

"Was he shy? A misogynist? Questioning his sexuality?"

"Just busy," Bradley said, swallowing. "Married to this work. He started day trading in his twenties, and spent the next two decades doing it. There was no time for a wife."

"Day trading?"

Bradley nodded, his hand descending into the bread basket again. "Playing the stock market."

"Did he do well?"

"Well enough to leave a couple million dollars when he died," Bradley said, dunking another piece of bread in oil. "Maybelle would have gotten it all, except my dad insisted on a prenup. Said he knew a gold-digger when he saw one. Uncle Joshua wasn't very happy about that, but he didn't expect to die anytime soon, and he said he'd tear it up on their tenth wedding anniversary. Dad told him that if she stuck for ten years, she would have earned half of everything."

"But she didn't."

Bradley shook his head. "Two and a half years later Uncle Joshua was dead. And Auntie Maybelle was half a million dollars richer."

It wasn't two million, but it wasn't anything to sneeze at, either.

"How did it happen? Your uncle's passing?"

"He died quietly in his own bed," Bradley said. "Heart attack in his sleep. After, apparently, an evening of passionate lovemaking."

He grimaced, as if the idea was unwholesome, and popped another piece of bread into his mouth.

I felt a *frisson* go down my back. That was exactly how Detective Grimaldi had described Harold Driscoll's demise, almost word for word.

"What?" Bradley said thickly, watching my face. I guess he still knew me well enough to be able to tell when something was going on in my head.

I shook it. Bradley's a lawyer; there was no sense in giving him ideas. Where Carolyn Driscoll wouldn't automatically think of causing a stink if she suspected something criminal, Bradley might. "Do you have any idea where they met?"

"Sure," Bradley said, swallowing. "A cruise. New Orleans to Mexico. Uncle Joshua needed a break from the stock market. Everyone said he was working too hard, and he needed to relax. So he booked a cruise. By the time he got back a week later, they were engaged."

He reached for the bread basket. When he relinquished it, I snagged a piece of bread for myself, figuring it was the only way I was likely to get one. "What did you think of Maybelle?"

"To be honest," Bradley said, dragging his piece of bread through the oil dish, "I didn't know her well. She didn't seem to like us, and of course mother hated her."

"Did you go to the wedding?"

He shook his head. "It was a private ceremony. Just the two of them."

"I guess Maybelle didn't care about making nice with Uncle Joshua's family."

"No," Bradley said, lifting the piece of bread, "but I don't know that I can blame her, the way my dad was going on and on about the prenup. Not that he was wrong." He popped the bread in his mouth and chewed.

"Anything else you can tell me about her?"

Bradley pondered while his jaws kept chomping. I nibbled daintily on my own piece of dry bread while I waited. "Can't think of anything," he finally said when he'd swallowed. "But you might check into her former husband."

Another one?

"Supposedly," Bradley said in response to my query, leaning back from the table as the waiter appeared with two steaming plates of food. He deposited them in front of each of us and stepped back, running an experienced gaze over the table for refills.

"A little more bread?"

Bradley glanced at the basket, which was empty, and then at me. "Savannah?"

"That would be lovely," I said, and did my best not to feel resentful that Bradley had tried to make it look like I'd been the one who had eaten all the bread.

The waiter removed himself and the basket.

"Any idea who her first husband was?" If Maybelle had married Uncle Joshua while still in her twenties, surely whoever she'd been married to beforehand would have to have been her first.

"No," Bradley said, eyes on his food, "but I can find out. After dinner."

"How?"

He glanced up. "My dad did a background check on her, when she first showed up. He'll have it somewhere."

"How about now?" It's rude to make a call while you're sitting down to dinner with someone else, but we were divorced; those courtesies didn't really matter. He'd already broken the big one by cheating on me with Shelby. And if we waited, it might be too late. John wasn't known for keeping late hours.

"He'll be at dinner," Bradley said and reached for his fork. "And besides, the food will get cold." He dug in. I smothered a sigh and did the same.

HE DID MAKE THE CALL, BUT not until we were back in the car on our way home. By then, my former father-in-law had finished dinner as well, and was relaxing in front of the TV. Or so Bradley reported after getting off the phone with him. "The information is at the office. He'll look for it in the morning."

"I appreciate it," I said, since it was the only thing I could say.

He sent me a sideways look. "What are you trying to accomplish with this, Savannah?"

"I'm not entirely sure," I admitted. "Steven Puckett's daughter is afraid that something bad will happen to her dad if he marries Maybelle. I started out with the idea that Maybelle may have caused her last husband's heart attack. But it doesn't seem that way. So I guess I'm just winding up threads, really. One thing leads to another. From Harold to Uncle Joshua to—maybe—a former husband."

Bradley nodded. "And what do you plan to do with the information once you have it?"

I didn't know that either. Although— "I have a friend in the police department. If I discover anything that seems significant, I'll let her know. Maybe there's something she can do about it. And if not, I can at least let Steven Puckett know. He might change his mind about marrying her if he realizes she's been married several times and they've all died."

"You're being careful, aren't you?" Bradley asked. He looked a little uncomfortable, I noticed. "I know we're not married anymore, but I don't want anything bad to happen to you."

"That's sweet." Even if I knew it was motivated mostly by guilt. I was a poor divorcée with no man to take care of me, and it was all his fault. "I'm doing my best."

Bradley nodded. "It was nice to spend time with you again, Savannah."

"You too," I said politely, since it hadn't been too painful, everything considered. And the food had been good. I hoped he hadn't gotten the impression that it was something I wanted to continue doing, though. I guess it was good that we'd put the past behind us and were able to be civil to one another, but I'd been happy not seeing him for the past couple years, and would be happy to continue in that same vein.

Bradley hesitated. "Are you seeing anyone these days?"

Just in case this was the opening volley in an attempt to talk me into going out with him again, I said firmly, "Yes. Todd Satterfield and I see one another occasionally. He has proposed."

Bradley's brow furrowed as he thought about it. "He was at our wedding, right?"

I nodded. We'd gotten married in the church in Sweetwater, and mother had invited everyone who was anyone to the wedding, including my old boyfriend. "He's the assistant D.A. for Maury County. I've known him my whole life."

"Did you say yes?

I shook my head. "Not yet."

"Why not?"

"I'm also seeing someone else. Someone you've never met."

"And has he proposed, too?" Bradley wanted to know.

No, and he wasn't likely to. And even if he did, I probably shouldn't accept anyway. Marrying Rafe would be awful. I'd always worry. If he were ten minutes late for dinner, I'd be in a panic, certain that he'd never come home again.

"Well," Bradley said, effectively stopping the conversation dead, "I hope you'll work it out. And that you'll be happy. I never wanted to hurt you, Savannah."

"I'm sure you didn't," I said. "Don't worry about it, Bradley. It's in the past. Forgotten."

"Thank you," Bradley said.

We drove the rest of the way in silence, until we pulled up to the curb outside my building. Bradley cut the engine.

"Don't worry about walking me up," I said. "I can manage."

"Are you sure?"

"Of course. I come and go all the time by myself. I'm sure you're eager to get home. Shelby might be there soon."

Bradley nodded, a flicker of guilt crossing his face. I guessed he might be wondering whether she could already be there, and what he'd say if she asked him where he'd been.

"You'll call me tomorrow, right? To tell me what your father says?"

He promised he would. I was just about to say goodbye and open the car door when it opened on its own.

I jumped, and I think Bradley did too, although I wasn't looking at him.

"Ready?" Rafe's voice said, his tone unusually tight. I took his hand and let him help me out of the car. My skin tingled where I touched his.

"Savannah?" Bradley said from inside the SUV, and I turned to see a worried expression on his face as he leaned across the passenger seat to stare at Rafe.

I smiled. "It's all right. You should get home to Shelby."

"Will you be OK?"

"I'll be fine," I said, although given the look on Rafe's face, maybe not. "Just call me tomorrow, OK?"

Bradley hesitated, but eventually he nodded and put the car in gear. I slammed the door and waited for him to pull away from the curb before I turned to Rafe, my heart beating faster. "What are you doing here?"

He didn't answer, and I wasn't surprised. Instead, he glanced at the taillights of the car disappearing down the street before turning back to me. "Shelby?"

"His wife. I told you he got remarried."

"Who?"

"Bradley," I said. "My ex-husband."

"That was Bradley?"

I nodded. Rafe's lips twitched.

"What?" I said crossly.

He shook his head. "What're you doing, dating your ex?"

"It wasn't a date," I said.

"Dinner at a nice restaurant? Just the two of you, without his wife? I'd call it a date."

Part of me wanted to ask if he was jealous, but what if he said no? "How do you know where we were?" I asked instead.

"Followed you," Rafe answered.

To Fidelio's? "Why?"

"Wanted to talk to you."

"So why didn't you come inside?" It couldn't have been any fun sitting outside in the car for the hour or more we'd spent lingering over dinner.

"Didn't wanna disturb you," Rafe said. "Just in case you got lucky."

"He's my ex-husband!" The guy I'd had to fake orgasms for during our entire marriage. A fact Rafe was perfectly well aware of.

"I didn't know that," Rafe said. "Wasn't like he had *loser* tattooed on this forehead."

That was true. He couldn't know whether Bradley was Bradley or someone else from looking at him. I conceded the point. "What did you want to talk about?"

"Carmen," Rafe said.

"Excuse me?" After all that effort—showing up at my apartment, following me to Fidelio's, and sitting outside in the parking lot before following me back home again—it would have been nice if he'd wanted to discuss something important. "Who's Carmen?" As if I couldn't guess.

"The woman you were following around this afternoon," Rafe said. "What the hell were you thinking, Savannah?"

Oops. The tone of his voice as well as the name—my own, as

opposed to the endearment he usually uses—told me how deadly serious he was.

"Did she see me?"

"No," Rafe said, with barely discernable patience, "I did."

"I didn't see you."

"You weren't supposed to," Rafe said.

Touché. Well, technically, he wasn't supposed to have seen me either. I guess I'm just not as good at sneaking around as he is.

"I just wanted to know who she was," I said.

"Uh-huh. Why?"

"Curiosity."

He nodded. "Sure."

"You don't think I have the right to be curious? A couple weeks ago we were up there—" I gestured to the second floor, where my apartment was, "—rolling around on my bed, naked. Now you're eating at Fidelio's with someone else. Someone you look at the way you used to look at me. And you didn't even have the courtesy to call and tell me you were back in town! After everything that happened, you couldn't do me that favor?"

His eyes softened, and I rushed on, before I could look too closely and see pity. "What's the big deal, anyway? So I followed your new girlfriend from the mall to her job. Why do you care, if she didn't even see me?"

"I don't want anything to happen to you," Rafe said.

That took some of the wind out of my sails, I admit. I fought against it. "Like you care."

His voice didn't change. "I never wanted you to get hurt."

"You should have thought of that before you walked out on me two weeks ago," I said.

And then, before he could open his mouth, I shook my head. "Never mind. Your girlfriend's safe. The next time I see her, I'll pretend I have no idea who she is. Just like I'm supposed to do with you. Anything else?"

He shook his head.

"In that case, I think this conversation had better be over. And next time you come to me and want to talk, I suggest you find something to talk about other than your new girlfriend!"

I stalked away from him, toward the gate. Part of me hoped he'd follow, and all of me was on the alert for a sound from behind, my body already jangling with anticipation... but it didn't come. By the time I'd unlocked the gate, stepped through, and closed it behind me, and looked back, he was gone.

Eleven

I'd barely had time to walk into the apartment and hang my purse on the hook in the hallway when my phone rang. For a second my heart jumped, and I was sure—I was absolutely certain—it would be Rafe.

It wasn't.

I punched the button and put the phone to my ear. "Heather?"

"Hi, Savannah," Heather Price's cool voice said. "What can I do for you?"

I blinked. That was certainly straight to the point. Then again, the last time I'd seen her, she'd been called away from the lunch table to be arrested, so I guess maybe the thought of me didn't inspire fuzzy feelings.

"I just had a quick question."

"What?" Heather said.

"About your boyfriend. Or ex-boyfriend."

She was silent, and I added, "Julio?"

"What about him?" Heather said.

"I just wanted to know whether he was still around. You know... out and about."

"He's in jail," Heather said. She didn't say 'thanks to you,' but her tone implied it.

"Does he still own that warehouse down by the river?" I twisted a tendril of hair around my finger. "I have a client who's looking for a commercial property like that."

"He never owned it," Heather said.

"He didn't?"

"That's what I said. It belongs to his boss. Julio was just running it."

"I see," I said. "What's his boss's name?"

"Hector," Heather said. "Hector Gonzales."

"What does Hector do?"

"Anything he wants." She chuckled, and it wasn't a nice laugh. I had my mouth open to continue the conversation, but she'd already hung up.

But at least I'd gotten a name. And as I wandered into the living room and sank down on the sofa, to relieve some of the stress on my feet from the high heels, I pondered. Julio Melendez was Hispanic. Hector Gonzales was a Spanish name. So was Carmen.

Come to think of it, Jorge Pena had also been Hispanic.

And then there was the nightclub in South Nashville, the one that must also be owned by Mr. Gonzales. It was called *La Havana*. Again, Spanish. Or perhaps Cuban.

I looked down at my lap, covered in red satin, and my feet, in strappy silver sandals.

I could go to a nightclub and not look out of place.

I didn't look even a little bit Hispanic, of course. But surely Caucasians went to *La Havana*, too? It couldn't just be Nashville's Hispanic population, could it?

Maybe it could. And if so, I guess I'd stick out like a sore thumb. But I'd never know unless I tried.

Five minutes later I was in the car heading for South Nashville. Twenty minutes after that, I pulled into the parking lot outside

La Havana. And by night, it was a very different place than it had been this afternoon. The parking lot was full, the building itself was literally vibrating with Latin rhythms, and the reinforced steel door was standing open, with people spilling out. The women were dressed much as I were, in skimpy dresses and high heels, while the men were more casual, in jeans or slacks, T-shirts or open-collared dress shirts.

Yes, they were mostly all Hispanic.

As I stood there, shivering in my satin, with goose bumps cropping up all over my arms, one of the men detached himself from the group and sauntered toward me, cigarette dangling in the corner of his mouth. "*Hola, senorita!*"

"Hi," I said. I took high school Spanish, but I wasn't about to embarrass myself by trying to use it.

He switched over to lightly accented English. "Looking for company?"

"Looking for a friend," I said, to give myself an excuse for being there.

He tilted his head. "What's his name, your friend?"

It just fell out of my mouth, I swear. "Jorge."

He grinned, putting a hand against his chest. "I'm Jorge."

"Another Jorge."

"Tell you something." He grabbed my elbow and led me toward the door. "I take you in. If your Jorge's not here, maybe I can be Jorge for you." He winked.

I smiled back, while I thought, *Not on your life.* He was several inches too short, a couple years too young, and his shirt was open halfway down his chest, which was scrawny. What I said was, demurely, "Thank you."

"*De nada,*" Jorge said, and stood politely aside to let me walk through the door first.

At first glance, *La Havana* didn't look too different from other establishments of its kind I'd seen in the past. There was a long bar along one wall, with a mirror behind it, and a couple of bartenders staying busy. There was a sound booth in the other corner, where someone was juggling CDs or songs on an iPod. There was no stage, and no live entertainment, just the music blasting from speakers at all four corners of the room, at eardrum-popping decibels.

Something else there wasn't, was seating. There were no chairs or tables anywhere, not even at the bar. People stood around talking or flirting, or they danced.

"See him?" Jorge asked next to me.

I looked around. "No."

"What's he look like, your friend?"

"Tall," I said, "dark hair, dark eyes, goatee, tattoo of a dragon on his back."

Fake, as far as I knew, since he hadn't had it the first time I'd seen him naked, and it had appeared pretty much overnight, which probably hadn't been enough time to have it properly done. The dragon was one of Jorge's distinguishing marks. Rafe only had one tattoo of his own: a viper curled around his left bicep. I added, "And a snake on his arm."

"I don't see him."

I didn't either. And given the fact that most everyone here was my height or shorter, he ought to have been pretty easy to spot.

"There are games in the back," my new friend told me, pointing in that direction. "Maybe he's there?"

"Maybe." I glanced down at him. "What kind of games?"

Jorge shrugged. "*Billar. Póquer.*"

"Billiards and poker?"

Jorge nodded.

Rafe played pool. I'd seen him. And I thought he might play poker as well. It was something I'd expect him to know how to do, plus, when I'd originally fetched up against him back in August, I'd Googled him, and someone with his name had turned up as a player in online poker tournaments. It could have been someone else, of course, although Rafael Collier isn't the most common name.

"I'll check there," I said.

"I'll wait here," Jorge answered and let go of my arm.

I made my way along the edges of the room, not wanting to push through the crush of bodies on the dance floor. The space was so tight they were all just bumping and grinding, rubbing against one another, and the idea of having to get into the middle of all the gyrating, possibly being bumped and ground along the way, didn't appeal. I really am a prude, I guess. I don't think I'd mind bumping and grinding with someone I cared about, even in public, but I didn't want to do it with strangers. A few of the dancers were practically making love fully dressed, or so it seemed.

It was a relief to make it to the other side of the room, where a small doorway led into a second room. It was smaller than the first, and unlike it, there was plenty of seating. A couple of pool tables were set up in the middle, while all around the edges of the room, groups of men sat around round tables playing cards while well-dressed women hung over their shoulders.

And unlike in proper casinos—where I'd honestly never been, since gambling is illegal in Tennessee—they weren't playing for chips. Instead, there were stacks of bills in the middle of each table.

I stopped in the doorway, staring.

With all that money staring back—from the looks of it, enough to pay my bills for a year—it took me a moment to notice anything else. When I did, I looked up and straight into the eyes of a woman standing beside the nearest table.

I gulped. I had guessed that Carmen must have a connection with this place, since it was owned by the same corporation or entity that owned the warehouse where she'd spent the best part of the afternoon, but I hadn't actually expected her to be here. I guess perhaps I should have, but honestly, she hadn't even crossed my mind.

She was just as stunning up close as I had expected from seeing her at a distance a couple of times. Back inside the red dress she'd had on the other night at Fidelio's, she looked like all the money on every table put together and multiplied, and she managed to make me feel both dowdy and too conservative in my tight and backless red satin. That long, straight brown hair fell over her shoulders, and her face could have graced the cover of People Magazine. Huge, dark eyes, long lashes, and full, red lips.

I managed a weak smile. "Um... bathroom?" Throwing my mind back through the mists of time, I dragged a word up from the forgotten recesses. "*Servicio?*"

I'm sure my accent was atrocious. It was at least ten years since I'd had occasion to use the Castilian Spanish I'd learned in school.

Carmen rolled her eyes and muttered something. I didn't ask her to translate it, since I could hear from the tone that it wasn't complimentary. She pointed down the hall to the left.

"*Gracias,*" I said. And followed up with, "Thank you."

"*De nada,*" Carmen said. But she didn't seem to mean it, and when I pushed off from the doorway and headed down the hall to the left, she watched me until I was out of sight.

For that reason, I thought I'd better actually visit the *servicio*. So I checked my makeup in the cracked mirror above the sink, applied a little more lipstick, rinsed my hands, and managed not to squeal when I noticed a big cockroach lying on its back in the corner behind the commode, all six legs folded on its stomach.

That done, I opened the door again and headed into the hallway, my head twisted and my eyes still on the cockroach, just in case it decided to stop playing dead and come after me. I wasn't watching where I was going, and as a result I ended up walking straight into a hard, male body parked right outside the door.

I bounced back.

"I'm..." The rest of the apology froze on my lips when I looked up and met a pair of hard, black eyes. It was a long time since he'd looked at me with that expression, and my heart started thumping erratically. From nerves, in case you wondered. There's nothing sexy about Rafe when he looks like he wants to commit murder. He's just plain terrifying.

He opened his mouth, and as expected, it wasn't a friendly greeting. "What the hell are you doing here?"

His voice was pitched just high enough to carry above the steady thump of the music, and it was tight with anger.

"It's a public place, isn't it? Anyone can—"

I broke off with a gasp when he shook me. Actually, physically, shook me. Hard enough that the back of my head knocked against the wall. And before I'd recovered from that, he'd leaned down to where our noses were within an inch or two of one another. "Don't fuck with me, Savannah."

"I'm not," I protested, shaken as much by his tone as by the combined use of a four letter word—something he tends to avoid around me, unless he's really, really upset—and my name. "I had no idea you'd be here."

He eased back a fraction of an inch. Not enough to really make a difference, but I was able to draw breath again. "You still following Carmen?"

I shook my head. "No. I swear."

"How d'you know about this place, then? And don't try to tell me it's a coincidence."

"I checked the ownership of the warehouse where Carmen went this afternoon," I said. "The same people own this, along with that warehouse in East Nashville where Julio Melendez ran his import/export business before he was arrested. Remember?"

"I worked with the man," Rafe said, "I ain't likely to forget."

"I can't get into any of the warehouses. But I could just walk in here. So I did."

"Gonna get yourself hurt," Rafe said.

I rolled my eyes. "Who's going to hurt me?"

He didn't answer, just arched a brow, and I scoffed. "You won't hurt me. Not that way."

"You have no idea what I'll do if I have to," Rafe said, and looked around. "You gotta get outta here."

"Why? I just got here. And I'm not bothering anyone."

"You're bothering Carmen. She told me to get rid of you."

I chill went down my spine, although it could just have been the cold cinderblock against my bare back. "What do you mean, get rid of? Permanently?"

"Right now," Rafe said, "just getting you outta here will do. If you come back, then yeah. Permanently."

"Do you always do what Carmen wants?"

"Don't be an idiot," Rafe growled, his hands tightening on my upper arms. "You know I ain't gonna hurt you. Not that way, whatever the hell that means."

I opened my mouth to tell him exactly what it meant, but he shook his head. "Save it. Damn, I wish you wouldna done this!"

"I'm sorry," I said, since he seemed sincerely upset. Disproportionately so, if you ask me. A whole lot more upset than the situation warranted. I mean, it wasn't like anything was liable to happen to me. The place was full of people, most of them probably quite nice, like my buddy Jorge. So what if they were gambling in the back room? It was none of my business. It wasn't like everyone else here hadn't already seen it. And if he didn't want me here, I could just walk out. Right?

No sooner had I thought the thought than there was a noise from the front of the building; a shrill whistle loud enough to cut through the music and the buzzing of voices.

"Damn," Rafe said.

"What?"

He shook his head, just shoved me ahead of him toward the end of the hall and the fire door—*Salida de Emergencia Solamente*. As he fumbled with the heavy iron bar keeping the door closed, a chattering wave of panicked humanity started pushing at us from behind. I don't speak much Spanish anymore, but I recognized words like *polizia* and heard others like *redada* and *prisa*.

"What's *prisa*?" I asked over the din of buzzing of voices.

"Hurry," Rafe said, lifting the bar lock on the door and pushing it open. An alarm started shrieking, adding to the chaos. The mass of people surged forward, pushing me forward too. I grabbed hold of him so I wouldn't lose him in the crush.

"What about *redada*?"

"Raid," Rafe said. He got an arm around my waist and pulled me out of the way of the stampede. It took everyone a second or two to realize that we'd all rushed straight into a flood-lit back parking lot and that we were surrounded on all sides by... I did a quick left-to-right count—at least a dozen official vehicles: black and white police cruisers, unmarked police cars, recognizable by their extra mirrors and antennas that civilian vehicles don't have, and sleek black SUVs with the logo of the Tennessee Bureau of Investigations and the FBI. Along with the cars, there were dozens of police officers and agents with guns trained on us, hands braced on car roofs and doors. Someone with a foghorn kept shouting orders to stop—"¡*Alto ahí!*"—in Spanish and English.

It was like a scene from a television show, and for a second I think my heart stopped. I've never had reason to be afraid of the police before, not even when Spicer and Truman caught me coming out of Maybelle Driscoll's house last week. I knew I'd broken the law, but it never occurred to me to fear for my life or my freedom. Spicer and Truman knew me; they'd know I hadn't done anything wrong.

This was different. These were cops I didn't know and couldn't recognize, scary in their black caps and bulletproof vests with SWAT written across the back, and they were holding guns. Guns that were aimed at me.

I must have made a noise, or maybe Rafe noticed my instinctive move to burrow into his side, because his arm tightened. I felt him draw breath, but before he could give voice to anything he might have thought of saying, Carmen burst out of the door and got caught in the floodlights. I glanced at him to see what he'd do, whether he'd drop me like a hot potato to rescue her.

He didn't. Or maybe he didn't have time. One of the spotlights swung toward us, and the next second we were lit up like a Christmas tree, outlined against the black wall of the nightclub.

The second after that, my breath went again.

Two things happened simultaneously: the guy with the foghorn yelled, "There he is! I see him!" while all the guns swung in our direction. The next moment, I found myself in front of Rafe with no real idea how I got there. I suppose it's possible that he pulled me around from his side to his front, but knowing him, I doubt it. It's more likely that I stepped in front of him. I'd done it once before: put myself between him and what I perceived to be danger. Then, I'd had a gun. Now I didn't. Although it seemed he did, because before I knew what was happening, a muzzle was pressed to my head, while his other arm crossed my body, pinning my arms to my sides.

I think I gasped. It was so sudden and so shocking—I hadn't even realized he was carrying a gun!—and the muzzle was cold against my temple. My knees buckled, and only Rafe's arm held me upright as I sagged against him.

"Don't shoot! Don't shoot!" Another figure in SWAT black ran out in front of the others while the crowd, squealing wildly, scurried in the other direction. "I need him alive. Don't shoot!"

Carmen glanced at Rafe over her shoulder and must have decided to abandon him to his fate, because she ran after the rest of the crowd as quickly as the four inch patent leather heels allowed.

Rafe muttered something.

"What?" I managed through the chattering of my teeth. Between the December nighttime chill and the fear, I was shivering like a Chihuahua.

"C'mon." He started inching along the wall toward the corner of the building, dragging me along with him.

"Is the safety on?" I croaked as I concentrated on shuffling my feet along. Since I was wearing high heels of my own, it wasn't easy. It didn't help that the ground along the back of the building was littered with debris: empty bottles, crumpled paper bags, and cigarette butts.

He chuckled. I felt the vibration against my back more than I heard the sound. "Course, darlin'. Don't worry."

Right. I had a gun pointed to my head, and a dozen or so other guns pointed at the man behind me, and we were outlined against the wall like ducks in a shooting gallery. Nothing to worry about. Nothing at all.

"Where's your car?" Rafe asked in my ear. We'd gotten to the corner, only to find that the other side of the building was also surrounded by every law enforcement agency in Nashville. They had rounded up the fleeing patrons and were herding them onto a big bus. I saw my buddy Jorge peering out the window, his eyes huge when he recognized me.

"To the right. Halfway down the row." I'm pretty sure my voice hitched on every other word. I couldn't seem to draw a deep breath.

Rafe's voice was level and perfectly calm, low and steady in my ear. "When we get there, scoot across the gearshift and into the passenger seat. Let me drive."

I nodded. "I'm scared."

"Don't be. I won't let nothing happen to you." It might have been my imagination—it probably was—but I thought he might have dropped a kiss into my hair before he raised his voice. Then again, maybe not. "Listen up!"

The buzz quieted down as everyone did as he said.

"We're gonna get into this car over here." There was a hint of a Spanish accent to his voice that he didn't usually have, something he'd affected to pretend to be Jorge Pena. "Don't nobody try to stop us, or I swear to God, I'm gonna put a bullet through her brain!"

His voice hardened on the last few words. He tightened his arm around me, and I squeaked. Everyone tensed.

That same black-clad figure from earlier had followed us around the corner, and spoke up again, both hands up and empty to show the lack of a weapon. "What do you want, Mr. Pena? Whatever it is, you got it."

The voice was female, and even through the terror, I recognized it.

Rafe chuckled. "A million dollars and a helicopter would be nice, but I'll settle for nobody trying to stop me."

"Why don't you just let her go? She's an innocent bystander. Not a part of this."

Thank you, I thought. Nice of Grimaldi to reinforce the idea that I was nobody, and so not worthy of retaliation if any were to come down from this.

"She's my ticket outta here," Rafe answered, his voice clear and carrying. "You ain't gonna shoot me while I got her. At least I hope you ain't stupid enough to try. Cause if I die, she dies too."

He pulled me along, step by step closer to the Volvo. I fumbled in my bag for the key, and undid the alarm and the locks just as we reached the car.

"Open the door," Rafe said in my ear. "Get in. Scoot across. Hurry."

He crouched as I did it, so as not to give anyone a target to fire on. By now, I was reasonably sure that no one would fire even if they had a clear shot, but I guess he did what he had to do. I scrambled across the gear shift and into the passenger seat, and half a second later he was inside the car with me, with the door locked behind him, holding his hand out for the keys. I dropped them in his palm and watched him insert the car key in the ignition and turn it. The car roared to life under us. Rafe's hand didn't even shake when he moved the gear shift. When he reversed out of the parking space at fifty miles an hour, narrowly avoiding taking out a police cruiser and Tamara Grimaldi, I couldn't hold back a terrified squeak.

He glanced at me. "Relax, darlin'. I know how to drive."

He stepped on the gas and we barreled toward the road leaving rubber on the pavement behind us, dodging cars and agents.

"I know," I managed. He drives like Mario Andretti on speed. But he hadn't killed me yet. Although this might be the time he did. I clung to both sides of my seat when he squeezed the Volvo through a narrow space between a cruiser and an SUV with the FBI logo on the door, and took the turn onto Nolensville Road on two wheels. "God!"

Rafe grinned. I smiled weakly, all the while waiting for the sound of shots or sirens from behind us. They didn't come, although in the rearview mirror I could see a dark shadow emerge from the parking lot we'd just left, and turn into a pair of headlights on the road behind us.

"They're following," I said.

"Let'em," Rafe answered. "Strap in, darlin'. It's gonna be fast."

He turned the Volvo onto Harding Road in the direction of the interstate, and lowered his foot on the gas pedal. The car jumped forward.

Twelve

Four minutes later we were on I-24. It had taken me that long to catch my breath.

"That was interesting," I said eventually, neutrally, when I thought I could speak without squeaking again.

Rafe glanced at me and grinned. "You did great. For a second there, when I saw you, I thought everything was gonna blow sky high. But then I realized Tammy musta sent you in."

"No," I said.

He shot me another look. "Tammy didn't send you in?"

I shook my head. "I told you what happened. I looked into the ownership of the warehouse, and—"

"Hold on. If Tammy didn't send you, what happened back there?"

"I didn't want them to shoot you," I said.

"They wouldna shot me. It was a set-up."

"I figured that out. Eventually."

He was quiet for a second. "So when I grabbed you, you thought I was taking you hostage?"

"That's why I asked you if the safety was on," I said.

"And you took my word for it?"

"I told you. I know you won't hurt me."

"Right. Not that way." He slid another look my way, out of the corner of his eye, while most of his attention was on maneuvering the Volvo through the late night traffic. He kept the car moving at a pretty good clip. Somewhere behind us, I figured the FBI vehicle followed, and he might be trying to lose it. Or not. "You wanna explain that to me now?"

Not really. I was used to blurting out truths when I spoke to him, usually without thinking, but right now I was in control of myself, and I had a question. "You first. Who's Carmen?"

That earned me another flash of dark eyes, incredulous this time. "You're worried about Carmen? Christ, Savannah; what's wrong with you?"

I'm in love with you, I thought, but I didn't say it. Not quite ready for that confession yet. Not out loud and no holds barred like that. "I'm not worried about her. I just want to know who she is."

"Her name's Carmen Arroyo. She's Hector Gonzales's right hand man—or woman—in Nashville."

"Hector Gonzales owns the warehouses, right?"

"Hector Gonzales," Rafe said, "owns a lot more than that. He runs the biggest SATG in the southeast."

I loosened my death grip on the seat and folded my hands in my lap. "What's a SATG?"

"South American theft gang. Organized crime. South American variety."

"Drugs?" That's what the South Americans do, isn't it?

"Not so much," Rafe said. "Smash and grabs of jewelry stores, hold-ups of armored cars, hijacking of tractor trailers and cargo boxes." He glanced in the rearview mirror before changing lanes. "The TBI's been working to shut them down for years. But I never got past the periphery. They're suspicious of anyone who isn't Hispanic. We got a couple of their minor players once in a while, but I never made it far enough into the organization to take down anyone worthwhile. Till August."

"What happened in August?"

"I talked Julio Melendez into hiring me for those open house robberies." He veered left, to pass an eighteen wheeler that wasn't moving fast enough, and zipped back into the lane in front of the tractor trailer again as soon as we were clear. He checked the rearview mirror, and I did the same. There was no sign of the SUV. "And I woulda been able to do a better job back then if goddamn Perry Fortunato hadn't gotten in my way."

I had no fond feelings for Perry either.

"Instead," Rafe continued, his hands tightening on the steering wheel as if around something soft, like Perry's throat, "I ended up blowing my cover and killing the son of a bitch. Not that he didn't deserve it, but I woulda had Carmen and Hector and everyone else back in September if it hadn't been for Perry. Instead, somebody sent a goddamn hitman after me, and more people ended up dying. People who shouldn't have died. And then I had to kill him too!"

"I'm sorry," I said, since there wasn't much else I could say. He hadn't had any other choice, really: it had been between Jorge and him, and between Perry and me, and I for one thought he'd done the right thing. I'd much rather be alive than not, and I wanted him to stay that way too.

He glanced at me, chagrined and maybe even a little embarrassed.

"So Carmen works for Hector," I added, bringing the conversation back to where it had derailed.

He nodded. "Hector's based outta Atlanta. That's where I've been the past couple months. Hector never met Jorge Pena, so he bought that I was him. When he hired Jorge to kill me, because Julio told him to, it was all done by phone and wire transfer. After Jorge was shot, we used his own phone to take a picture of him—after we shaved him—and then we sent it to Hector as proof that the job was done. When I showed up in Atlanta, Hector had no reason to think I wasn't Jorge. I had the man's phone and all the information. So he put me to work cleaning house."

"Cleaning house?"

"Getting rid of anyone Hector don't like," Rafe said. "There's a house in Cobb county where half a dozen of my targets are in house arrest, waiting for Hector to get taken off the streets so they can rejoin the world of the living."

"And will he be taken off the streets? He wasn't there tonight, was he?"

He shook his head. "He's still in Atlanta. But the police there moved on Hector at the same time as the MNPD and TBI moved on us. I don't think anybody had the chance to call and warn him."

"So they got him."

"I hope they did," Rafe said. He entered the ramp to take us from I-24 over to I-40, and looked in the rearview mirror again. I did the same. Still no sign of the SUV.

"Where are we going?"

He glanced over. "I'm taking you home."

"And?"

"Someone'll come get me."

"I see." The last time he'd driven me home, we'd barely made it upstairs without scandalizing the neighbors.

His voice pulled me out of my reverie, just as things were heating up in my mind. "You ever gonna tell me what 'not like that' means?"

"Oh." Well, that brought me back to earth with a thud.

But we had to discuss it, and now was as good a time as any. Might as well get it out in the open. We'd had tricky conversations in the car before; maybe it would be easier to talk when I wouldn't be looking him straight in the face.

I took a deep breath and squared my shoulders, figuratively, before plunging in. "Remember last month when you were here? When David went missing?"

"Hard to forget," Rafe said.

"After we found him, we went home and... um..."

His lips curved. "Hard to forget that, too."

True. Even if my memories of the event were tainted by what happened afterwards, what happened before had certainly been memorable.

"You found that pill on my kitchen counter." The morning-after pill. Mifepristone. Also used for first trimester at-home abortions.

The smile disappeared. "Yeah."

"And then you left and came back and I'd started bleeding and you had to take me to the emergency room."

He nodded, tight-lipped.

"You left me there." My voice shook, and I had to make an effort to firm it. "I was in the hospital having a miscarriage, and you left."

"I waited for your family to get there," Rafe said.

"I didn't want my family."

"What about Satterfield?"

"I didn't want him either." When I'd discovered that mother had brought Todd with her, I'd been mortified. "I wanted you. And you didn't stick around."

"It wasn't my place—" Rafe began.

"How can you say that? You had more right to be there than anyone!"

He shot me a glance. "What's that supposed to mean?"

I blinked. Something was wrong here. He sounded sincere, like he really didn't understand what he'd done. In deference to his obvious cluelessness I kept my words simple. "I lost your baby, Rafe. How is that not your place?"

He turned to look at me, for long enough that I had to remind him to keep his attention on the road so we wouldn't crash.

"What?" he said, facing forward again.

"I lost your baby. And you left me there. Alone."

He shook his head. "That can't be right."

"What do you mean, it can't be right? I was there; you did it. Or are you questioning my knowledge of whose baby I was carrying?"

"Satterfield—" Rafe said, and that's when I lost it.

"Don't you dare try to blame Todd for this! What did you think, that I was sleeping with both of you at the same time?"

He opened his mouth, and I cut him off before he could say it. "I'd gone through weeks of agony over that baby. You were gone, and I didn't know whether you'd ever come back. You told me you'd only be gone a few weeks, and it had been two months. You didn't call and you didn't write. You never promised me anything, and you sure as hell hadn't signed on for fatherhood."

By now I had tears spilling down my cheeks, and I was too upset to care. "I had no idea whether I could count on you and I wasn't sure I could handle the responsibility on my own. So I went to see the doctor. She gave me that pill you saw, so I could get rid of the baby if I wanted. I'd had it for almost a week and I never took it. Because I wanted that baby. I may have been anxious and worried and scared out of my mind, but there wasn't a single second when I didn't want it. And after all that, when I lost it anyway, and you just walked out, like nothing had happened...!"

"I didn't know," Rafe said.

"Yes, you did!" I dashed the tears off my cheeks with the backs of my hands. "I sent Catherine after you. My sister. I told her to ask you to come back. And you didn't!"

He shook his head. "She didn't tell me it was my baby."

That took the wind right out of my sails. I dropped my hands to my lap. "She must have."

His voice took on an edge, too. "Why else would I leave, Savannah? You think I didn't wanna be there?"

"You could have asked me," I said.

"Sure I could. But why?"

"You knew it could be your baby. I'd slept with you. Without protection."

"If it was my baby," Rafe said, his hands so rigid on the steering wheel his knuckles showed white, "I figured you'd have told me. You didn't."

OK, so that hit home. And stung. I'd had plenty of time to tell him, but I had chosen not to. What was he supposed to think?

"I was in the middle of telling you in the hospital," I said, "but then my mother showed up..."

"And you acted like you couldn't get rid of me fast enough."

"I'm sorry about that. I just..."

I trailed off. There was no excuse I could make, really. Mother had walked into the room and I'd snatched my hand away from his without thinking. I had regretted it immediately, but by then it was too late.

"When I got out in the hallway Satterfield was there," Rafe said, his voice tight, "and he told me it was all my fault."

"What was your fault?"

"I didn't ask. But since we'd done what we'd done that afternoon, I guess I figured he was blaming me for the whole thing."

"What we did had nothing to do with it," I said. "I told you so. I would have lost the baby anyway."

"Yeah," Rafe answered, "but I'd just figured out you were pregnant, and you hadn't told me it was mine, so I figured it had to be his, and he was blaming me for causing the miscarriage because I didn't keep my pants zipped, and it all just added up..."

"So you hit him." I nodded. Understandable, under the circumstances. "He didn't mean that, though. Todd knew it wasn't his baby."

"You sure about that?"

"Of course I'm sure," I said. "Todd knows I've never slept with him."

"Never?" He sounded surprised, the bastard.

"No. Never." I glanced over at him, debating. In the end I figured I might as well just tell him the truth. "I've only ever slept with two people. You and Bradley."

He looked at me, shocked.

"What?" I said. "Did something about me give you the idea that I have a habit of sleeping around?"

"You slept with me."

"And it took you two months to get me into bed. Does that say promiscuous to you?"

"I never thought you were promiscuous," Rafe said. "Just that you'd been sleeping with Satterfield. He asked you to marry him."

"Without sampling the goods. Mother always told me a man won't pay for the cow if he can get the milk for free."

He smiled. "You gave me free milk."

"Yes, I did."

I waited for him to ask why. He didn't. We were close to home, and he focused on maneuvering the Volvo through the quiet East Nashville streets toward 5th and East Main while I focused on wiping my face. Once we got there, he pulled up to the curb outside the condo complex and cut the engine. I thought about telling him to pull into the garage, but I decided it wasn't worth the trouble. The car would be OK on the street for one night.

He turned to me, and I waited for him to speak. When he did, it wasn't what I expected to hear. "D'you know someone who drives a white compact?"

I blinked, switching mental gears as quickly as I could. "I'm sure I know a lot of people who drive white compacts. It's the most common car on the road, isn't it?"

He didn't answer, and I added, "Why do you ask?"

"The one across the street's been following us since we got off the interstate. Prob'ly before that, too. I think I saw it outside Fidelio's earlier."

"You're kidding." I stretched my neck to look past him and across the street. "Are you sure?"

"Pretty sure," Rafe said. "But I can find out." He opened the door. I opened my mouth, to ask him what he was planning to do, but before I got the words out, he was jogging across the street toward the white car, gun in hand.

Whoever was in the compact must have taken a single look at him and decided that retreat was the safest option, because the next second, the car had peeled away from the curb with a squeal of tires. Rafe had to throw himself out of the way to avoid being hit. The compact took off up the street, and I took off too, out of the Volvo and over to where Rafe was just picking himself up.

"Are you OK?" I started patting him, to make sure he wasn't hurt.

"Are you crazy?" He pushed me behind him with one hand and scanned the street in both directions.

"Nobody's going to hurt me," I said. "You scared him away, whoever he was. Or she. Let's just get inside."

He let me tug him along, through the gate and across the courtyard, but he didn't put the gun down until we were upstairs, inside my apartment with the door locked and bolted behind us, and he had walked into every room and made sure it was empty. He even looked behind the shower curtain and opened my closet door and moved the clothes around to make sure no one was hiding inside. Once that was done, he laid the gun on the dining room table and turned to face me.

"What've you been up to, darlin'?"

"Other than following Carmen around?" I said. "Not much."

"You musta done something, to make someone take this kind of interest in you."

I shook my head. "I can't think of anything. Isn't it more likely someone's following you?"

"In my line of work, people tend to be better at surveillance. If someone was following me, we prob'ly wouldn't see 'em."

"Maybe it was someone who trailed us from the nightclub. Trying to be a hero, you know? He's probably on the phone with the police right now, telling them where we are."

"Maybe." He thought for a second. "Your ex got remarried, right? You think it could be the wife?"

"I doubt it," I said. Shelby wouldn't be caught dead in an economy compact, at least not if I were any judge of character.

Although she might be smart enough to realize that's what I'd think, and so she'd rented or borrowed a simpler car to throw me off. If Rafe had first noticed the car outside Fidelio's earlier, that led some credence to the idea that it might be Shelby. She'd probably started out by following Bradley, and when he dropped me off and went home, she decided to follow me instead. If memory served, he'd started sleeping with her around the time I got pregnant. Maybe he'd picked up another mistress now that Shelby was expecting. Or maybe he hadn't, but Shelby just thought he had.

"Whoever they are, they're long gone." Rafe walked to the sofa and made himself comfortable. "Mind if turn on the TV?"

He reached for the remote, muscles moving smoothly in his arm under the short sleeve of the black T-shirt. My mouth went dry. Until he opened his. "I wanna see if we made the news."

"Oh, God." That possibility blew anything else right out of my head. If my mother saw me on the news, facing a firing squad with a gun to my head, she'd have all sorts of fits. "Please do."

He'd already turned the TV on, and as soon as the picture came into focus, he started flipping channels. We hit pay dirt on Channel 4. "...latest from the hostage situation in South Nashville," the perky blonde anchor said, "we'll go to Chip, live at the scene. Chip?"

"Brandy." Chip nodded. He was blond too, and looked a bit like a King Charles spaniel. "We're here, outside *La Havana* nightclub off Nolensville Road in the Tusculum area, where earlier tonight, federal and local authorities cracked down on what they say is an illegal gambling parlor and money laundering facility with ties to organized crime."

Over Chip's shoulder, we could see that police and agents in SWAT black were still milling around the parking lot outside the nightclub. I guess I shouldn't be surprised at that. It felt like an eternity had passed, but in reality, it was just about an hour since we'd stood face to face in the hall outside the bathroom. Chances were there'd be law enforcement in and around the nightclub until morning.

"Several arrests were made," Chip continued, "and more than a hundred witnesses and suspects were carried off in buses, to be processed at an undisclosed location. Meanwhile, everyone is still closemouthed about the hostage situation a few witnesses have told us took place earlier."

And then the TV cut to what looked like it might be cell phone footage: jumpy, grainy and dark. Rafe leaned forward with a soft curse. I leaned back, and although I didn't curse, I wanted to.

There we were, the two of us, outlined against the purple wall, lit up by spotlights with our shadows making strange and grotesque shapes behind us. Thank God whoever had shot the video had done so from a distance, but even so, it looked horrifyingly real. I was pale, my eyes huge, as I stumbled along, and when Rafe started calling out demands that nobody try to stop him or I'd end up with a bullet through my brain, he sounded all too serious.

The clip ended with the Volvo fishtailing out of the parking lot with a federal SUV in hot pursuit, and Chip came back onscreen. "The identity of the hostage has not been released by authorities, but the kidnapper has been identified as Jorge Pena, a resident of Miami and a suspect in several local, national and international homicides. If anyone sees this man, you are advised to keep your distance and call 911 immediately. Do not attempt to engage the suspect, who is described as armed and extremely dangerous. Brandy?"

Chip disappeared, and Brandy came back on, only to promise more news after a short break. The news gave way to a commercial about yoghurt, and Rafe turned it off. He didn't look at me, just kept staring at the blank screen. I did the same, since I couldn't think of anything to say to make him feel better.

"You think your mother saw it?" he asked eventually.

"I hope not." Although if she had, chances were she would have tried to call me by now.

He shot me a quick look out of the corner of his eye. "Looked pretty bad, didn't it?"

"It looked real, if that's what you mean. Obviously everyone there thought you were holding a loaded gun to my head."

"I *was* holding a loaded gun to your head," Rafe said. "And before you ask, yeah, there were real bullets in the guns the police and TBI had, too."

"But they wouldn't have shot us, right?"

He shook his head. "It was choreographed. All of it except you. I was just supposed to get swept up along with everyone else, but then you showed up, and I figured I'd take advantage of the situation to get you outta there."

"I would have been arrested, too?"

"Yes, darlin'," Rafe said, "you woulda been arrested. You were hanging out in an illegal gambling den."

"So you saved me from having to spend the night in a cell with a lot of prostitutes? And Carmen?"

He nodded.

"My hero," I said.

He shook his head. "Sometimes I wonder about you, darlin'."

Sometimes I wondered about me, too. But I was feeling just a little giddy and giggly, like I'd had a glass of champagne too many, and I didn't feel like pretending otherwise. "I do know I'm supposed to stay away from you, you know."

I thought he might smile at that, but he didn't. "You'd be safer if you did. People wouldn't try to shoot you."

"On the other hand, Perry Fortunato probably would have strangled me—after he raped me—if you hadn't been there to take care of him, so it worked out well enough."

We looked at one another in silence for a moment.

"If you know you're supposed to stay away from me," Rafe said, "why don't you?"

"I guess because I like you."

He nodded. "I like you too."

"I assumed you did. You slept with me."

"Darlin'," Rafe said, "that don't mean I like you. I've slept with lots of women I didn't like."

My eyes narrowed. "Like who? Carmen?"

His voice didn't change. "I was thinking of Elspeth Caulfield."

"So you didn't sleep with Carmen?"

For a second he just looked at me. "Don't worry about Carmen," he said at last. "She was part of the job, nothing more."

So he had slept with her. And it had been in the line of duty, so I couldn't even make a fuss the way I wanted to. And—point to him—he didn't lie about it.

"I know I have no claim on you," I said, striving to keep my voice steady and realizing I was giving myself away with every word I uttered. "You're a free agent, you can sleep with anyone you want... but I really don't like that!"

"If it helps, I don't plan on doing it again."

"You'll have to," I said, my voice taking on a shrill edge. "They'll keep sending you undercover, and you'll have to do whatever you have to do to do the job. Even if it's sleeping with the people you're trying to arrest."

He shook his head. "I'm done after this. My cover was blown. I got another few months by becoming Jorge, but once this sting's over, I'm finished. No more undercover work for me."

I blinked. "What will you do?"

He shrugged. "Not sure yet. Might be kinda hard getting another job, what with a criminal record and all."

"Surely they'll strike everything you did while you were undercover off your record?"

"Sure," Rafe said, "but I earned that assault and battery conviction all on my own. Two years in medium security."

"You were eighteen. And there were mitigating circumstances."

He shrugged.

"Can't they find something else for you to do?" Somewhere out of harm's way? Where he wouldn't have to sleep with the suspects? It seemed the least they could do after ten years of faithful service and putting his life on the line every day.

"Wear a suit and tie and ride a desk?" He shook his head. "Not sure that's for me, darlin'."

"I've seen you in a suit and tie. You look good."

And if he had a normal life, with a normal job, maybe he could have a normal relationship, too. Feeling a little like I was taking my life in my hands, I added, recklessly, "I could meet you at the door with a pipe and slippers at five o'clock."

"If I want someone to bring me my slippers, I'll buy a dog," Rafe said, and then added, when he saw my expression, "I didn't mean it like that."

"Of course not."

"I didn't. Listen, darlin'," he leaned forward, "I've spent ten years never knowing when someone might pull out a gun and shoot me. I get up in the morning never knowing if I'm gonna live through the day. I'm afraid if I make plans, something bad'll happen."

I guess I could understand that. "I'm sorry."

"It ain't that I don't want to. Just that I never thought I'd survive long enough to have any kind of future. I still might not. The job ain't over."

"I understand," I said, as a knock on the door heralded someone's arrival. As I got up to answer it, I added, over my shoulder, "Just... keep it in mind, OK? I'd like another shot at that baby."

I didn't give him time to answer, just opened the door.

"Evening, Ms. Martin," Tamara Grimaldi said.

Thirteen

She was still dressed in SWAT black, with gun belt and heavy boots, and she didn't look happy to see me. Or perhaps it was Rafe she was unhappy to see. She scowled past me into the apartment. "Is he decent?"

"Of course." I may have wanted to rip his clothes off, but I hadn't actually done it. "Come on in."

"I need to take him with me. He has to show his face in night court so everyone can see we got him."

"I'm sure he'll be happy to go to night court," I said. "Whatever it takes to put this whole mess behind us, right?"

Neither of them answered me. Grimaldi brushed past me into the apartment, and came face to face with Rafe in the living room. They stared at one another for a long moment before Grimaldi broke the silence, her voice tight. "What the hell were you thinking, dragging her into the middle of that?"

"I didn't drag her anywhere," Rafe answered, in the same tone. "She showed up. I had to get her outta there before something could happen to her. I did the best I could."

"Why are you talking about me like I'm a potted plant?" I wanted to know. "I'm standing right here. And if I remember correctly, *I* was the one who stepped in front of *him*."

They both ignored me.

"For your information," Grimaldi said, hands on her hips, "that idiot stunt got you national news coverage. By tomorrow, it'll be on every news channel in the country and all over the internet. If you had any hope of salvaging your career, you just blew it sky-high."

"My career was over long before tonight," Rafe answered calmly. "I blew my cover months ago, and you know it. By now, everyone knows who I am."

"You do realize her family's having collective fits, don't you?"

"They haven't called," I said.

Grimaldi turned to me. "Everyone called your brother. Then he called me. He was unhappy. And that makes me unhappy. His wife died just a few weeks ago, and here is his favorite sister, a hostage in a police-standoff, with a gun to her head!"

"Catherine is his favorite, not me. And if he recognized me, he would have recognized Rafe too."

"Your faith in Mr. Collier is touching," Grimaldi snarled, "but your brother doesn't share it. He's upset."

"I'll call him."

She shook her head with a sigh. "I talked him down. He's fine, really. He knows you weren't in any danger."

"Thank you."

"Don't thank me yet. I have to arrest your boyfriend." She reached for the handcuffs hanging from her belt.

"He's not..." The denial was automatic, and I bit it off. After losing the baby—and Rafe—I'd promised myself I'd never again try to deny how I felt about him, and that automatic denial of him as my boyfriend had to go. "Can we have a minute first?"

Grimaldi paused with the cuffs in her hand, looking from me to

Rafe and back. "You've already had plenty of time to figure things out. He needs to get to night court so there's no question that he's under arrest."

"Just one minute. Please."

She sighed. "Fine. One minute. I'll wait in the hallway."

"Thank you."

I waited until she was outside with the door closed before I turned to Rafe. He was grinning. "What's the plan, darlin'? You want me to jump off the balcony and take off down the street?"

I shook my head. "I know you have to go. I just wanted to say goodbye in private."

The grin widened. "Planning to do something you don't want anyone to see?"

"We don't have time," I said, and had the pleasure of hearing him actually laugh out loud. I added, "You'll come back, won't you?"

"I've always come back before."

I shook my head. "Not this time. You came back without telling me."

"I woulda told you eventually. I was trying to keep you out of it."

I'd already figured that out. "You'll be careful, right?"

"I'm always careful," Rafe said.

No, he wasn't. He was rarely careful. Although he usually managed to survive with his skin intact.

"I'd really like you to kiss me goodbye," I said; he smiled, "but I'm afraid if you do, Detective Grimaldi will have to pry my fingernails out of your skin. And probably put the handcuffs on me just to keep me from trying to hold on to you."

He laughed. "I'll risk it. C'mere, darlin'."

He reached out a hand. I took it, and he pulled me closer. I thought he might embrace me, but he didn't, just kept our fingers entwined while his other hand came up to cup my cheek. I leaned into the touch, and lifted my free hand to wrap my fingers around his wrist. The steady beat of his pulse against my fingertips was reassuring. Things could be worse. He might be leaving, but he was alive. And for once, hopefully not heading into anything too dangerous.

When his head descended, my eyes fluttered closed, and when his lips brushed mine, my knees turned to water. It had always been that way. At first I'd told myself it was terror; now I knew it was just the way I responded to him. Breathless and weak in the knees, like the heroine in one of Barbara Botticelli's bodice rippers. I swayed toward him and felt his chest move when he chuckled. And then his lips came back, and everything faded to black.

It must have lasted more than a minute, because when I came back to myself, Tamara Grimaldi had opened the door and was telling Rafe he'd had enough fun and it was time to go. I opened my eyes reluctantly, and I'd been right about the death-grip: at some point I'd let go of both his hands and latched onto his shirt, and I was bunching fistfuls of material, practically trying to crawl up his body to get closer.

"Let go, Savannah," Grimaldi said; one of the few times she'd used my first name. "I need to take him."

I let go, with a bit of effort, and did my best to smooth out the material. It didn't work, and the pull of hard muscles under the fabric was distracting. Rafe was grinning, as if he knew what I was feeling. I managed a weak smile in response before I turned to Grimaldi. "You'll make sure nothing happens to him, right?"

"He'll be fine." She twirled the handcuffs. "Hands behind your back, please."

I watched, wincing, at Rafe obediently put both hands behind him and let Grimaldi snap the handcuffs on.

"Are there cameras outside?"

She shook her head. "Not here. Outside night court, yeah. You never know who might have gotten caught driving drunk."

"Try to stop them from getting a good picture of him," I said. The identity situation was still a problem. To most people, Rafe Collier was dead. If they saw his picture in the paper, they'd wonder what happened.

And even if the caption said his name was Jorge Pena, a few of them would probably recognize him for who he really was. And I had no idea how the TBI planned to handle that aspect of things, whether he'd get to go back to being Rafe Collier again, or whether he'd become someone else entirely. He couldn't continue to be Jorge, since Jorge was wanted for multiple homicides here and abroad. "You'll make sure they know he's not really Jorge Pena, right? I don't want him extradited anywhere to stand trial for someone's murder that he didn't commit."

"I'll take care of him. Don't worry." She gave him a nudge toward the door.

"See you around, darlin'," Rafe said.

"I'd better." I followed them to the door and stood and watched them walk down the hallway to the stairs. Only when I couldn't see either of them anymore did I close and lock the door. And then I went out on the balcony.

I'd expected a police car. Flashing lights, maybe. A few cops with guns trained on the door. A smaller version of the scene outside *La Havana.*

There was nothing like that. Just an unmarked car waiting at the curb. When Rafe and Grimaldi came out of the courtyard, a man in black—Rafe's handler, Wendell Craig—opened the car's back door and kept his hand on Rafe's head while the latter got in. He looked up once before the door closed, and shot me a grin when he saw me standing there, arms wrapped around myself against the chill. Grimaldi turned too, but she didn't smile or wave. Wendell gave me a nod, and then they all piled into the car and drove off down the street. I waited until the red of the taillights had faded into the distance before I went back inside and closed the balcony door.

THE FIRST THING I DID was get undressed and in the shower. My red satin dress had taken quite a beating tonight. Between dinner with Bradley and the crowd in the nightclub I reeked of a mixture of Italian spices and cigarette smoke, and then there was Rafe's treatment during the hostage situation. The dress was wrinkled and stained, and it desperately needed to go to the dry cleaner. My hair smelled pretty ripe too, and the shampoo and warm water felt nice. I came out feeling somewhat refreshed, as if I'd washed away a few weeks worth of stress and anger along with the bad odors. It didn't matter what Rafe and Carmen had done after dinner on Friday; whatever it was, it had been in a day's work for him. He kissed *me* because he wanted to.

Actually, he'd kissed me because *I* wanted him to. Because I'd asked him to. But he'd wanted to, too. At least I thought so.

Or maybe he was just really good at pretending.

He *was* really good at pretending. He'd have to be. He must have been convincing when he was with Carmen. Maybe he hadn't neglected to contact me because he wanted to keep me out of what he was doing; maybe the real reason really was that he was through with me. The baby situation may have been too much for him. Especially my statement that I wanted to try again. Most single men would run like the wind if a woman they'd bedded twice talked about slippers and pipes and babies.

I might not ever hear from him again. And not because he was dead; because he didn't want me.

But somehow I didn't think so. Somehow, I managed to hold on to the belief that he'd be back. Probably because if I didn't, I'd be halfway to night court by now, ready to handcuff myself to him.

I really was pitiful.

Curling up on the sofa, I grabbed my phone and dialed my brother's number. "Howdy," I said when he answered.

"Are you OK?"

"Of course I'm OK. It takes more than a few guns pointed my way to scare me."

"Ha-ha," Dix said coldly. "If you had any sense at all, you'd stay far away from that guy. Ever since you hooked up with him it's been nothing but trouble."

"This wasn't his fault," I said. "I shouldn't have been there."

"No," Dix agreed, "you shouldn't."

"They had it all worked out, and I stumbled into the middle of it. It was my fault."

"Uh-huh. If I didn't happen to know that you're telling the truth, I'd tell you to stop making excuses for him."

"I'm not trying to make excuses for him." And then what he said registered and I added, "What do you mean, you happen to know I'm telling the truth? How could you know?"

"I spoke to Detective Grimaldi," Dix said.

Of course. "She said you'd called her." And she must have laid the blame for what happened firmly where it belonged. On my shoulders. I made a mental note to thank her. My family has enough hang-ups about Rafe as it is. "Although I don't need you to check up on me, Dix. I'm twenty seven. I'm capable of taking care of myself."

"Of course," Dix said. "That's why you found yourself with a gun to your head on national news this evening. Because you're so good at taking care of yourself. You just be grateful mother didn't see it."

"I am. Believe me."

"So how are you? Really?"

"I'm fine," I said, leaning back. "I really am. It was scary for a minute or two, though. I knew Rafe wouldn't hurt me, but I wasn't sure about the others. There were a lot of them. With guns. It took me a while to realize that they knew what was going on and they really weren't there to shoot him." My mind probably hadn't ticked over too swiftly, what with the stress and all.

"What happened after you left?"

"He drove me home," I said. "And then Tamara Grimaldi and Wendell came and picked him up, to take him to night court. Apparently they want to make sure everyone sees him there, so there's no question about the fact that he got arrested, too."

"It's a tricky situation," my brother answered. "Nobody else was there last time he was shot, but everyone believed that he was dead. They wanted to avoid a similar situation this time. They wanted to actually show, publically, that he was arrested along with everyone else."

"It makes sense." And quite interesting how he knew so much about it. "You and Tamara Grimaldi must have talked a lot."

I heard what I can only describe as an audible squirm. He didn't say anything, didn't make a sound, and I couldn't see him, but I knew he was wiggling like a worm on a hook.

I grinned. That was new, and rather fun for me. I don't often get to see my brother ill at ease—he's much too well brought up to do anything embarrassing—and after all the squirming I'd done myself lately, while dodging pointed questions about my love life and my involvement with Rafe, it was nice to be able to play tit for tat. "What have you been up to, Dixon?"

"Nothing," Dix muttered.

"You seem to know a lot about it for someone on the outside."

He took a breath. "Fine. I've been talking to Tamara. On and off."

My eyebrows zoomed halfway up my forehead. "Really?"

"We were having dinner when you called me a few nights ago."

"When you told me you were doing a favor for a friend?" He didn't answer, and I added, "What kind of favor?"

"She needed a date," Dix said. "One who didn't look like an undercover cop."

And she'd called my brother? Interesting. "So it really was a date. You said it wasn't."

"It wasn't. Not really. And I did it for you."

"How do you figure that?"

"We were keeping an eye on your boyfriend," Dix said. "And that woman he was with."

"Carmen." For a second I saw green. "He slept with her."

Dix hesitated. "Did he tell you that?"

Not in so many words. "He told me he'd done what he had to do for the job, but that I shouldn't worry because she wasn't important."

"That doesn't mean he slept with her," Dix said.

"Of course it does." What else could it mean?

There was another pause while Dix pondered my answer and—probably—tried to come up with something to say without putting his foot in his mouth. "How do you feel about it?"

"Fine," I said. "If I ever come face to face with her, you'll probably have to hold me back, but I believe him. He did what he had to do to get the job done. And he's a man, right? Men can do that sort of thing."

While women, for the most part, read emotions into sex, men can have sex for the sake of having sex, with no emotions required. Can't they?

Dix made a non-committal sound in his throat.

"I'm upset," I admitted. "I hate the idea that he slept with someone else. Even if it was just part of the job. And even if we aren't together in any sort of relationship. It's not like he's exclusively mine. He never said he was. He never pretended to be. We never discussed it. But dammit, Dix, I want to kill her!"

"Good," Dix said. "For a second there I was worried. You sounded so reasonable."

"Please don't tell anyone. Especially mother. Or Todd. They'll just see it as another reason why I need to give up on him."

"We don't discuss Rafe Collier," my brother said. "Both mother and Todd prefer to pretend that he doesn't exist. And they do have a point, you know."

"I know." I should give up on him. I knew it. I just couldn't.

There was another moment of silence. "Did you talk about the baby?" Dix asked, his tone diffident.

I told him we had. "And that's another thing. Do you remember when he and Todd got into that fight in the hospital, and Rafe decked Todd, and I asked Catherine to go after him and bring him back? And he didn't come? Well, it's no wonder. She didn't tell him the baby was his. He thought it was Todd's."

"Oops," Dix said.

"I know. Why would she do that?"

"I'm sure she didn't do it on purpose. Catherine loves you. She wouldn't lie about something like that. Had you told her?"

I said I hadn't. "I assumed you had."

"In front of mother? No, sis. I told you, if you decided to keep the baby, you'd have to tell everyone the news yourself. Including whose baby it was."

So Catherine might sincerely not have known the truth. "I'm still going to talk to her."

"Of course," Dix said. "I should probably let you get to it. I'm glad you're all right."

"I'm fine. And not that you asked, but Rafe is fine too. And Tamara."

"Good," Dix said. He was probably referring to Tamara Grimaldi being fine, and not Rafe. "And good luck with Catherine. Don't be too hard on her. She loves you."

"I know she does," I said. "I'll be nice."

"I'll call you tomorrow."

I thanked him again and hung up. And then I poured myself a glass of wine and dialed my sister's number.

Catherine is four years older than me, while Dix is roughly halfway between us. He and I have always been closer than Catherine and I. It's partly the age-difference, I think—not that four years is a lot— and partly just the fact that Dix and I are more alike than Catherine and I. Or Catherine and Dix, for that matter. Physically as well as emotionally, my brother and I take after mother's family, the Georgia Calverts. Blonde, blue-eyed, docile and reserved. Catherine is named for mother's grandmother, Catherine Calvert, but she looks more like the Martins. My dad had dark hair and a stockier build than the

Calverts. Dix has inherited dad's physique, and so has Catherine. She also has his dark hair, sallow complexion, and stubborn streak. When I divorced Bradley, Catherine represented me in the divorce, and she would have nailed his hide to the wall and taken him for half of everything he owned if I hadn't held her back. At that point I just wanted to be free of him; as far as I was concerned, he could keep all the stuff. Having it around just served to remind me of him anyway. But Catherine was out for blood, and would have gotten it if I hadn't persuaded her it wasn't necessary. She loves me, she's fiercely loyal to both me and Dix, and when I got pregnant, I'd felt fairly certain I could count on her support. I hadn't told her about it, no... but then I hadn't told anyone else, either. Including Rafe.

"Savannah! Are you all right?"

While I cogitated, Catherine answered the phone, her voice as close to hysterical as I'd ever heard it.

"Of course I'm all right," I said. "I guess you watched the news."

"Yes! Oh, my God, what happened?"

"Nothing much. The police and TBI raided a nightclub I happened to be at. It was my own fault."

"He held a gun to your head!" my sister shrieked.

"Not really. He wouldn't have shot me."

"You don't know that!"

"Of course I know it," I said. "I love him. He'd never hurt me."

"He...!" She stopped. "What?"

"I love him."

There was silence. Then Catherine said, her voice carefully calm, "I don't think I understand the situation."

"No," I agreed, "I don't think you do, either. And on that note, I have a bone to pick with you."

"Why?"

"Last month, at the hospital, when I asked you to go after him? He said you neglected to tell him that the baby I lost wasn't Todd's."

"It wasn't?" And then she caught on. "Oh, God. Savannah..."

"Yeah, yeah. I slept with Rafe Collier. I didn't make sure I used protection. I got pregnant out of wedlock. I brought shame on the family."

"No," Catherine said, "that's not it."

"It's not?" I'd expected to hear at least one of those.

"You can sleep with anyone you want. Even Rafe Collier. It's none of my business." She hesitated. "Although..."

"Yes?"

"I remember what he was like in high school. Are you sure getting involved with him is a good idea?"

"Positive," I said. "If Rafe's not the problem, then what is?"

"You sent me after him," Catherine said, "and you didn't give me the information I needed. So instead of helping, I went out there and broke his heart."

"Excuse me?"

"Didn't you see the look on his face?"

"Of course I did," I said. It had been the reason I'd asked Catherine to go after him in the first place. Part of the reason. The other part was that I just wanted him back. But he'd looked so upset, so angry, that I'd been worried.

I heard the sound of Catherine's earring click against the receiver. "I never thought I'd feel sorry for Rafe Collier, but I did that night."

I winced. "Did he... say anything?"

"Not much," Catherine said. "I had to run to catch up with him, and he was already unlocking the door of the car by the time I got there. It wasn't a long conversation."

"Was he rude?"

"Not at all," my sister said. "I'm sure he would have preferred to leave without talking to anyone, but he was polite."

"So what happened?"

"I told him you sent me after him," Catherine said, "to make sure he was all right. He told me he'd survive."

Ouch.

"I asked him to come back inside," Catherine continued, "but he said no. He had to get back to work and besides, you didn't need him, you had your family there."

"He was wrong," I said.

"Yes, Savannah," my sister answered patiently, "but I didn't know that then. Nor, I assume, did he."

I mumbled a shamefaced no.

"Why didn't you tell him?"

"I was scared," I said. "I never expected to get pregnant. It never even crossed my mind. And when I did, I didn't know what to do. I didn't know if I could handle having a baby on my own. Any baby really, but especially his. Mother would have had a fit if I showed up with Rafe Collier's baby."

"She would have gotten over it," Catherine said. "And Dix and I would have supported you."

"I figured you would. Once you got used to the idea. But everyone would have been shocked. And I didn't want to be a single mother, and he never promised me anything..."

Then again, he never made plans, as he'd told me earlier. Suddenly the fact that he hadn't said anything about the future didn't seem so monumental. He'd been happy to see me again when he came back last time. There'd been no indication that he didn't want to keep seeing me.

"I'm an idiot," I said.

"Yes, you are," my sister agreed.

"It's just... I love him, Catherine. And the idea of telling him that I was pregnant, and having him look horrified, because all I really was, was a few hours of fun between the sheets; he certainly didn't want me having his baby—or worse, to have him ask me to marry him, not because he wanted to, but because he thought he had to, after knocking me up... all because I was too stupid and inexperienced to make sure I didn't get pregnant in the first place..."

I trailed off, having totally lost the thread of my soliloquy.

"He wouldn't," Catherine said. "He cares about you. Any idiot can see it. You'd have seen it too, if you weren't so neurotic."

"You think?"

"Yes," Catherine said, "I think. He told me he hoped you and Todd would be very happy together. And not to bother sending him an invitation to the wedding."

"I hope you told him I have no plans of marrying Todd."

"I had no idea whether you planned to marry Todd or not," Catherine said, "since you hadn't talked to me about it. So I did my best to let him down easy. You and Todd have been friends forever, there's always been an understanding between you, I'm sure you didn't mean to hurt him, blah blah blah..."

"Oh, God." And he'd come back to Nashville three weeks later and found me with Todd. I'd done everything wrong.

"Listen, Savannah," my sister said. "God knows I have no reason to want you to get involved with Rafael Collier. Not aside from the fact that you seem to want to be. But if you plan to keep him around, and it sounds like you do, you'll have to make sure mother knows he's off-limits. She'll give him hell if you don't. She loves Todd. She's always wanted you to marry him. And you remember how she treated Jonathan in the beginning."

I nodded. "She stopped once you married him, though."

Catherine allowed that she had. "Are you planning to marry Rafe?"

My mind blanked for a second, rebelling against coming right out and saying it. Then I reminded myself that I'd promised there'd be no more prevarication. "If he wants me. If he doesn't, I'll take whatever I can get."

Catherine was quiet for a second. "I just want you to be happy, Savannah. We all do. Even mother. If he's who you want, then more power to you. As long as he doesn't hurt you, I have no problems with him."

"He won't hurt me. Ever." In fact, he'd taken great pains not to hurt me. Had blown his cover and risked his life with Perry Fortunato back in September, so I wouldn't get hurt. I hadn't realized before how much I'd been a part of screwing up his life and his career. It was my fault his cover was blown. My fault he'd be unemployed soon.

I shook the thoughts off. There'd be time for them later. "Tonight wasn't what it looked like. I walked into the middle of a raid, and he was trying to get me out."

"With a gun to your head?" my sister asked.

"I know it looked bad, but they wouldn't have shot him, and he wouldn't have shot me, and it took me just a few seconds to figure out what was going on. It looked good, though, didn't it?"

"It looked scary," Catherine said. "I thought you were going to die."

"Convincing, do you think?"

"Yes," Catherine said, half-choking, "it looked convincing."

"Good. That way, maybe nobody will realize that Rafe was in on it all along. I'd hate for something to go wrong and for someone to send another hitman after him. It's not fair to make him keep killing them."

"No," Catherine said, in the voice of one humoring the mentally deficient, "of course not."

"You think I'm crazy, don't you?"

"No," Catherine said. "I think you're in love. And maybe a little crazy. I mean... Rafe Collier? Have you lost your mind, Savannah?"

"You don't know him," I said. "He's wonderful. I know he isn't 'our' kind of people. Mother will have all sorts of fits. Todd won't ever forgive me. And most of Sweetwater will probably snub me when I come home to visit. But I love him. It'll be worth it."

If he'd have me.

"If that's how you feel," Catherine said, "then it'll definitely be worth it. Tell him I'm sorry."

"I would, but he's in jail right now."

"Of course he is." Her voice was amused. "The next time you see him will be soon enough. Make sure he knows I didn't know any better. If you're bringing this guy into the family, at least let him know I'm on his side. Or your side."

I promised I would.

"And make sure he knows that if he hurts you, I'll nail his hide to the wall," Catherine added. "I know you think he won't, but just make sure he knows."

"You can tell him yourself. If he ever comes back."

"He will," Catherine said. "And don't think I won't."

Fourteen

The phone calls continued as soon as I woke up the next morning. First it was Tamara Grimaldi, and as always when I saw her name on the caller ID, I felt a little stab of fear. When she called it was rarely good news, and I'd spent enough time worrying about Rafe's safety to be able to let go of it easily. At this point he should be safe, but what if something had gone wrong?

"Detective?"

"Ms. Martin." She sounded exhausted. As well she should, considering that she'd had a lot to do last night, and presumably a lot of people to process. I doubted she'd gotten to bed at all yet.

"Is everything all right?"

"Yes and no. I'm calling to update you."

"I appreciate that," I said, leaning back against the pillows and smoothing the comforter across my lap. No, I hadn't gotten out of bed myself, it was that early. "Although the 'yes and no' has me a little worried. What's wrong?"

"The Atlanta PD screwed up," Grimaldi said. "They let Hector

Gonzales slip through their fingers."

Uh-oh. "That's not good. Is it?"

"No," Grimaldi said, "it isn't."

"Do you think he might come after Rafe?"

"If he has any sense," Grimaldi said, "he'll run in the opposite direction."

"But?"

"He doesn't seem to."

I could feel myself turn pale. "He's coming here? Why?"

"Because," Grimaldi said, "instead of sticking to the plan, your idiot boyfriend staged a kidnapping and got himself all over the news. As soon as Hector realized it, he called."

"Why?"

"That's what we don't know," Grimaldi said. "Could be he wants to compare notes, to see if he can figure out what went wrong."

"Or?" I had a feeling I wasn't going to like what was coming next. I was right.

"Or he could have realized that your boyfriend isn't actually Jorge Pena and that's how the whole thing unraveled."

"You mean he's coming to kill Rafe." My voice was remarkably steady, considering.

"It's possible," Grimaldi said.

Possible? It seemed pretty certain to me, and I said so. "I suppose you've got him staked out somewhere, just waiting for Hector to drop in and snuff him out?"

The answer to that question was so obvious that the detective didn't even bother to respond. "Hector might not have realized it," she said instead. "He might just want to combine forces and rally the few troops he still has. And he might think the fact that they have a hostage could play in their favor."

"What do you mean, they have a hostage? I'm right here!"

"Megan Slater is playing the hostage," Detective Grimaldi said.

Someone else was playing me?

"Isn't she the same girl who stayed in my apartment back when Jorge—" the *real* Jorge, "was looking for Rafe?"

"That's her."

"Todd says she looks like me." He had shown up at my place for a date I'd totally forgotten about, and had met Megan Slater. I hadn't had the pleasure myself; I just had his word for the resemblance.

"She does," Grimaldi confirmed. "Enough to fool anyone who doesn't know you."

"I don't suppose you'll tell me where they are?"

"I don't suppose I will," Grimaldi said.

"I just want to make sure he's all right."

"I'm sure. But you have to trust me on this. He needs you like he needs a hole in the head right now. Let him concentrate on doing his job. Which he can't do if you're there, distracting him. You'll be doing him a favor by leaving him alone."

Probably. But I still wanted to see him. "You'll tell me the minute you catch Hector, right?"

She promised she would. "By the way, your boyfriend happened to mention that the two of you had company last night. Any ideas on who might have been following you?"

"Probably just someone who trailed us from the nightclub, thinking they'd be a hero," I answered. "But when they saw Rafe coming, whoever it was took off instead of risking a confrontation."

I'd have done the same thing. If Rafe Collier had been coming towards me with a gun in his hand, I'd have made tracks as fast as I could in the opposite direction, too. But it was probably better not to mention the gun to Detective Grimaldi. I added, "It couldn't have been Hector. Not unless he was already in Nashville last night."

"He wasn't. The Atlanta PD saw him at eight PM. He wouldn't have had time to get to the nightclub by the time everything happened. Any other ideas?"

"Rafe suggested it might have been my ex-husband's current wife. Bradley has a history of cheating. Maybe she thought he was having dinner with someone else, instead of with me."

"Does she drive a white compact?"

"I have no idea what kind of car she drives," I said, "but I doubt it. Then again, she'd probably realize that she couldn't trail her husband in her own car, and arrange for a substitute. She's not stupid." Much as I'd enjoy thinking so.

"Did your ex have any of the information you were looking for?"

"Some of it." I told her what Bradley had said about Maybelle meeting Uncle Joshua on the cruise ship and marrying him, and about the prenup Bradley's father had insisted Uncle Joshua sign. "He died of a heart attack too, after they'd been married a few years."

Grimaldi's voice sounded a little easier now that we were off the subject of Hector Gonzales. "Would the prenup prevent her from receiving half of everything if they divorced?"

"So I assume," I said. That's what a prenuptial agreement is for, right?

"How much did she inherit when he died?"

"She didn't. That's the thing. According to Bradley, the prenup covered that, too. She got a quarter million, I think, but nothing like what she would have gotten without it."

"Then I doubt there's anything there," Grimaldi said. "If she knew about the prenup, and that she wouldn't inherit, she had no reason to do away with him."

Sadly, she was probably right. "He's supposed to contact me with the name of Maybelle's first husband."

"Another one?"

"So it seems. Once I get it, do you want me to let you know?"

"You can," Grimaldi said, "but there's no hurry. I'll have my hands full until we catch Hector, and to be honest, I don't think there's anything I can do about any of this. There's no law against marrying rich men with bad hearts."

There wasn't.

"You don't mind if I keep looking into it, do you?"

"If it means you'll stay out of my hair," Grimaldi said, "and away from my stakeout, you can look into anything you want. At least this way I don't have to worry about anything bad happening to you. I had to tell your boyfriend you got yourself shot last month, and he wasn't happy. I don't fancy having to do it again."

If he'd been unhappy about me getting shot, he hadn't mentioned it to me. "I'm more concerned that you'll call me and tell me *he's* been shot."

"We'll try to make sure that doesn't happen," Grimaldi said and hung up before I had time to tell her that she'd better do more than just try.

I leaned back against the pillows, chewing on my bottom lip. Dammit, why couldn't fate just be kind for once? Was it too much to ask that things just go according to plan? My own interference last night notwithstanding, Rafe had done enough to bring down Hector Gonzales and his organization. Why did he have to put himself in danger again?

But as Detective Grimaldi had said, it was what he did. He'd chosen this. I couldn't change him, and I wouldn't if I could. He was who he was, and that's who I'd fallen in love with.

Nonetheless, the situation was scary. To distract myself so I wouldn't stay in bed and fret all day, I forced myself to think about Alexandra's situation instead.

When Bradley told me that Uncle Joshua had died of a heart attack, just like Harold Driscoll, I'd been so sure there was something to it. But Grimaldi was right: there's no law against marrying rich men with bad hearts. As long as you don't kill them, and there was no proof that Maybelle had. Grimaldi had checked on Harold Driscoll's death, and had found no suggestion of foul play. And knowing my ex-father-in-law, Bradley's dad, as I did, if there'd been anything suspicious about Uncle Joshua's death, John Ferguson would have had Maybelle slapped in chains so fast her head would have spun. No, they had been heart attacks, pure and simple.

Hopefully Stephen Puckett didn't have a weak heart.

I swung my legs over the side of the bed and put my feet on the floor... and the phone rang again. The floor was cold, so I pulled my feet back under the covers as I answered. "This is Savannah."

"Morning, darling," a male voice said.

I snuggled into the blankets. "Hi, Tim."

"Was that the scrumptious Mr. Collier you were with last night?"

He must have seen the news, too. My phone would probably be ringing off the hook today. "Not at all," I said. "Didn't you hear the news anchor? They said he'd been identified as Jorge Pena, international hitman."

"No offense, darling, but I've met the man. And he's not someone I'd forget."

"I'm sure," I said. Tim had developed a crush on Rafe the first time he saw him—on TV—and the fact that Rafe is a hundred percent heterosexual didn't deter Tim in the least. They'd come face to face a couple of times, and it had been entertaining, if slightly annoying, to watch Tim practically turn himself inside out to be charming. Not that Rafe had minded; he'd flirted right back.

"I assume he's in jail? Since you're home and seemingly safe and sound?"

"He is. And he'll be there a while. And if you don't mind, I'd prefer not to talk about it. Is there something else I can do for you?"

"Yes, darling," Tim said, "you can tell your clients that my clients have countered their offer. I've sent the counter to your email, but I thought I'd call and give you a head's up, too."

So he could ask about Rafe, of course.

"Thanks," I said. "What's the counter?"

He told me, and all in all it wasn't too bad. Tim's clients would sell Aislynn and Kylie their house for a few thousand dollars more than the girls had offered, and they had countered a few of the other details in the contract too. But the differences seemed like they could be worked out, assuming Aislynn and Kylie still wanted the house. With what had happened, and Kylie in the hospital and medical bills and having to buy a new car, things might have changed.

"I'll let them know," I told Tim, "and get back to you."

"You do that, darling. And one of these days, I expect you to tell me the whole story about Mr. Collier. Because I think there's more to it than what you've shared."

"Of course," I said, crossing my fingers. It would be a cold day in hell before I told Tim anything. "I'll let you know what my clients say."

I hung up before he had the chance to respond. Unforgivably rude, of course—mother would have had something to say about it—but she wasn't here.

I made another attempt to get out of bed, and this time made it all the way into the bathroom before the phone rang again. This time the caller was Alexandra Puckett.

"Oh my God, Savannah, are you all right?!"

"I'm fine," I said, taking a seat on the toilet lid and digging my toes into the fluffy bathroom rug. "It wasn't what it seemed."

Her voice turned diffident. "It looked like Rafe."

Like Tim, Alexandra had met Rafe during the week or two after her mother's murder, and like Tim, she had developed a schoolgirl crush on him. Unlike Tim, she didn't flirt, and she had also been more upset when I'd told her he was dead. Tim might have been shocked and dismayed, but I doubted there'd been any real mourning going on. Alexandra had cried.

"It was," I said.

"You told me he was dead."

"I lied." I heard her draw breath, and hurried on before she could start yelling at me. "It wasn't just you, OK? I lied to everyone, even my own family. Nobody knew he was alive."

Alexandra sniffed. "Why?"

"Someone sent a hitman after him. He got shot. He pretended he was dead and then he went undercover to figure out what was going on."

"Oh." She sniffed again. "Is he back now?"

"No," I said. "He's still undercover. As far as everyone else knows, he's dead. You can't tell anyone that he isn't. If everything works out, he'll be back. If not, I'm not sure what'll happen."

"Wow." Alexandra was quiet for a moment. "Um, Savannah...?"

"Yes?"

"Have you figured out anything about Maybelle? Something I can use to stop her from marrying my dad?"

"Not yet," I said apologetically. "I'm sorry. I'm trying. I did track down the husband she had before Mr. Driscoll. He's dead, too. Another heart attack. And I think she may have had another husband before that. I'm trying to find out. How's your father's health?"

"Fine," Alexandra said, "as far as I know."

"Does he take any kind of medicine?"

"He has high blood pressure," Alexandra said.

That was related to the heart, wasn't it? My dad died from a heart attack, and he'd had high blood pressure. Then again, he'd also been a lawyer, and lawyers statistically have high levels of stress.

"I'll let you know if I find out anything else," I said, "but I don't know what good it'll do, to be honest. I've been talking to my friend in the police department, and she says there's nothing she can do about any of it. Harold Driscoll died of a heart attack, and so did the previous husband. There's no proof that Maybelle did anything to either of them."

"She's up to something," Alexandra answered darkly. "She's been gone half the weekend. I've hardly seen her at all."

"Christmas shopping?"

"Maybe. But I think she's plotting something."

"She's probably just planning the wedding," I said. "But I'll keep digging, OK? If I learn anything else, I'll let you know."

"OK, Savannah," Alexandra said. And hesitated. "Savannah?"

"Yes?"

"I'm glad Rafe's alive."

"I am too," I said.

"Are you gonna marry him?"

"If he asks me," I said.

"I knew it!" She hung up.

I did the same. Poor Alexandra, I felt for her, really. The idea of acquiring Maybelle Driscoll for a stepmother would be enough to throw me into a tizzy, as well. There was just something about her, about that placid, sweet face, and those guileless blue eyes, and that demeanor of helpless feminine docility, that screamed at me like nails dragging across a chalkboard. I had no problem imagining Maybelle as a murderess. I'd considered her the front-runner in Brenda's murder. She was just the kind of woman I could picture taking out a rival and then showing up at the memorial service to console the grieving widower, all womanly flutters and concern.

But she hadn't killed Brenda. And she probably hadn't killed her late husbands, either. Enthusiastic sex isn't a crime. If it were, many more of us would be dead. Harold and Joshua had probably died happy. And if he married her, Steven Puckett might die happy, too.

The phone rang again, and I picked it up without checking who it was.

"Good morning, darling," my mother's voice said.

I winced. A lot of people call me darling. I live in the South, after all. Tim does it, girlfriend to girlfriend. Todd's dad Sheriff Satterfield does it, to the daughter of the woman he's dating. Rafe does it, his voice alternately amused and heated enough to curl my toes. And my mother does it, with a well-bred coolness that almost belies the endearment.

Almost.

It isn't that she doesn't love me. I know she does. But the way she talks sometimes conveys those feelings of exasperation and disappointment I'm sure all parents occasionally feel toward their children, especially when those children get romantically involved with screw-ups like Rafe Collier.

"Mother. Hi." I exited the bathroom and went back to the bed, curling up on top of the comforter. If I crawled back underneath, I probably wouldn't get up for a couple of hours, and I had things I needed to do.

"Are you all right, darling?"

"I'm fine," I said, for what felt like—and probably was—the seventh or eight time since the events last night.

"The phone has been ringing off the hook, darling. People are worried about you."

"My phone's been ringing, too. But it's nothing to worry about. I'm fine. So is everyone else."

Mother was quiet for a moment, probably assessing her angles of attack. "Would you like to tell me what happened?"

Not really. But I felt I owed it to her, so I went over the events of last night again, making sure to emphasize the fact that it had been my own fault that I was there, that I hadn't been in any danger, that Rafe hadn't hurt me and never would, and that everything was fine now; I was home, safe and sound, with everything back to normal.

"And young Mr. Collier?" mother said.

It would be nice if she got used to calling him Rafe, since I planned to keep him around, but I supposed that was too much to ask, too soon. "The police have him. He's in a safe house somewhere, staked out as bait for a crime boss."

There was a pause. "I see," mother said.

"I'm sorry. It sounds crazy, I know. But after this is over, he's done. He'll be able to have a normal life again. You can get to know him." And fall in love with him, the way I had. If he came back to me, of course. But he would. He had to.

"Lovely," mother said, sounding like she had a hard time getting the word out. I took pity on her.

"I know it's a lot to process. But you'll get used to it. I love him."

"So you said," mother managed.

"You do want me to be happy, right?"

"Of course, darling."

"He'll make me happy." When he didn't drive me out of my mind with worry.

"If you say so, darling," mother said. When I didn't answer, she added, "I just wanted to make sure everything was all right. I didn't see the news myself last night, but after everyone called..."

"Everything's fine. The news made everything sound worse than it was. You know you can't trust the news."

"Of course not," mother said. "All right then, darling..."

"Right. Places to go, people to see. I'll call you later."

"All right," mother said. As she hung up, sounding rather subdued, I wondered what my involvement with Rafe would mean for my family in the future. Not so much for me and him—because I'd deal with it, whatever it was, if he'd stick around—but for the rest of them. So far, I'd only considered things from my own perspective: how my family's reaction to Rafe would impact him and me. Now, for the first time, it crossed my mind to wonder how my involvement with him would affect everyone else.

Fifteen

When I walked into Kylie's room at Vanderbilt Medical Center, she was sitting up in bed, in earnest conversation with Aislynn and...

I blinked. "Officer Spicer?"

He looked up from the notepad in his lap and brushed a hand over his thinning ginger hair. "Miz Martin."

"What are you doing here?"

A glance around showed me that Truman was hanging out over by the window, as far from the bed as he could get while still staying within the same room. Maybe Kylie's injuries made him uncomfortable, or maybe he was still young enough to be embarrassed about a woman in a bed.

"Taking a report," Spicer said. "You know anything about what happened the other night?"

I shook my head. "Just what Aislynn and Kylie have told me. The brakes on the car gave out and they had an accident."

Spicer nodded. "Didn't expect to see you here, Miz Martin."

"Kylie and Aislynn are trying to buy a house."

"That have anything to do with this?"

I glanced at Aislynn and then at Kylie. "I can't imagine how."

Spicer kept the pencil poised over the notepad. "No bidding war? Nobody who'll get the house if your clients were out of the way?"

"Gosh," I said, "I don't think so. Tim didn't say anything about anyone else having made an offer."

"Tim?"

"Timothy Briggs. My broker. He's the listing agent."

"M-hm," Spicer said and wrote the name down. "Phone number?"

"For Tim?" I rattled it off. "Do you plan to call him?" He might not be happy about that.

"If I have to," Spicer said. "For now, we're just gathering information." He got up from the chair. "I'll be in touch."

"Thank you, officer," Aislynn said. After the two policemen had exited the room, she turned to me. "Do you have news about the house?"

"We have a counter offer." I relayed the information Tim had told me, and gave them the printed counter I had gotten off my email. "Look it over and decide what you want to do. If you still want the house, you can accept their counter or counter back with your own terms. If you don't... just let me know you've decided not to move forward, and we'll reject their counter and leave it at that."

They looked at each other for a second.

"We still want the house," Aislynn said, turning back to me. Kylie nodded.

Nice, how they communicated with just glances.

"Great." I smiled. "Talk about the counter, decide what you want to do, and let me know."

They nodded.

"How are you feeling today?"

"Better," Kylie said. Her voice was less hoarse, and her bruises had faded from black and dark purple to yellow and green. The neck brace was also gone. "If all goes well, I'll be going home tomorrow."

"That's wonderful." If a little scary, how quickly the hospital wanted to get rid of her. I'd noticed the same thing myself, when I was in the hospital last month: as soon as you could survive on your own, they kicked you out. "Do you need a ride?"

Getting to go home was one thing; getting there on the back of Aislynn's scooter was something else.

"We can take a cab," Kylie said. She tried to move down in the bed and winced. Aislynn rushed to help shift her.

"Don't be silly," I said. "I'll be happy to drive you home. It's the least I can do."

"Thank you, Savannah," Aislynn said. Easing Kylie back down against the pillows, she glanced at the clock above the door. "I need to go soon. Sara Beth opens at eleven."

"I'll give you guys some time to talk about the house," I said. "Call me when you know what you want to do. Anytime today will be fine."

I turned toward the door and then did a Columbo. "Um... what's going on with the car? And the police?"

"The auto shop notified them," Kylie said. "The brakes on the car may have been compromised. The police wanted to know whether we had any enemies. Anyone who might be trying to cause an accident."

Good Lord. "Do you?"

"Not that we know of," Aislynn said.

"Have you been arguing with anyone? One of the neighbors? Taking his parking space, or something? Or did someone complain about the bill at the café? Did you foreclose on anyone's house?" Kylie's work in the bank might have precipitated something like that.

She shook her head. "Not that I can think of."

"Me, neither," Aislynn said. And added, her tone almost apologetic, "the officer said it might be a hate crime."

I blinked. "How so?"

"Well, we're two women together, right? And this is the buckle of the Bible belt. People are conservative here."

"Not all people," I said, since most of the people I know, at least in Nashville, couldn't care less about Aislynn and Kylie and what they chose to do behind closed doors.

"But some people mind. And the police thought it might be someone who saw us together and thought they'd strike a blow for heterosexuals everywhere."

It was possible, I supposed. Although I thought heterosexuals everywhere were more inclined to just want to leave Aislynn and Kylie alone. Most of us are too preoccupied with our own sex-lives to take that much of an interest in someone else's.

"When do they think it happened?" How far could someone drive with punctured brake cables? Half a day? Or just a few blocks?

"Most likely at the coffee shop," Kylie said. "It was dark by then, and we were parked out of the way. Not as far out of the way as you, but not right in front either. Someone could have paused for a minute next to the car and no one may have noticed."

"That's awful."

They both nodded. Then Aislynn's face lightened. "But at least we had insurance. And the settlement will pay for another car. As soon as Kylie's back on her feet, we're going car-shopping."

"Good for you." I opened the door again. "I'll give you guys some time to discuss the offer on the house. Just give me a call when you're ready. And let me know when you need to be picked up tomorrow to go home."

They promised they would, and I left. Only to walk into Spicer and Truman as soon as I got to the lobby.

"Gotta few more questions," Spicer said.

"Of course." I looked around and spied a conversation area off to the side. "Why don't we go sit down." I had a few questions myself.

"So what's going on?" I added when we were comfortably

positioned, Spicer and Truman in two blue armchairs while I had the matching sofa to myself. I folded one leg over the other and smiled across the table at Truman, who blushed.

"Auto repair contacted us," Spicer grunted. "Said it looked like the car had been tampered with."

"That's not good, is it?"

He shook his head. "Seemed like a couple of nice girls. Can't imagine why anyone'd wanna hurt either of'em."

"I can't either." Nor could they, it seemed.

"Have you known'em long?"

I said I hadn't. "Aislynn and I met a couple of weeks ago, when my sister-in-law was killed. She works at Sara Beth's Café in Brentwood, and Sheila had lunch there the day she died."

"This don't have nothing to do with that, does it?" Spicer said.

"I can't imagine how. Sheila's killer is behind bars, and it isn't like Aislynn knew anything about it." I thought for a second. "Kylie told me she has an ex-husband. Damian, I think she called him. They got divorced a few years ago, before she met Aislynn, but I suppose a certain type of man might feel resentful about being replaced by a woman."

"We'll look into that," Spicer said, making a note. "She mentioned him, but said they parted on good terms."

"They may have. I wouldn't know. I'm grasping at straws here. I mean, I don't know them well, but I can't imagine why anyone would want to harm either of them. Are you sure about the car?"

"The auto repair people seemed sure," Spicer said and changed the subject. "You still driving a Volvo, Miz Martin?"

I wrinkled my brows. It was just a few days since he'd seen my car, parked in Maybelle Driscoll's driveway. "Yes. Why?"

"Just thinking. The car those girls were driving was a Volvo too, wasn't it?"

"So? If you're thinking I'd know how to do something to a Volvo because I own one...!" I stopped when Spicer shook his head.

"You sure this don't have nothing to do with you, Miz Martin?"

Oh. "You mean, someone was trying to disable my car and got theirs instead?"

"It could happen," Spicer said, and Truman nodded. "Specially considering the company you keep."

"Rafe? I don't see why..." But I stopped before I said anything else, because the theory made a lot of sense.

No one seemed to have a reason for going after Aislynn or Kylie; I was a much more likely choice, to be honest. If the sabotage had taken place Sunday night, outside the coffee shop, then it was possible that someone had been aiming for my car and had gotten Kylie's instead. They'd both been there: two blue Volvos, very similar in appearance and age. Someone might have been excused for mistaking one for the other, especially in the dark. Whoever it was might not have watched me park; had just seen me at the coffee shop and attacked the first blue Volvo they got to. Which would have been Kylie's. Mine had been tucked away all the way at the back of the lot, beside the dumpster.

"I can't imagine who I might have upset lately," I said. "I suppose Carmen Arroyo might have noticed me Friday night at Fidelio's." I'd certainly noticed her. I hadn't seen Rafe glance my way at all in the restaurant, though—I'd gone home thinking I'd dodged a bullet—but I supposed it was possible Carmen had picked up on something I hadn't. But it had to have been blatant for her to go to the extreme of trying to get rid of me, and I doubted Rafe was ever that transparent. Especially with someone he knew was a criminal.

"Anyone else?" Spicer had his pencil poised.

"I spoke to Heather Price the other day. Remember her? She was dating Julio Melendez back in September, when you arrested him for those open house robberies? I guess it's possible she blames me for that."

"We'll look into it," Spicer said, writing it down.

"What are you two doing down here in the first place? This isn't your usual beat, is it?"

Lyle Spicer and George Truman were patrol officers, and their beat was East Nashville. Vanderbilt University Hospital and the south side of town, where Kylie and Aislynn's accident had happened, were out of their area. So, frankly, was the questioning they were doing.

"When the report came in from the auto shop," Spicer said, "it got flagged for the detective's attention."

'The detective' is his name for Tamara Grimaldi, as if she were the only member of the Nashville PD with that title.

"Why?"

"Cause of the St. Jerome's investigation," Spicer said. "Miz Turner's name's in the file cause of your sister-in-law."

Of course. Aislynn had been interviewed in connection with Sheila's death since Sheila had been at Sara Beth's for her last meal. The Nashville PD must have automated their process enough that when another report involving Aislynn Turner came in, a red flag went up.

"Do you know anything about what the detective's up to?" I asked. Innocently, since I didn't want them to think I had anything invested in the answer.

They exchanged a look. Truman tried to hide his grin but Spicer didn't even bother.

"Fine," I snapped, even as I could feel myself blushing, "so I'm worried. I don't want anything to happen to anyone."

"Anyone?" Spicer looked like he was enjoying himself a little too much, and Truman could hardly hold back his laughter.

"Rafe," I snarled. "I don't want anything to happen to Rafe. Or anyone else either, but mostly Rafe. Do you know if anything's going on?"

"No," Spicer said, taking pity on me. "Last we heard, nothing's going on. Every squad car in Nashville's keeping an eye out for Hector Gonzales, but nobody's seen him. And he ain't been in touch."

"They have some protection where they are, right? He and Megan Slater?"

"Your boyfriend can take care of himself," Spicer said. "So can Officer Slater. Plus they've got the detective and her team standing by, and a taskforce from the TBI. They'll be fine."

"Have you been over there?" *And while you're at it, why don't you tell me exactly where 'there' is?*

"No," Spicer said, "and you ain't going, either."

"Of course not. I wouldn't dream of it."

"Right," Spicer said and didn't try to sound like he believed me. "We'll look into Miz Price. Meantime, why don't you just try to stay outta trouble, Miz Martin? Just in case someone's gunning for you, too."

I promised I would, but between you and me, I was still more worried about Hector Gonzales looking for Rafe than I was about someone hypothetical possibly trying to get at me.

"Wilkins," my ex-husband said.

"Excuse me?"

"That was Maybelle's last name when she married my uncle. Wilkins."

Of course. "Your dad called?"

"I called him," Bradley said.

"Did he have any information on Mr. Wilkins? First name? Cause of death? Did he die from a heart attack, too?"

I was in the car, on my way back home after leaving the hospital, and while we were talking, I was navigating down the highway in the direction of home with one hand and holding the phone to my ear with the other. It had started sleeting while I was inside, which didn't help matters. The road was slippery and the other drivers were alternately slowing to a crawl or pretending it was a bright, sunny day with no road challenges whatsoever. I wasn't sure which segment of the driving public was more annoying at the moment.

"Lenny," Bradley said. "Lenny Wilkins. Might be Leonard, might not."

I nodded. In the South, it's hard to be sure. People really do name their children Lenny.

"And I don't know what he died from," Bradley added. "All I know is they got married in Florence, Alabama. But I'm sure dad would have checked to make sure Lenny was really dead. If my mother could have annulled Uncle Joshua's marriage for polygamy, she would have."

Having known Althea, I didn't doubt it.

"I'll try to track down the information myself," I said. After all, it wasn't fair to expect my ex-father-in-law to have suspected Maybelle of any wrongdoing beyond being after Uncle Joshua's money. "I appreciate the help." I put on my turn signal and moved ponderously over in the right lane.

"Glad to do it," Bradley said. And hesitated. "Are you all right, Savannah?"

"I'm fine," I said. "Traffic's a little difficult right now, but I'm holding my own."

A four wheel drive SUV with big, beefy tires zoomed by with a beep of his horn and a squirt of wet matter that hit my windshield. I resisted the temptation to make a rude gesture, mostly because both my hands were occupied.

"I felt bad leaving you with that guy last night," Bradley said. "I know you said it would be all right, but..."

"Oh." Right. He'd dropped me off outside the condo after dinner, long before any of the events happened at *La Havana*. And he must not have been watching the news. He was just concerned about having left me with Rafe. "It was. All right, I mean."

There was a tentative pause before he continued. "That man... was he a friend of yours?"

"Boyfriend," I said, looking left and right and left again before merging onto the ramp for I-65 north.

Bradley was silent, and part of me really wished I could see his face. The tone of his voice made up for it, to some degree. "Excuse me?"

I managed to restrain my giggle, but just barely. "I've known him for years. We went to high school together."

"He's from Sweetwater?"

"Uh-huh." The ramp was ending and Interstate 65 was coming up; I concentrated on merging and cutting across a couple of lanes to put me in the right position to merge onto I-40 up the road.

"I don't remember him from our wedding," Bradley said.

There was a good reason for that. Mother would never have invited Rafe to my first wedding. If she could, she'd do her best to keep him out of my second, too.

"He wasn't there. He was in jail by then. Or in Memphis." It was probably Memphis. I was pretty sure he was out of jail by the time I was out of high school. Several years before I married Bradley.

"Jail?" Bradley echoed.

"For assault and battery. It's a long time ago." And none of his business. "He only served two years of a five years sentence. Time off for good behavior." Ostensibly. In reality, it was because the TBI recruited him and sprung him from Riverbend Prison so he could go undercover for them. I didn't tell Bradley any of that. "I'm fine. I'm always fine when he's around."

"I see," Bradley said, sounding a little like he was choking. "Um... he wasn't upset, was he? He looked upset."

"He was, a little." But that was before everything else happened, while he was warning me away from Carmen.

And then I realized what Bradley was afraid of. "Oh, don't worry. He wasn't upset with you. Or about you. It had nothing to do with us having dinner together."

"Oh," Bradley said, his relief palpable. "Good."

I grinned. No, Rafe knew Bradley's inadequacies much too well to be worried about us carrying on a torrid affair. "Speaking of significant others, I hope Shelby didn't give you a hard time last night?"

"Not at all," Bradley said complacently. "She got home a little after

I did. Nothing to worry about, Savannah. She doesn't suspect a thing."

As if I cared what Shelby thought or suspected. "What kind of car is she driving these days?"

"Excuse me?" Bradley said.

"Her vehicle? What is it?" It was time to merge with traffic on I-40, and I looked around, head swiveling, to make sure I didn't get myself into trouble.

"Oh," Bradley said. "Um... I'm buying her a new car for Christmas. A minivan. For the kids, you know."

"Of course." And wouldn't she be thrilled? I mean, that's what we all want, isn't it? Minivans under the Christmas tree? "What does she drive right now?"

"An Audi," Bradley said. "Sports car."

That made the minivan sound even better. Part of me wished I could be there to see Shelby's face when she saw it. "What color is it?"

"Red," Bradley said, sounding like he was humoring the crazy lady.

"Neither one of you has a white economy compact, do you? A Toyota or Honda?"

"No," Bradley said, and I could imagine the curl of his lip. "Why?"

The sleet was getting heavier and the road more slippery. The ramp to merge with I-24 was coming up. It's a tough place to navigate, because the next exit comes up really quickly. I'd have to merge while simultaneously cutting across three lanes of traffic to get into the exit lane, and the other drivers aren't always observant or willing to let me over. I slowed down. "Someone was following me yesterday. I thought maybe it was Shelby. That she'd figured out you were having dinner with someone else and was having you followed."

Maybe that was the explanation: Shelby had hired a two-bit PI to follow Bradley around, and when he'd dropped me off, the PI had decided to follow me instead.

"I can't imagine why she would," Bradley said, sounding worried.

"You cheated on me with her. Maybe she's afraid you're cheating on her with me. Or someone else."

"I would never," Bradley said, offended. "I love Shelby. And I can't think of anyone we know who drives a white Toyota."

Naturally not. He was a lawyer, and Shelby was a lawyer's wife: I'm sure all their friends drove Audis and Mercedes.

"Thanks anyway." I took my hand off the steering wheel to flip on the turn signal. Out of the corner of my eye, I saw a blurred shape to my left, a touch too close: a car in the next lane, trying to merge into mine. There was a blinking yellow light in my peripheral vision. At the same time, an eighteen wheeler was coming up from behind in the right lane, the one I was trying to get into. It was going a little too fast for comfort, considering the conditions and the poor visibility. I wasn't sure I'd have time to get in front of it. A quick glance in the rearview mirror showed that I had a car behind me, too: some sort of work-van. All I could see was the color—pale blue—and the bumper and headlights; that's how close it was.

The car to my left nudged me. I don't know what the problem was, whether the driver just didn't notice me or perhaps thought I had moved over already. In either case, the Volvo slid sideways in a maneuver I hadn't planned, straight into the path of the tractor trailer.

Sixteen

The driver of the truck laid on the horn, a deep bass rumble that rattled through my bones. I had no time to respond, or glare at the careless driver to my left: all my efforts went into keeping the Volvo out of the path of the tractor trailer bearing down on it. The phone went flying, with Bradley's voice still quacking out of it, and I clamped both hands around the steering wheel as sweat broke out on my forehead in spite of the chilly weather.

A few other horns joined in the chorus as I slammed on the brakes and slid on the slick roadbed. The tractor trailer skimmed by, continuing its bone-shaking bass honk, the back tire scraping along the side of the Volvo. Somewhere in the recesses of my mind I hoped there wouldn't be scratches in the paint, but it was the least of my concerns. Behind me, the van was trying desperately to avoid rear-ending me, fishtailing on the slick road. It managed to squeak by with just a gentle nudge of my bumper and a scream of the horn. I saw the driver's face, eyes wide and mouth open, going by in a flash. He looked as terrified as I felt. In front of me, the driver of the car that had caused the whole thing put on a burst of speed and hustled out of the way of the van. All I noticed was a flash of taillights disappearing through the sleet.

There was space behind the tractor trailer, and—heart pounding and hands shaking—I stepped on the gas again, and managed to get myself and the Volvo across three lanes of traffic and into the exit lane on the far right. Nothing seemed to be wrong; the car was handling just fine. A minute later I was off the interstate, pulling to a stop on the shoulder of the exit ramp. And there I sat, shivering, until I became aware of a strange quacking sound. I had just isolated it as coming from the cell phone on the floor when the blue van bumped to a stop behind me and the driver jumped out and came running. I rolled down the window, in time to hear, "Holy hell, are you all right, lady?"

He was young, probably even younger than Truman, with brown, shaggy hair and acne, dressed in some sort of navy blue coverall. A fuzzy strip of hair on his upper lip was an attempt to grow a mustache, and I could see moisture on his skin through the hairs. He must have been as scared as me.

"I seem to be," I said as I bent to retrieve the cell phone from the floor of the car. "Excuse me a second, would you? I'd better take care of this first. Bradley?"

"What happened?" my ex-husband's voice yelped. "Are you all right?"

"I'm fine," I said, my refrain over the past twenty four hours. "I just had an almost-accident on the interstate. The weather is bad and the roads are slick."

"Did you hit someone?" Bradley asked, his tone vaguely disapproving.

"We're not married anymore," I reminded him, since I recognized the attitude from when we had been. Hopefully he had the good grace to blush, although of course I had no way of knowing. "No, I didn't hit anyone. And no one hit me. But it was a close call. And on that note I should go. There's someone who's waiting to talk to me. Thanks for the information."

"Call me if you need anything else," Bradley said. I promised him I would, and he hung up. I did the same and turned to the young man outside the window.

"Sorry about that. Are you all right?"

"I ain't worried about *me*," the young man said. "*I'm* fine. A little shook up. But nothing happened to *me*. *You're* the one I'm worried about."

"Nothing happened to me either."

"No thanks to that idiot in the other car!" the young man said. "Fool didn't even have the sense to stop and check that everything turned out all right."

"Not everyone is as civic-minded as you are. I appreciate you coming back to check on me."

"Holy *crap*," the young man said, "it's the *least* I can do, innit? I damn near knocked you into the river!"

"I think I was probably in more danger of being mowed under by the eighteen wheeler, to be honest."

The young man nodded. "Saw him bumping along the side of you. Car all right?"

"I haven't checked," I said, reaching for the door handle.

"Stay there. I'll do it."

He jogged around the car and inspected the damage before coming back. "Don't look too bad. Rubber residue from the tires, mostly. You should probably go through a car wash and see what comes loose before you start worrying about taking her to a body shop."

'Her' being the Volvo, I assumed. Men call their cars, their horses, and their guns 'she,' don't they?

"I'll do that," I said. "Thank you."

"Name's Eddie." He handed me a business card with that name and a phone number, plus the information that he was an electrician. "Don't know if it'll do any good to file a report, but if you do, you can give the cops my number. I'll tell 'em what happened."

"I'm not really sure what happened," I admitted. "It went so fast. I was getting ready to merge, and the car in the lane next to me was too close..."

Eddie spat. "Women drivers!" And then he seemed to think better of it. "No offense, lady. You did good. But the driver of that Toyota—"

"It was a Toyota?"

He nodded. "Lady was probably talking on her cell phone." His glance fell on mine, and he added, "No offense."

"None taken. I shouldn't have been on the phone. But that wasn't the problem."

"No," Eddie agreed, "problem was the lady in the Toyota not paying attention. Looked like she didn't realize you were there."

"Maybe I was driving in her blind spot."

Eddie shook his head, tossing droplets of water. He was getting soaked standing out there. "You were right next to each other. She'da seen you if she looked out the window. Guess she didn't bother."

Guess not.

"You should get back in your car. You're getting wet. But before you go... I don't suppose you caught the license plate?"

"Sorry," Eddie said. "It all went too fast. All I saw was it was a white Toyota. Or maybe off-white, or something."

"How do you know it was a woman driving?" If he'd been behind me, and she'd been ahead and to the left, how would he have seen her? Especially with the weather so bad and the visibility so poor, and everything happening so quickly.

"She passed me," Eddie said. "Just before it happened. I looked over. Couldn't see her face—my van is higher than her car—but I saw her legs. Hose and high heels."

But no actual description. Oh, well.

"Thanks," I said. "I appreciate you stopping to check on me. I'm glad we're both OK."

"Me too." Eddie nodded to the business card still in my hand. "You got my number. Take care of yourself."

I said I would, and he jogged back to his van and started up. I watched him pull out and go past me and up the incline to Shelby Avenue, where he waited for the light to change before cutting across the street and getting back on the interstate.

I stayed where I was. My hands were still a little unsteady, and I had a lot to think about.

I know that accidents happen. The weather was certainly yucky enough to be a contributing factor. Visibility was poor and the blacktop was slick. Traffic was snarly, as it always is at that particular juncture of interstates. I'd had trouble there before. And I had been on the phone. It might have contributed to my being unobservant. The truth was that I'd escaped with my life and health, along with most of my sanity, so I had no real cause for complaint. It was just interesting how, so soon after Kylie and Aislynn's accident, I'd almost had one myself. Especially considering Lyle Spicer's suggestion, that the earlier accident could have been meant for me instead of Aislynn and Kylie.

And now there was Eddie's mention of a white or off-white Toyota. There'd been a white car following us home from the nightclub last night too. As well as...

I thought back. Yes, a white car had narrowly escaped hitting me on South 5th Street a few nights ago. I'd been on my way home from the coffee shop when I'd gotten Aislynn's call about the accident, and I'd done a U-turn across a bunch of lanes. There'd been a white car right there, that had almost hit me. I'd chalked it up to crazy driving on my part and lack of attention on theirs, but what if it had been deliberate? What if the driver of the white car had been following me then, too?

That knocked Shelby Ferguson out of the running, anyway, along with any second rate PI she might have hired. Kylie and Aislynn's accident had happened Sunday night, long before Joshua Rowland's name had come up in connection with anything. I hadn't heard from Dix until Monday morning, and had put off calling Bradley until after noon, since I didn't fancy talking to him. So anyone or anything to do with the Fergusons was out.

Carmen Arroyo drove a red Mercedes, and she had definitely not been following Rafe and me the night of the raid. The police might have let him—and me—slip through their fingers, but that was only because they knew we weren't who they were after. They wouldn't have let Carmen get away. And anyway, if they had, Tamara Grimaldi would have told me. So it couldn't have been Carmen.

Heather Price, then? She might have been hanging around *La Havana* the night of the raid, and when we fishtailed out of there, she might have followed. I'd called her that afternoon: she was the one who had told me about Hector Gonzales. It was possible she resented me—and even more so, resented Rafe—for her boyfriend ending up in prison. She might have wanted to hurt me because of it, both for my own part in Julio's arrest and to upset Rafe. Most people had probably figured out by now that going after me would bother him. And she might have been hanging around before the night of the raid. She'd probably seen Rafe during the open house robberies a couple of months ago. He'd been working with, or for, her boyfriend. Maybe she'd seen him again recently, in his Jorge Pena guise, and had recognized him. She could have started following him around. And of course she knew that the two of us had a thing going. She and I and the late Connie Fortunato had discussed it back in September.

I HAD TALKED TO SPICER AND Truman about Heather. They were looking into her. But maybe I should pay her a visit anyway. If nothing else, I could at least scope out what kind of car she drove. And it would give me something to do, apart from spending the day fretting about Rafe and Megan Slater and Hector Gonzales.

Ten minutes later I was on my way, after calling Brittany at the office and begging her to look up Heather Price's home address for me.

And I was driving slowly, staying off the interstates and using the back roads instead, keeping an eye out for white Toyotas as I went.

I didn't have far to go. Heather lived just a few short miles north of downtown in Germantown, an old industrial and warehouse area that had been converted to a hip urban neighborhood over the past ten years.

When I pulled up to the address on Monroe, I saw that Heather lived in an old Folk Victorian cottage, brick construction and stained glass windows with a wrap-around front porch, a hundred and some years old. She shared it with the business she ran: a sign in the miniscule front yard said *The Right Price Interior Design and Real Estate Staging Company*. There was no parking save for on the street, and not much there. With just a bit of difficulty—I don't like double-parking—I slotted the Volvo into a barely-sufficient space on the other side of the street, behind an SUV with Georgia plates. There were cars parked all up and down the street, as well as cruising by, but I looked around carefully, and there was no sign of a white Toyota. Which might mean A) that it didn't belong to Heather, or B) that it did, but she wasn't home. In either case, it seemed safe to cross: the Toyota wouldn't appear out of nowhere and try to mow me down.

At first I didn't think she'd answer. I knocked on the old carved-wood door, and heard nothing. Next I spied an old-fashioned doorbell, the kind you twist, and twisted it. It rang through the house, but didn't bring anyone to the front. Gaining a little courage from that, I pressed my nose to the hand-blown glass panel in the door and squinted inside.

The interior was dark, but I saw enough to distinguish dark wood floors, high ceilings, and plaster walls in traditional Victorian jewel colors. Heather's place reminded me of Mrs. Jenkins's house in East Nashville, if on a much smaller scale. They were both brick Victorians, probably built within a few years of each other, and both had the traditional features of the era: Heather because she'd painstakingly restored them and Mrs. J because she hadn't messed with them in the first place.

A movement in the recesses of the house caused me to jump, and a good thing too, because a second later, the movement turned into a shadow, and then into the outline of a woman coming toward the front door. I stepped back, feeling a little guilty about my unbridled curiosity. If I'd realized she was here, I wouldn't have been so bold.

By the time she reached the door, I'd recognized Heather, and by the time she'd twisted the locks and pulled the door open, I'd managed to affix a friendly smile to my face.

"Hi. Sorry about that. I thought the place was empty."

"No problem," Heather said with a glance over her shoulder. She stepped through the door onto the porch and pulled it shut behind her. "What can I do for you?"

"Nothing, really. I was just in the neighborhood and... um..." *Wanted to see what kind of car you drive and whether you tried to kill me earlier.*

She didn't look like she'd been outside the house so far today, to be honest. Her red hair was a tangled mess, her face was bare of make-up, and she was dressed in shapeless gray sweatpants that did nothing for her derriere, and a stretched-out and faded blue T-shirt I would have turned into dust rags, had it been mine.

"Where's your car?" I asked.

She looked at me as if she thought I was crazy, but she pointed down the street. "Right there. The van."

I turned to look at it. Dark blue. "I thought you drove a white Toyota."

"No," Heather said. "I use the van to transport my staging stuff. There's not enough room in a sedan. Or even an SUV. I could really use a bus." She smiled, although it looked a bit forced.

"Sorry," I said. "I guess I must have been confused."

Heather nodded. And shifted her feet for a second before she said, "I saw on the news last night how the police raided that nightclub. The one you called and asked me about. Hector's place. *La Havana.*"

I nodded.

"Did you know that was going to happen, when you called me?"

"No," I said, "I had no idea."

"Did you tell them to do it?"

"Of course not," I said. "I'm a real estate agent. I don't tell the police what to do."

"But you were there, weren't you? I saw the video."

There seemed no point in denying it. "When I went there, I had no idea what was about to go down, though. I just wanted to see the place. If I'd known, I'd have stayed away."

She wrapped her arms around herself. "That guy you were with in the video... it wasn't really Jorge Pena, was it?"

She was probably cold, and no wonder, with her arms bare and the temperature in the thirties.

"Do you want to go inside and sit down?" I asked. "I have a few minutes, if you want to sit and talk."

She shook her head. "I'm fine. It didn't look like Jorge. It looked like that guy who used to work for Julio."

I didn't answer, and eventually she must have taken my silence for acceptance, same as in a real estate contract.

"I thought he was dead," Heather said. "Didn't Jorge kill him?"

Not quite. Although he tried.

"Did he kill Jorge instead? Because somebody got killed, didn't they? A couple of months ago?"

She waited until I nodded.

"Shit," Heather said, with another glance over her shoulder. "So has he been pretending to be Jorge this whole time? Where is he now?"

"The police have him."

"He's in jail?"

I shook my head. "The police in Atlanta were supposed to arrest Hector Gonzales last night. They let him get away instead. The police here think he's on his way to Nashville, and they're hoping he'll get in touch with Rafe when he gets here."

"Rafe." Heather nodded. "That's his name. I remember now. You two had something going, right?"

I shrugged.

"So where is he?"

"I don't know," I said. "All I know is that the police and TBI are keeping him somewhere until they catch Hector. I don't know where."

Heather nodded. "Thanks for letting me know. You know, about Hector and everything."

"No problem." I looked around. There was no activity on the street, and no white Toyota. "I should go. Thanks for talking to me."

"You're welcome," Heather said and reached for the door handle. "Take care of yourself."

"You, too." I headed down the stairs toward the street. When I hit the bottom step, I could hear the lock slide home behind me, and then the rattle of chains and deadbolts. It seemed like Heather was taking precautions. Maybe the idea of Hector Gonzales worried her too.

I SAT IN THE CAR ON the other side of the street for a minute before driving off. The weather was still bad, and there wasn't much else I could do out here, so I should probably just head home. In my hurry to get to Heather, however, I had neglected to follow up on the information Bradley had given me, so I took a minute to call 411 and ask for listings of people named Wilkins in Florence, Alabama. There turned out to be many of them. As the operator read down the list for me, I listened with half an ear while the other half tried to figure out what to do next. It took a second for my ears to catch up with my brain, so by the time I said, "What?" the operator had already reached the Ns.

"Norma, Oliver, Penny..."

"No, no. Before that."

"Leonard," the operator said.

"Leonard Wilkins?"

"Is that who you're looking for?"

It had to be. I replied in the affirmative and got connected. The phone rang a few times on the other end, and was answered. "Body shop."

I smiled. The greeting brought back memories. Back in August, whenever I'd call the only telephone number I'd ever had for Rafe, now disconnected, Wendell Craig would answer, and he'd always say something different. It had been a car lot once, a grocery store, and— if memory served—a pool hall. Of course it was neither; it was just Wendell's throwaway cell phone that he used to keep in touch with Rafe and the TBI.

"I'm looking for Leonard Wilkins," I said.

"Speaking."

The voice was male, but sounded too young to have been Maybelle's husband, who at any rate was supposed to be dead.

"I'm looking for information about the Lenny Wilkins who used to be married to Maybelle Hicks," I said.

There was a pause. Then— "Who's this?"

I introduced myself and explained the situation. "Did you know Maybelle?"

There was a pause. "No," the young man said, "I didn't have that pleasure."

It might have been my imagination that supplied the sarcasm, but I don't think so.

"Did you know Lenny? Was he your uncle or something?"

"Something," young Lenny agreed. "Don't remember much about him, though. I was just a couple years old when he died."

"I don't suppose you remember Maybelle either, then."

"No," Lenny said, "can't say as I do. Where d'you say you was calling from, again?"

I told him I was calling from Nashville. And since I assumed he might have been too surprised by my call to process a few of the other salient details as well, I also recapped what I'd said earlier. "Maybelle is set to marry the father of a friend of mine. I'm looking into her past and finding a lot of ex-husbands."

"You don't say?"

I said I did. "After your... uncle?... she went on to marry a stockbroker from Natchez, Mississippi, and after he died, a CPA in Nashville. Now she has her eye on a financial planner."

"Moving up in the world," Lenny said.

"What did Lenny do? The original Lenny?"

"Used to be his body shop," the new Lenny said, with—I imagined—a look around. "After he died, his brother took over. I started working here when I was fifteen, part time. Now I run the place." I heard a faint note of pride in his voice.

"Good for you," I said. He sounded pretty young to be running his own business. "Would you mind telling me how Lenny died? The original Lenny?"

"House fire," Lenny said. "Trailer burned to the ground with him in it."

"That's horrible." But I also wasn't surprised Maybelle had left Lenny if he lived in a trailer. Rafe had grown up in a singlewide trailer in the Bog, the Sweetwater mobile home park, and I wouldn't wish his upbringing on my own worst enemy.

"Imagine so," Lenny said.

"Was it an accident? Was he smoking or something?"

"That's what they say," Lenny said. "What did you say your name was, again?"

I told him my name was Savannah Martin. "I don't suppose there was anything suspicious about the fire?"

"Suspicious?"

"You know, like maybe it wasn't an accident. Maybe someone torched the trailer."

"Who'd wanna do that?" Lenny wanted to know.

"I certainly can't imagine. I thought maybe you could."

He didn't answer, and I added, "Thank you very much for your time. I appreciate it. Would you mind giving me a call if you remember anything you think might be helpful?"

"Sure," Lenny said, but judging from the tone of his voice, I was pretty sure I'd never hear from him again. Since there wasn't anything I could do about it either way, I hung up the phone and put the car in gear. Glancing across the street as I pulled away from the curb, I saw the curtains in Heather's house flutter. She must have been standing at the window watching me.

Seventeen

Instead of going home once I'd crossed the Cumberland River, I took a quick left up Dickerson Pike, past the bronze buffalos at Dickerson and Grace Street, outside the old Salvation Army headquarters. Dickerson Pike was a buffalo trail back in the old days, hence the statues.

Dickerson Pike is where Rafe and I had broken into a storage unit one night back in August to look for evidence of Brenda Puckett's murder. And it's also where Jorge Pena's motel room was, at the old Congress Inn on the corner of Hart Lane. I'd gone there once, after Jorge was dead, to say goodbye to Rafe and tell him that he had a son no one had bothered to mention.

Mrs. Jenkins's house was nearby, and after a few blocks on Dickerson I took a right and cruised down Dresden Street, over to the Milton House, the old folks' home where Mrs. Jenkins lived when I first met her. At the four way stop at the entrance to the Milton House, I turned left up Potsdam.

101 Potsdam Street, Mrs. J's house, is a three story brick Victorian with a circular tower on one corner, a ballroom that takes up the entire

third floor, and a library on the first floor where Rafe and I had found Brenda Puckett's butchered body the first Saturday in August.

In October, while Jorge Pena was gunning for Rafe and someone else was taking potshots at me because I was involved with him, Rafe had arranged for Mrs. Jenkins to go to a safe house somewhere. The house on Potsdam was supposed to be empty. It had crossed my mind to consider whether Tamara Grimaldi and the TBI might be using it to try to lure Hector Gonzales into their trap, and since I was out driving anyway, and on this side of town, I figured I'd drive by and scope things out.

The area isn't the best, so I wasn't surprised to see a couple of homeboys in saggy pants hanging out down on the corner, probably waiting to either buy or sell drugs. It was also not too surprising to see a young woman in super-tight jeans and a short, furry jacket walking slowly down the other side of the street, long, blond hair swaying and hips swinging. She stared intently at every car that drove by and was probably looking for business, too. The homeboys catcalled something at her, and she flipped her hair over her shoulder and answered in kind. At the bus stop across the street from the house, an older black man was sitting on a bench, shoulders hunched and chin pulled into the collar of an oversized corduroy jacket. I couldn't see his face, but the sun shone on grizzled hair. He looked cold, and no wonder: it was chilly out, just above freezing, and he looked like he'd been sitting there a while.

There's a circular driveway that goes up to the house, and I turned in, hearing the gravel crunch under my tires. It brought back memories of the first time I came here, on a hot August morning, after getting a phone call from a potential client telling me that Brenda Puckett had stood him up for an appointment. He hadn't introduced himself, and at that point I'd had no idea he was someone I'd gone to school with. My first sight of him—astride that big, black Harley-Davidson, with sunglasses covering his eyes and the viper tattoo peeking out from underneath the sleeve of a T-shirt that might as well have been painted on his body—had inspired something roughly halfway between instant attraction and instinctive recoil. I'd noticed he was gorgeous—what woman wouldn't?—but that edge of danger, of ruthlessness, had warned me off. He'd been a big ethnic-looking guy with lots of muscles and a tattoo, and he'd scared me.

Amazing what a few months can do for someone's perspective.

He wasn't here today, nor was the Harley. The driveway was empty. I pulled to a stop at the bottom of the stairs and contemplated getting out and knocking on the door. But it was cold and I didn't think I'd get an answer even if someone was here. So I sat a minute and then put the car back into gear and drove off. If he was inside, at least he'd know I was thinking about him.

I was two blocks away, headed back in the direction of Dresden, when my phone rang.

"What do you want?" Tamara Grimaldi demanded.

"Excuse me?"

"Didn't I tell you to let me handle this?"

"Um…" Yes, she had. Seemed like maybe they were at the house on Potsdam after all, or at least that the detective kept it under surveillance. "Sorry."

"I'm sure you are. He's fine, and I'll make sure he stays that way. Go home. Stay out of trouble. I'll call you when it's over."

She hung up without waiting for my answer. I did the same, grimacing.

WHEN THE PHONE RANG AGAIN a minute later, I thought it might be Tamara Grimaldi calling back. Or—my heart skipped a beat at the thought—Rafe himself wanting to reassure me. But instead it was Heather Price's number I saw on the caller ID.

"What are you doing?" was her greeting when I answered the phone.

I wrinkled my brows. "I'm still in the car. Why?"

"I need to talk to you." She lowered her voice. "About Hector."

Hadn't we just talked about Hector a few minutes ago? "What about him?"

"Not on the phone," Heather said.

I sighed. What could be so important that she couldn't tell me over the phone? "I'm not too far away from you. I'll just turn around and drive back. It'll just take a few minutes."

"No!" She sounded upset at the idea. "I'll meet you somewhere."

"You want to grab some lunch?" It was getting on for that time of day, and I could definitely eat. "There's a place just down the street from your house that—"

"No," Heather said. "Somewhere where there are no other people."

I blinked. "What is it that's so important you can't tell me where someone else might overhear?"

"He contacted me," Heather said.

"Call the police."

"I can't!" She took an audible breath, and when her voice came back, she sounded a little calmer. "I'm afraid, OK? He knows where I live, so I don't want to stay here. Or anywhere nearby. Can't we just meet somewhere? Please?"

I hesitated, and she added, "He told me to meet him. He wants my car so he doesn't have to drive around in his. If I don't meet him, he'll be angry. But you can call the police and get them out there..."

"Where?"

"I'll tell you when we meet," Heather said. And added, "I want to get somewhere safe first."

Fine. Maybe she'd tell me where Hector was, and then I could call Tamara Grimaldi and tell her I'd done her job for her. And get Rafe back. "Do you know where I live?"

"I can find it," Heather said. "Give me the address."

I did. "I'm on the second floor. Just park on the street and hit the bell by the door. I'll buzz you in."

"I'll be there in fifteen minutes." She hung up. I did the same, arching my brows. Hector really must be a scary dude, if just a phone call from him could get her this worried.

I DID CONSIDER CALLING TAMARA GRIMALDI again, to tell her what Heather had said. But she had her hands full, and she was already miffed at me, so she might not appreciate it. Plus, I didn't want to distract her unnecessarily. Or worse, distract Rafe. And it wasn't like I'd be in any danger. It was just Heather—who really hadn't tried to run me down; the white Toyota belonged to someone else—and she'd sounded pretty terrified on the phone. I'd go home, calm her down, find out what she knew, and *then* I'd call the detective.

Pleasant thoughts of solving the case, of having Heather tell me where Hector would be, of arranging for Grimaldi and her crew to be there to nab him, and of having Rafe be safe, finally, played through my head on the drive home. Since I didn't have anything scheduled for the rest of the day, I drove the car into the underground parking garage when I got there, instead of parking on the street the way I do when I know I'm going back out again. The sleet had turned nasty, and I don't like to get wet.

I parked in my usual, designated space, and got out of the car. I was bent over, reaching for my purse, when I heard the scuff of a shoe behind me. The next second, before I even had a chance to straighten up and look behind me, something hard connected with the back of my head, and everything turned black. A black that was a lot less enjoyable than the black that accompanied kisses from Rafe.

I CAME BACK TO MYSELF SLOWLY. The first thing I became aware of was that my head hurt. A lot. Enough that I felt nauseous. Lifting my head increased the pain, so I kept it hanging, even if that was uncomfortable, as well. And opening my eyes hurt, with bright flashes of light stabbing my retinas.

Everything spun for a few seconds while I swallowed nausea. Once I managed to focus, I realized I was looking at my own lap. I recognized the purple and gray skirt I'd put on this morning. Or maybe it had been yesterday morning, depending on how much time I'd lost being unconscious.

The circular swirling pattern made the nausea worse, so I closed my eyes again for a while, trying to focus on whatever else I could discern about my situation instead.

I was sitting, obviously, if my head was hanging and my lap was down. The chair was hard, wood or metal, not cushy against my posterior. I could rock it back and forth a little, so it wasn't bolted to the floor. I couldn't move my hands or my feet, however. When I tried, my ankles stayed together, and so did my wrists. Someone must have tied me up, and had probably tied me to the chair, too.

Where was I? The last thing I remembered was pulling into the parking garage at home, and then... nothing.

Was I still there? In the parking garage?

Probably not, I decided, nostrils quivering. There was no smell of oil or gas. And although it was chilly, it wasn't as cold as the garage would be.

But I also wasn't at home. My apartment smells of gardenia and a hint of Chanel No 5. This place smelled of...

It didn't smell of anything much, actually. A little musty. Dusty. With just a hint of metal and perhaps wood.

I opened my eyes again, just a slit. The chair under my butt was metal, and the floor below was concrete. No wood in sight, although the smell was there, in the air. When I squinted around, I saw I was in a dusky, cavernous room with enormously high ceilings, under which ran heating and cooling ducts and something that might have been plumbing pipes. There were a few dusty windows here and there, letting in gray-streaked daylight, but I estimated them to be at least fifteen feet above ground. I couldn't have reached them even if I hadn't been stuck to the chair.

That's as far as I'd gotten when a voice said, "Look who's awake. Good morning, Sleeping Beauty."

If it had been Rafe, the voice would have been ripe with innuendo. It wasn't. There was an undercurrent of excitement, but not—thankfully—the kind of excitement I'd heard in Perry Fortunato's voice back when I'd been half naked and tied to the headboard in his bedroom. Whatever else this guy had planned, it didn't sound as if rape was part of it.

I squinted up at him, my eyes narrowed and my head still pounding. "It's morning already?"

"Well, no." He sounded apologetic. "It's still afternoon. Two thirty."

That was a little better. I'd been out cold just over an hour. "You hit me."

"Sorry about that." He didn't sound sorry.

"Hector Gonzales, I presume?"

He nodded. "A pleasure."

Sure. "Where's Heather?" I looked around, carefully. I was starting to feel a little better, but with the way my head hurt, it seemed better not to tempt fate.

"She left us." He smiled. His canines were a little too long, giving him the appearance of a vampire, or perhaps a dog.

Aside from the teeth and the fact that the smile didn't reach his eyes, there was nothing too terribly off-putting about him. He was around forty or forty-five, with straight black hair and brown eyes, and he was tall for a South American. Six feet, give or take, dressed in slacks and a white shirt, a little worse for wear. I surmised he might have been wearing the same clothes since leaving Atlanta in a hurry last night. He looked like he'd slept in them. He also hadn't shaved in a while, and there was a distinct shadow outlining his jaw. I wouldn't call it a beard, not yet, but it was on its way there. And he smelled bad, a combination of perspiration and fear, with a dose of anger thrown in for good measure.

"Is she all right? You didn't hurt her, did you?"

"Don't worry about Heather," Hector said. "She's fine. All snug at home. And you have enough worries of your own. Don't you?"

I guess I did. Nonetheless, I did my best to keep my voice steady. "I'm afraid I'm not sure what's going on. Would you mind telling me what I'm doing here? Wherever here is?"

Hector smiled. It wasn't a friendly smile. "Don't you recognize it?"

I looked around again. It looked like an empty warehouse. One I'd never seen before. "Julio's warehouse? Down by the river?"

It seemed most logical. Hector owned another, but it was further away from my apartment. Would he have risked taking me halfway across town?

He didn't confirm it. Then again, he didn't deny it either, so I thought I was probably right.

"What do you want with me?" I asked. I could guess, but I wanted him to say it.

"We have a friend in common. A very close friend."

"Heather?"

"No," Hector said, "someone else. Let's not beat around the bush, Ms. Martin. We both know what this is about."

"I don't," I said. "Explain it to me."

"You're gonna call him."

No, I'm not. "I don't have the number."

Hector looked disbelieving, and I added, "I really don't. The only number I had was disconnected months ago."

"What do you do when you want to talk to him?"

"I wait," I said. "If he wants me, he knows where to find me."

Which made me pretty pathetic, come to think of it. Not at all the modern woman I'd imagined I'd become. Just the same old Southern Belle, sitting at home waiting for her beau to phone in.

Hector smiled unpleasantly. "Good thing I know where to find him." He pulled out his phone.

I'd hoped he was kidding, that it was another way of trying to get me to admit I knew the number all along, but unfortunately it wasn't. He dialed and put the phone on speaker. It rang once, and then Rafe's voice came on. "Hector. Took you long enough."

"Been busy," Hector said and gave me a nasty little smile. "Been spending some time with a friend of yours. She wants to say hello."

He held the phone up to my mouth. I shook my head. Hector added, "Looks like she's gonna need a little convincing, though. Hang on."

He took a step closer. I figured he'd just threaten me, but instead he hit me. Not hard—it wasn't a punch or anything, just a slap across the cheek with the flat of his hand—but it was loud, and it hurt. My head snapped sideways, and I could feel my cheek turn hot. It didn't do my headache any good, either. Tears stung my eyes, but I managed to keep my mouth shut.

"Looks like I might need some help here," Hector told the phone. "Your girlfriend don't wanna talk to you. I can keep hitting her till she does, or you can talk some sense into her yourself."

There was a beat of silence on the other end of the line, and then Rafe's voice came back. He still sounded calm, but I could hear the anger underneath, that edge of stone-cold fury. "What do you want, Hector?"

"I wanna kill you," Hector said pleasantly, "but since it looks like I can't, I'll settle for killing your girlfriend instead. I'll keep the line open so you don't miss nothing."

Oops.

There was another pause. Then— "Where are you?"

"Can't tell you that," Hector said. "You'll try to stop me."

Well, duh.

"I don't even know who the hell's there with you. And if you can't make her talk..."

"She'll talk," Hector said, and stuck his hand in his pocket. When he brought it out, he held a knife. The light glinted on the blade when he leaned down and held it in front of my face. Suddenly his voice was neither suave not friendly. "Listen, *puta*. You don't do what I want, I'm gonna cut you. *Comprende?*"

I nodded. I understood perfectly. Judging from the look in his eyes he'd do it, too. I cleared my throat. "Rafe."

There was a beat. "Yeah." I wondered if Hector heard the difference in his voice. Up until now I guess he'd been hoping I was someone else.

"I'm sorry," I said. "I should have been more careful."

"You all right?"

"So far." Although I guessed I probably wouldn't continue to be. Hector was grinning unpleasantly, twisting the knife back and forth as if admiring the play of light along the blade. I averted my eyes for the next little bit of conversation. This might be my only chance to say these words and I'd just as soon forget that we had an audience. "Listen. It looks like I might never get the chance to say this again, so... um... I love you."

He didn't respond, and after an awkward silence I added, "I'm sorry it took me so long to admit it. Listen..." I had to stop and swallow something that felt like my heart, beating at the top of my throat. "Remember that afternoon a couple months ago, in the car, when you offered to let me tie you to the bed and have my way with you?"

I waited for him to answer this time. "Yeah."

"I'm sorry we didn't get there." I emphasized the last two words as much as I thought I could without attracting Hector's attention. "I'm sorry for a lot of things I didn't do. Tell my mom I love her, OK? And my brother and sister."

He didn't answer. "Hector still there?"

Hector grinned and lifted the phone to his own mouth. "I'm here, '*mano*."

Even though the phone had been taken away, I could still hear Rafe's voice. He was making no attempt to control his emotions this time, and anger vibrated down the line. "Listen, fucker. You hurt her, I swear to God, I'll find you and kill you if it takes the rest of my life. You'd damn well better hope the cops get you first, cause if I ever see you again, you're a dead man."

The next thing I heard was silence.

"What the—?" Hector said and stared at the phone. He even shook it. Then he redialed the number, only to get a busy signal. Again and again. It was almost funny, or would have been, if I hadn't been duct taped to a chair, stuck in this life-and-death situation with a man who looked more and more unhinged with every second that passed. His face got purple and his jaw tight, and he kept stabbing the buttons as if it were the phone's fault he couldn't get through.

I counted seconds, wondering how long it would take him to decide to kill me anyway, even if Rafe wasn't on the other end of the line, listening.

The answer turned out to be roughly four minutes. That's longer than you might think. My life didn't exactly flash before my eyes, but I spent the time thinking about some of the things I'd miss when I was gone. My family in Sweetwater. Dix and the girls; Catherine, Jonathan and their kids. Mother and Bob Satterfield. I even thought about Todd.

And Tamara Grimaldi, who was probably cursing the day she met me.

And Rafe, who might be cursing me too.

He hadn't told me he loved me. I'd said it to him, but he hadn't said it back.

Did that mean he didn't? Or did it just mean he wouldn't say it in front of Hector?

Honestly, if I was going to die anyway, he might just have told me he loved me whether it was true or not. At least that way I would have died happy.

Eventually my time was up. Hector glared at the phone, which kept giving him the busy signal, and threw it at the wall. It hit with a crack, and fell to the floor. I swallowed convulsively when he turned on his heel and stalked toward me, black eyes feral and lips curled back from his teeth, vampire style.

"What did you tell him, *puta*?"

"You heard every word I said," I protested. "I didn't tell him anything."

Except that I loved him.

And yes, I might have reminded him of a conversation we'd once had, sitting across the street from this warehouse, waiting for Julio Melendez to show his face. If he remembered the details, he might have figured out where I was. That's what I was hoping for. It wasn't as if I'd bring up something so unladylike otherwise.

However, that was if I'd guessed right about the warehouse. If I was in the one in South Nashville instead, or a different warehouse entirely, one I didn't know about, all bets were off. Saving myself might be up to me, and if so, I wouldn't give a whole lot for my chances. I was strapped to this chair, in an empty warehouse in an industrial area with no close neighbors, and Hector had a knife. He could amuse himself for hours, and no one would hear me scream.

"There's something I don't understand," I said. If I kept him talking, maybe I'd gain a few more minutes of life, or a bit more time for Rafe to come to my rescue. If he was on his way, as I hoped he was.

"What's that?" Hector was testing the point of the knife against his thumb.

"How do you even know who I am? Or that I have any connection at all to Rafe? I didn't know anything about you until last night."

"I didn't know anything about you either," Hector said, lowering the knife, "until you were nice enough to tell me."

"Excuse me?"

He smiled. "I heard you talking to Heather. Very kind of you to warn her that I was coming to Nashville. Even if I was already here."

"You were there?" A little belatedly I realized that yes, he'd been inside the house while Heather and I had been talking on the porch. It explained the frequent nervous glances she'd shot over her shoulder and why she hadn't invited me in. She'd been afraid I'd see him. I'd even parked the Volvo behind an SUV with Georgia plates, and hadn't considered the possibility that Hector might already be there.

Stupid.

"I drove up last night. Just barely got outta Atlanta with my skin." His face darkened.

"Sorry," I said, inanely. Sometimes those good manners that mother instilled in me can be misplaced.

He smiled. "I was gonna hook up with my good buddy Jorge. Until Heather told me that Jorge ain't who I thought he was."

Oops.

"Thought I got rid of him once already," Hector added, sort of pensively, without looking at me. "Guess he wasn't as easy to kill as I thought. And now it's too late. But I've got something better." He grinned at me.

I smiled back, weakly. "Killing me isn't going to make any difference. It won't ruin his life. I'm just not that important to him."

"He sounded like you were important," Hector said.

I shook my head. "Not so much that you'd notice. Those couple of months he spent in Atlanta after Jorge was killed? I didn't even hear from him. And when he came back here, he spent all his time with Carmen."

Hector's face darkened. "Stupid bitch," he said, and I don't think he was referring to me. "So busy getting it on with the help that she didn't look out for my investment."

His hand tightened around the handle of the knife and I was profoundly grateful that it wasn't me he was upset with. Until I remembered that he'd kill me anyway, whether he was upset or not. I swallowed. "He meant what he said, you know. If you hurt me, he'll find you."

"I'm not so much worried about that," Hector said, "since I'm a lot harder to find than he expects."

I opened my mouth to argue—if something happened to me, Rafe and Tamara Grimaldi would find him; there was no doubt in my mind—but before I could speak, there was a booming sound off in the recesses of the warehouse, and we both looked in that direction.

Hector didn't move.

"Aren't you going to answer it?" I asked.

His lips tightened. "Shoulda known he'd find his way here."

"It might not be him. Maybe it's Heather."

"Heather wouldn't come back here," Hector said, but he sounded unsure. Before I could reinforce the idea that it was Heather and he needed to open the door for her, however, the person outside started yelling as well as kicking, and then there was no doubt who it was.

"Open the fucking door, Hector! Or I swear to God I'm gonna kick it down!"

Eighteen

Hector's face turned purple. I held my breath while I waited to find out whether he'd choose to put a bullet in my brain before going to answer the door, or whether I'd actually survive another day. Or hour. Few minutes.

Eventually he said, "Don't go anywhere," and stalked off in the direction of the door. I went to work trying to loosen my hands, but without much to show for it. I couldn't see what was going on behind my back, but from the feel of things, Hector had fastened my wrists with duct tape, and there's just no way to loosen something like that.

All too soon he was back, walking backwards, gun up and pointed.

I looked past him and wasn't sure whether to be relieved or upset.

Rafe looked just like the last time I'd seen him, still dressed in the black cargo pants and black T-shirt he'd worn to play bouncer at *La Havana*. Like Hector, he must have spent the night in them. Unlike Hector, he still managed to look fresh. And that was in spite of still looking like Jorge: his hair gelled, with the earring and goatee. He wasn't wearing a coat. I wondered if that was deliberate or whether he'd really just run out of the safe house without a jacket in order to get here.

He was unarmed, hands up and out, empty. If he'd had a gun when he arrived, Hector had taken it.

What had Tamara Grimaldi been thinking to let him walk in here alone and unarmed? Hector would kill him. He'd already said he wanted to.

Hector stopped halfway into the cavernous room, and perforce, Rafe stopped too. He looked around and found me, and then looked me up and down, from disheveled hair to bound ankles, before his eyes came back to linger on my cheek, where he could probably see the results of Hector's slap. I saw a flash of anger, but when he turned back to Hector, his eyes were the same flat, expressionless black again, and his voice was controlled.

"Cut her loose."

"Or what?" Hector taunted.

Rafe's voice stayed level. "You wanted me, not her. And I'm here. Let her go."

Hector contemplated me, his head tilted. "I don't think so."

"She ain't part of this. You shoot me, it's business. You'll still go down for it, but it's different. But if you hurt her, they'll nail you to the wall."

Hector shook his head.

"Why the hell not? You got me; I'm what you wanted."

"I'm trying to decide," Hector said.

"Decide what?"

"Do I kill her first, so you can watch, or do I kill you, so she can? After all, she loves you!" Hector grinned offensively.

Rafe glanced at me, but try as I might, I couldn't see anything in his eyes this time. He turned his attention back to Hector. "You don't kill her at all. Your business is with me. You cut her loose and let her walk outta here."

"Can't do that," Hector said.

"Then you kill me first. And when I'm dead, you let her go. You won't need her then."

"Works for me," Hector said with a shrug. He raised the gun.

"No!"

There was nothing I could do but scream, so I did it. "Stop it, you bastard! I'm not going to sit here and watch you shoot him!"

Hector grinned. "Would you rather I shoot you first, *querida?*"

"Yes! I don't want to watch him die!"

"Fine with me," Hector said. The gun swung back in my direction.

"Hell, no." Rafe ignored it to step in front of me. "You wanna shoot her, you do it through me."

"No!" I swear I could see Hector's finger tightening on the trigger. "Don't be stupid, Rafe. Get out of the way!"

The situation was weirdly familiar. We'd been here before. I'd been strapped to the bed in Perry Fortunato's bedroom, and we'd managed to distract Perry with talk, and then Rafe had taken him down, with a little help from the knife he'd had in his pocket. Even if he had one this time, I didn't think it would do us much good. Hector wasn't likely to be swayed by a mock argument.

Although he might be swayed by something else. Or if not swayed, at least distracted for long enough that Rafe had time to make his move.

Unfortunately, there wasn't much I could do to create a distraction. I was stuck to the chair. I couldn't stand. I couldn't go anywhere. And although I had use of my mouth, it was already obvious that Hector was impervious to anything I said. Although the chair he'd taped me to wasn't bolted to the floor. I tested it to make sure. It wobbled.

I took a deep breath—this wouldn't do my headache any good—and flung myself backwards, praying for the best.

There's something very disconcerting about freefalling back, knowing your head is about to meet the concrete with the kind of crunch that could knock you senseless. Under normal circumstances, it was something I'd never do. I was never one of those children who throw themselves on the floor or practice fainting or getting shot. I was a proper little girl, sitting around with my ankles crossed and my hands folded in my lap, playing with Southern Belle Barbie.

In this case I did my best to keep the back of my head from hitting the concrete too hard—a second knock on top of the one Hector had given me would only reinforce the concussion I suspected I might have—but I did lift my feet to make sure the skirt slid as far up my thighs as I could manage. Hector was a guy and according to Rafe I have good legs—I thought it might be enough to catch his attention.

My back hit the floor with the bone-jarring crunch I had anticipated, and the skirt slid up almost to my crotch, my taped legs waving in the air. Hector glanced my way and I saw his jaw drop. Then I didn't see anything else, since I was flat on my back on the floor. I did hear things: a sort of whoosh through the air, an exclamation of pain from Hector, and a second later, the sound of something heavy and metallic hitting the floor. I surmised from the evidence that Rafe had indeed taken advantage of Hector's momentary distraction to—perhaps—kick the hand holding the gun. The gun had gone sailing through the air, hitting the floor, and I guess I should be grateful the bullet missed me. It pinged off something overhead, but didn't hit any of us.

The fight wasn't over, however. Just because Hector was now gun-less, didn't mean he was down and out. He still had his knife somewhere, and he also had fists.

There was the sound of blows, of feet scuffing across the floor, grunts and curses in Spanish and English. I tried to shift my weight— and that of the chair—so I could see what was going on. At the moment, all I was looking at was my own bare knees, and more of my thighs than I was comfortable with.

I needn't have worried. They didn't stay in one spot for long. Pretty soon they'd moved around to where I could see everything that was happening, and believe me, I wished I couldn't.

Rafe's in good shape. I've had the chance to personally inspect every inch of him, and believe me, there's nothing about that man that isn't physically perfect. He's tall, he's strong, he's beyond fit, and he has learned how to fight. He's also not afraid to fight dirty, which can be a real asset in a situation where your opponent is trying to kill you. I'd put my money on him against anyone pretty much anytime.

This time, I was a bit concerned.

Oh, he was still tall and strong and fit, and he definitely had the motivation to fight, and to use any trick he could to win. Hector would kill him—kill us both—if he didn't. But Hector was a formidable opponent. I hadn't expected them to be so evenly matched. Hector was at least ten years older and a bit shorter, as well as a little thicker around the middle, and I'd thought Rafe would have an advantage. But Hector must have been just as motivated, what with the rage of losing his business empire, the knowledge that he was on his way to prison, and the more personal realization that Rafe had fooled him, and fooled him good, for several months. They went at each other like two junkyard dogs, snapping and growling, in what I sincerely hoped wouldn't turn out to be a fight to the death, but which—given Hector's need to survive and escape—might just end up that way.

While I was stuck on the floor, taped to my chair, upside down like a turtle.

I wiggled and jostled, wriggled and squirmed, but try as I might, I couldn't get loose. My hands were now under me, but still tightly fastened together, and on top of that they were going numb. Trying to move them hurt.

All around me, the fighting went on. Hector hit Rafe, who hit him back. Twice. And fighting dirty was no asset this time; Hector fought just as dirty as Rafe did. That whole thing about honor among thieves? I guess it goes out the window when a lengthy prison term is at stake.

There was nothing for me to do but what I was already doing. So I did, praying for a game-changer, some sort of intervention that would tip the scales in our favor.

And that's when Hector got tired of the scuffling and brought out the knife.

"I'LL TAKE HER HOME," RAFE said.

It was fifteen minutes later, and I was upright and mostly all right. My wrists and ankles still smarted from where the duct tape had been ripped off, but it was no worse than a bikini wax.

Rafe was not so lucky. He had bruises coming up all over his arms and face, and a cut at the corner of his eye that I'd been worried about until one of the paramedics slapped a butterfly band-aid on it and declared him good to go. His knuckles were bruised and bloody, and the paramedic had poured some disinfectant over them, but Rafe had refused bandages. I think I was the only one who noticed that his right wrist seemed to be bothering him. He'd sprained it once before, in another fistfight at eighteen, so maybe it was weaker than his left. Since he didn't mention it, I didn't either. I kept an eye on it, though, and if it started swelling up, I'd definitely tell him to do something to it.

Hector was on his way to the hospital in an ambulance, with a cop and an FBI agent riding shotgun. To go back to the fight for a second, even if I'd really rather forget about it: Rafe hadn't seemed surprised to see the knife, so perhaps he knew that Hector carried one, or he'd surmised as much when he'd overheard Hector threaten to cut me during our phone conversation earlier. I had hoped Rafe might have had a knife of his own tucked away somewhere, but no such luck. So for a minute or two, Hector kept lunging at Rafe with the knife, while Rafe did his best to avoid getting cut. They circled around the floor a bit, but he always seemed aware of where I was, and always veered off in the other direction if they threatened to come too close.

Eventually he must have gotten tired of weaving and dodging, because he waited for Hector to strike again, knife extended, and then, instead of moving away, he got in closer, bending his knees and then knocking

Hector's knife arm up with his shoulder. The knife went flying, same as the gun had earlier. Rafe followed up with what I can only describe as a wicked punch to the throat, and Hector fell to his knees, choking.

Rafe went to scoop up the gun and knife. While Hector was clutching his throat, trying to catch a breath, he used the knife to cut the tape around my wrists and ankles, and then told me to go open the door to let 'the others' in. I did, and was practically stampeded by a horde of alphabet agents and cops, with Wendell Craig in the lead, closely followed by Tamara Grimaldi.

And now here we were, with Rafe offering to drive me home.

Detective Grimaldi squinted at me, up and down and up again. "Don't you think she should go to the hospital instead?"

I shook my head. "No more hospitals." Between the miscarriage and getting shot and what happened to Aislynn and Kylie, I'd seen enough hospitals lately to last me a while. And besides, that's where Hector was headed, and I didn't want to be in the same building with him.

"One of the paramedics looked at her," Rafe said, ignoring me. "He said she'll be all right."

Grimaldi sighed. "Fine. Take her home."

"Her car's outside. I'll use that. I'll need a ride back."

Grimaldi nodded. "I'll come get you. Call when you're ready."

"Thirty minutes," Rafe said.

I pouted. If he wanted to be picked up in a half hour, that meant he had no plans of indulging in hanky-panky once we got to my place. Hanky-panky, at least with Rafe, takes longer than thirty minutes.

Grimaldi nodded. "I'll see you in thirty."

Rafe nodded too, and turned to me. "Let's go."

I went. Through the warehouse, where the TBI and police, and for all I knew the FBI too, were processing the crime scene. He kept his hand on the small of my back, a sort of intimate gesture I hoped meant something other than just the fact that I was wobbly.

The ambulance had already left, with Hector inside. He'd survive, but his larynx might not; the paramedic who looked at him said it might have been crushed. Sad to say, I couldn't find it in myself to care. Rafe was safe; that was all that mattered to me. Oh yeah, and I'd survived with my skin intact. That was also something to celebrate. Except it didn't seem like he wanted to. In fact, he'd hardly looked at me at all since he cut me loose from the chair. Or spoken to me. Or even responded when I spoke to him.

Was he angry with me?

"Are you sure you can't stay longer than thirty minutes?" I asked diffidently when we were on our way across the slick parking lot toward the Volvo. Hector must have hijacked my car for the ride here, probably because he didn't want to drive his own car with the Georgia-plates any more than necessary. I wondered whether he'd bundled me into the trunk or just kept me in the back seat for the drive.

Rafe glanced at me and the corners of his mouth turned up. My heart started beating again. "Once I get started doing what you want me to do to you, I ain't never getting outta here. And I've got places to go and people to see."

"Like who?" We reached the car and he opened the passenger side door for me and helped me in. I was still a little dizzy, and my head hurt from the whack Hector had given me, but the paramedic had shined a light in my eyes and declared I didn't have a concussion.

"Heather," Rafe said, his voice turning hard. "Tammy's going after Heather, and I wanna be there. And once the hospital releases Hector, I'm going back to Atlanta with him." He closed my door and walked around the car to the driver's side.

I don't want to let you out of my sight, I thought. What I said was, "What if you don't come back?"

"I'll come back. Keys?"

He held out a hand. I dropped the keys into it and watched him insert one in the ignition and turn the car on. After a few seconds to let the various fluids make their way throughout the engine, he backed out of the parking space and headed for the road.

"I'm afraid," I admitted.

He shot me a glance, a flash of dark eyes under long lashes. "Nothing's gonna happen. Hector's on his way to the hospital. And we'll get Heather. Everyone else is in jail."

I nodded. He was right, of course. But that wasn't what I was afraid of.

He still hadn't told me he loved me. Granted, in the warehouse with all the other cops and paramedics—and Hector—may not have been the best place for such a confession. I could understand why he hadn't broached the subject. But I wanted to hear it. I needed to hear it. And if he didn't say it... did that mean he didn't?

Yet I couldn't ask him. I'd said too much already. Asking a man straight out if he loves you, when he won't come out and say it himself, would be beyond mortifying, it would be contrary to everything mother always taught me about the relationship between the sexes. The man is supposed to do the pursuing, while the woman is the prize at the end of the hunt, sitting demurely on her tuffet waiting for appropriate proofs of adoration and worthiness to be placed at her feet.

I'd already blown that possibility by confessing my feelings before he did. But I wasn't about to compound the offense by begging.

So I sat, hands folded in my lap, while he maneuvered the Volvo out of the parking lot and onto River Road in the direction of my apartment. I was literally biting my tongue to keep from soliciting a response—any response—but I kept quiet.

He did, too, just kept his hands on the steering wheel and his eyes on the road. Until we'd driven a block or two, when I shot a glance at him—not my first one—and noticed a furrow between his brows.

I furrowed my own. "What's wrong?"

"Is that smoke?"

I leaned forward. It was hard to tell, with the general grayness of the weather and the light sleet that had picked up again during the hours I'd been inside the warehouse, but yes, something appeared to be leaking from underneath the hood of the car. "Oh, no. Is the engine overheating?"

That was all I needed. I had trouble enough just feeding myself; I had no money left over for expensive car repairs.

"No," Rafe said. "That's smoke, not steam." He made an abrupt right, pulling the car onto the gravel shoulder of the road and slamming on the brakes. "Get out."

"But—"

He shot me a look. "Out!"

"All right, all right." I opened the door and swung my legs out. "There's no need to be mean. I'm going."

I slammed the door and walked around to the front of the car. While I'd been taking my time getting up and out, he'd unlocked the hood latch. Now he lifted the hood. I gasped as a tongue of flame licked out at him, accompanied by a cloud of black smoke.

He took a step back. "Shit!"

"Oh my God!" I squeaked, hurrying closer. Only to be grabbed around the waist by an arm as hard as a vise. Nothing wrong with his wrist that I could discern.

"Stay the hell away from it!"

"But my car...!"

"I'll take care of the car." He let me go. "Gimme your coat."

"What?"

"Coat." He plucked it from my shoulders. Hector had removed it earlier, before tying me to the chair, and Rafe had recovered it and put it around me before we went outside, but I hadn't bothered to put my arms through the sleeves. He was able to just slide it right off.

I wrapped my arms around myself as the ice cold drizzle hit my bare skin. "What are you—?"

The answer to that question became evident when he turned toward the car. I almost lost my breath when he threw the coat—and himself—onto the engine.

Nineteen

I'm pretty sure I sounded like a banshee. I had no words, but I was shrieking at the top of my lungs. I may have been cursing him. And I grabbed him anywhere I could—shirt, pants, shoulders, around the waist—and tried to pull him backwards, away from the car and the fire.

I didn't stand a chance, of course, and I'm sure I made his job doubly difficult. But watching him disappear under the hood, into the smoke, all I could think of was that he'd catch fire and die. While I stood here and did nothing.

It didn't last long. Less than a minute before he turned on his heel. I thought he'd be angry, that he'd push me away and yell at me to stop making things harder, but he didn't. He just moved me back, at a safe distance from the car, before he wrapped his arms around me and pulled me close to his body and held me there, his nose buried in my hair. I'm ashamed to admit that I clung to him, my hands fisted in his shirt, pressing my face into his shoulder. I was shivering and sobbing, soaking his T-shirt with tears.

Eventually he raised his head. I raised mine too, and looked up into his face. I'm sure I looked like hell, even if my makeup was waterproof, but if I did, he didn't let on.

"You all right, darlin'?"

"Of course I'm all right," I sniffed, moving back reluctantly and wiping my cheeks with the backs of my hands. "I wasn't the one who threw myself on top of a burning car."

"I had to put the fire out."

He said it with the same sort of inflection as if he'd said he had to take the trash out. Like there was nothing to it, just one of those necessary chores he had to deal with once in a while.

"I thought you were going to die!" For the second time today.

"Takes more than that to kill me," Rafe said. "Although if we stay here much longer, I think I'll probably freeze to death."

He fished for the phone in his pocket. Once he got it out, he hit a button—speed-dial, I guess—and a few seconds later he was speaking. "It's me."

"What's wrong?" Tamara Grimaldi's voice said, faint and tinny.

"Had a little problem. We're gonna need that ride sooner than later."

Grimaldi's voice came back. I couldn't hear her words, but the question was obvious from Rafe's answer. "The car caught fire."

I couldn't hear Grimaldi's exclamation, but Rafe winced, so it must have been strong. "No. But I want it towed and looked at."

Grimaldi quacked, and he glanced down at me. "Yeah, she's fine. Same as she was five minutes ago."

Grimaldi said something else, and he added, with another grimace. "I know. I know! Just get over here. It's cold."

Grimaldi said something in goodbye, something Rafe didn't answer, and he pocketed the phone and looked at me. "She's on her way."

"I'm sorry," I said.

"It ain't your fault, darlin'."

"I haven't had the car looked at for a while. No money. Maybe if I had this wouldn't have happened."

That was three times today I'd narrowly cheated death. The almost-accident on the interstate, which could have gone badly wrong. Then the run-in with Hector, and now this. It was almost as if someone was gunning for me. Although it hadn't been Hector in the white compact; he hadn't known I existed then. And I doubted he'd gone outside to rig my car while I was unconscious in the warehouse. Why would he? He'd planned to kill me, so it wasn't like I'd be driving home afterwards. Unless he hoped that Rafe might be the one to drive my car after I was dead, but that was an awfully big chance to take. He might end up killing some totally innocent grease monkey who worked for Bailey's Towing instead. And whatever else I may have thought about Hector, he wasn't stupid.

"What happened?" I asked.

Rafe hesitated. "Looks like one of the fuel injection lines came loose."

"Wouldn't we have smelled gas leaking?"

He shook his head. "See, the gas starts out in the gas tank. When the fuel pump starts working, the gas goes through the fuel injection lines into the fuel distributor. If there's a loose connection, some of the gas is gonna splash on the engine. When the engine temperature gets high enough, the gas can ignite. But none of it's gonna happen until the car's running. And by then it's too late to notice any smell at all."

I blinked. "How big a deal is that? A loose fuel injection line? Is it a big deal?"

"Depends," Rafe said. "If you know what you're doing, not that big."

I nodded. He'd taken care of it quickly enough, anyway. "But you know a lot more about cars than I do. If I'd been alone..."

"Don't think about it."

"I have to think about it. Could it have been an accident?"

He shot me a look. "You think it wasn't?"

"It's the third time today I almost died."

He was quiet for a moment. "Hector. And what else?"

I told him what had happened on the interstate earlier. "It could have been an accident. But maybe not. The guy behind me, who stopped to check on me, said that the other car was a white Toyota. And..."

He nodded. "We saw a white Toyota the other night."

"That's why I went to see Heather in the first place. I thought maybe it was her car."

"But it wasn't?"

I shook my head. And then qualified it. "Not unless she has two. She pointed to a Dodge van. She said a sedan wouldn't be big enough for her staging supplies."

"But she might have another car. One she doesn't drive to work."

I nodded. She might. And she would have had time to mess with the Volvo while I was inside the warehouse with Hector. Maybe she thought that if I survived, I'd call the police and implicate her, and she was trying to avoid going to jail.

"Damn." Rafe looked around. "What the hell is taking Tammy so long? I wanna get you outta here and home. And then I wanna go find Heather Price and beat some answers out of her!"

"You don't know that it was her," I said.

His eyes were black with anger. "Maybe not. But by the time I'm done with her, we'll have some answers one way or the other."

He glanced over his shoulder again as a car came up the street. "Here she is. Let's get you home and warmed up."

"Can't I come with you to look for Heather? I'd feel safer with you." And my presence might keep him from losing it completely. I'd never thought he'd be the type to hit a woman, but he'd sounded serious about taking his fists to her to get answers.

"No," Rafe said and opened the back door of the unmarked police car for me, "you can't. You're going home, and you're going to bed, and you're gonna stay there. Where I won't have to worry about anything else happening to you."

He slammed the door and got in the front next to Tamara Grimaldi, who was watching me in the rearview mirror. I made a face. He could at least have stayed in the back with me.

"How are you?" Grimaldi asked, and I focused on her instead of my disappointment.

"Fine. I wasn't the one who threw myself on a burning car."

She shifted her gaze to Rafe. "You did that?"

He shot her same kind of look he'd given me. "Someone had to."

"You could have just let it burn," I said.

"No, I couldn't," Rafe said.

Grimaldi added, after a quick glance at him. "If someone didn't put the fire out, the car could have blown up."

For a second I was speechless. Then—

"You told me it was no big deal." My voice was at least an octave higher than usual, and could probably be heard by dogs in a wide area. Grimaldi winced. Rafe, of course, didn't. That didn't stop me. "You said it wasn't dangerous. And now it turns out the car could have exploded? And instead of leaving it alone and getting us both away from it, *you threw yourself on the engine*?!"

"Someone had to," Rafe said.

I huffed and sat back, folding my arms across my chest.

"So what happened?" Grimaldi wanted to know. I listened as the two of them, both obviously more knowledgeable about cars than I, discussed the mechanical ins and outs of what had just taken place.

"Well, could it have been an accident?" the detective asked.

Rafe shrugged. "Call the Volvo dealer and they'll tell you one of their fuel lines could never, ever work itself loose. But I'm sure it's happened. No way to know if it did this time."

"When was the car serviced last?"

I didn't bother answering, since I'd already told Rafe the answer. "She says it's been a while. But that don't matter. You call the mechanic and ask if he checked the connection, he's gonna say he did. Doesn't mean shit."

"Who'd know how to do this?" Grimaldi asked. "Anyone? Or does it take special knowledge?"

"More knowledge than some people have." I don't think I imagined the glance into the back seat. No, I would have no idea how to sabotage a fuel injector. In my world, women drive cars, men work on them. Rafe added, "Anyone with a basic understanding of how a combustion engine works woulda known what to do."

"Does it take much strength?"

He shook his head. "Wrench and the knowledge of where the fuel lines are located. And a few minutes of privacy."

Which he or she had had while I'd been tied up inside the warehouse.

It's just a mile or two from River Road over to Fifth and Main, so we were there within a few minutes. The conversation wasn't even over when Grimaldi pulled up to the curb outside the condo complex and moved the gearshift into park. "I'll wait. You take her upstairs and get her settled."

"It could take a few minutes," Rafe warned.

"No doubt. Just get back as quick as you can. The more time we lose, the more likely it is we'll miss Heather."

Rafe nodded and opened his door.

"You can come upstairs," I told Detective Grimaldi while I waited for him to open mine. Not only have I been brought up to wait, but it was a police car, so the inside back door handles were missing. "It's not like we'll be doing anything you can't see." Not with the way he was chomping at the bit to go after Heather Price.

The detective's lips twitched in the mirror. "Thanks, but I have a few phone calls to make. I want to see if Spicer and Truman have dug up any information on the accident the other day. Whether there's any connection to you."

God, yes. Aislynn and Kylie. Whom I had promised to drive home from the hospital tomorrow.

"When can I have my car back?"

"Not sure," Grimaldi said, as my door opened, and Rafe extended a hand to help me out.

I ignored it for the moment. "I promised Kylie Mitchell I'd drive her home from the hospital tomorrow."

"I'll send Spicer and Truman to do it," Grimaldi said. "Safer that way, anyway. For all of you. Until we figure this out, I want you to go inside and stay there. No wandering around on your own. No investigating anything."

"You're as bad as he is," I muttered, and took the hand Rafe offered. I did my best not to let the warmth and feel of his skin against mine affect me, although I didn't do a very good job. I could feel myself melting just from the brief touch. Since I didn't want him to know—as if there was any chance that he didn't already—I told him, snippily, "You don't have to walk me up. I can find my own way."

"Sure." He headed for the gate. "Yeah, I'm gonna leave you down here and drive off with Tammy. And when you get upstairs, Heather'll be there, waiting for you."

"Heather won't be there." But I didn't tell him again that he didn't have to walk me up. Not because I thought Heather might be there, but because I was afraid he might believe me and actually leave. And in spite of being miffed at him, and at his habitual need to put himself in danger, I didn't want him to go any sooner than he had to. Every minute was precious, and I didn't want to miss any.

We walked up the stairs in silence, and just like last time, Rafe made his way through the apartment room by room and closet by closet before declaring that it was safe. I followed him, three steps behind, and we ended up in the middle of the floor of the bedroom, facing one another.

I'd been unforgivably lax in getting up and out this morning. After Tim's call—and all the other phone calls, but especially Tim's—I'd been so excited about getting to the hospital to tell Aislynn and Kylie the good news that I hadn't bothered to make the bed. A horrible faux pas in mother's book of proper behavior, especially if there was a chance someone might stop by and notice my lack of housewifely instincts. Double strike if it was a man.

This man didn't seem to mind. The bed looked rumpled and inviting, and all I wanted to do was crawl under the covers, close my eyes, and sleep my headache away. Judging from the look on Rafe's face, he seemed to share the sentiment. His gaze snagged on the bed for a moment, and when he looked back at me, his eyes were darker than usual, filled with heat but also with something softer, something almost like longing. Like he too just wanted to crawl in, get close together, and rest. Whatever it was, it made the breath catch in my throat.

Of course, it could just have been a while since he'd had a decent night's sleep, but I wanted to believe he wanted what I wanted.

"You could join me," I said.

He smiled. "No, I couldn't. Tammy's waiting, and if I join you, I won't be leaving again today."

"You could come back after you catch Heather."

He shook his head. "I gotta go to Atlanta, darlin'. I'd stay if I could, but we'll all sleep better when Hector's back where he belongs."

True. "I guess this is it, then."

"Guess so." But he glanced at the bed again.

"Want to tuck me in?" I suggested. His lips curved at that, but he shook his head no.

"Better not. Tammy's waiting."

I nodded. "You should go. Make the world a safer place. And come back when you're done. I'll still be here. So will the bed."

He didn't say anything, just looked at me. So I took a couple of steps forward and went up on my tippy toes to press my lips against his for a second. I was on my way back down when he snagged me around the waist and kept me there, plastered against him, stomach to stomach and chest to chest.

"Thought for a minute I lost you, darlin'." The words were spoken into my hair; his cheek against the top of my head, as if he wanted to make sure I couldn't look at him when he spoke.

My heart was beating too hard to make answering comfortable. Although I did manage to utter a few words. "I thought so too." And not just for a minute. For weeks.

He lifted his head, and used a finger under my chin to tilt my face up toward him. "I ain't gonna come back and learn that you've gotten yourself engaged to Satterfield, am I?"

I shook my head. "But just in case, maybe you'd better give me something to remember you by."

He arched a brow. Just one. "You afraid you're gonna forget me?"

Never. But of course I didn't tell him that. "Better safe than sorry, right?"

"Damn right," Rafe said, and kissed me.

As always, it was an out-of-body experience. I floated, oblivious to anything but his arms around me and his mouth on mine. And when he lifted his head, after what could have been an eternity but which probably was just a minute or so, the dizziness from earlier had returned, full force. The room spun, and I swayed.

Rafe chuckled. "Lie down before you fall down, darlin'." He gave me a gentle push toward the bed.

I righted myself and did my best to gather the shreds of my dignity. "I'll see you out first. And make sure the door's locked."

"Fine. But then you go straight to bed. You need to save up your strength. I have plans for when I come back."

He grinned. I grinned back. It was nice to flirt again. This was how he used to talk to me, before all the angst of getting pregnant changed things. Maybe we'd be all right after all. Maybe he didn't love me, the way I loved him. Maybe he did. Maybe one day he'd tell me, one way or the other. But for now he liked me. And wanted me. And that in itself was a start. I could wait for the rest, as long as he stuck around. Or as long as he came back every time he left.

He passed through the apartment and out the door and stopped in the hallway outside. "I wanna hear locks and bolts before I leave."

"You will. Just promise me you'll be careful out there."

"I'm always careful," Rafe said.

No, he wasn't. But he also wasn't going to change. "Don't wait too long before you come back."

"A week. At most."

I could live with that. "And if you change your mind on your way down the stairs, just come back up. Tammy can handle Heather. I'd be happier to have you stay here."

"I'll keep that in mind," Rafe said. "Bye, darlin'."

"Goodbye." I closed the door. Slowly. To give him time to change his mind.

"Lock it," his voice said from outside.

"I know, I know." I flipped the lock closed and then slid the deadbolt. "Happy now?"

There was no answer. I put my eye to the peephole and saw nothing but empty space. He was already gone.

But he'd be back. And as I made my slow way toward the bedroom, shedding layers as I went, I thought about those plans he had for me when he got back. I'd been on the receiving end of Rafe's plans for me before, and the occasions had been memorable. I left my boots in the hallway, my skirt in the living room, and my blouse on the floor in the bedroom, and by the time I was ready to crawl under the covers in bra and panties, I was smiling. And that's when there was a knock on the door.

Twenty

M y heart jumped. He'd had just enough time to run downstairs, tell Tamara Grimaldi that he'd changed his mind about Heather, and hustle back up the stairs again.

I practically ran into the hall, all tiredness forgotten, without bothering to wrap anything around myself. He'd have me out of my lingerie in no time flat, and it wasn't like he hadn't seen it all before anyway. My hands fumbled over the locks and deadbolts, and I pulled the door open with a big smile. "I knew you'd—!"

Only to stop when I found myself looking into the muzzle of a gun.

My first thought was, *not again*!

Over the past couple of months, I'd seen more than my fair share of firearms. I wasn't as used to them as Rafe, who—frankly—acts like being faced with another gun doesn't bother him in the least, but it wasn't my first stick-up. There's something about it that never gets old, though. Each time is like the first time. Probably because each time can kill you.

I don't think what went on in my head could be called 'thinking' precisely, but a lot of things flashed through in rapid succession. Processing, forming theories and discarding them at the speed of light.

First of all, it obviously wasn't Rafe coming back for an interlude between the sheets. My second flash of insight, that Hector was back, came and went in a nano-second. I'd seen him driven off in the ambulance and there was no way he'd be upright and mobile so soon. Then Heather flashed into my mind: maybe she hadn't gone home, maybe she'd come here instead, to kill me if Hector didn't. Maybe she'd shot Rafe already; maybe he'd never made it back outside. He could be lying on the stairs, his blood soaking through the gray industrial carpeting. And I was here, at gunpoint, and couldn't help him, while Grimaldi was outside in the car, with no idea that anything was wrong. Unless Heather had killed her, too.

It was at that point that I managed to pull my attention from the gun up to the face of the person holding it, and my mind tilted again. "What—?"

"You're a lot harder to get rid of than I thought," Maybelle Driscoll said.

For a second I just stared. Then— "Where's Rafe?"

First things first, after all. And not only because I was worried for his health and well-being, but because I was worried for mine. If he was hurt, he wouldn't be able to come to my rescue.

"That young man who was here?" She wrinkled her nose. "Hardly the kind of man a young lady like you should be associating with, is he?"

"You sound like my mother." And there was something almost calming about it. "Where is he?"

"He drove off." She huffed. "I thought he never would."

So at least he wasn't bleeding to death in the hallway downstairs. That was the good news. The bad news was that he was gone, and I couldn't count on him or on Tamara Grimaldi to come to my rescue.

"He was only here a couple of minutes," I said. "Nowhere near as long as I wanted him to be."

Maybelle took a step forward, into the apartment. Since she had the gun, I didn't try to stop her. Maybe I should have. I could have tried to slam the door in her face, or on her arm, but I was afraid she'd shoot me if I did. So I just stepped back and let her walk inside.

We ended up in the living room, facing one another.

She was still wearing her coat, a peacock blue that set off her blonde hair and blue eyes. It was the same color as the almost-too-celebratory dress she'd worn to Brenda's memorial; I guess someone must have told her once she looked good in it.

I, on the other hand, was wearing considerably less. I was practically naked, just dressed in a lavender lace bra and matching panties. Maybelle looked me up and down. "Put on some clothes, for God's sake."

I did, not because I cared that I made her uncomfortable, but because I didn't want whoever found me after she shot me to find me in my skivvies. It's like mother always said: be sure to put on clean panties in case you're in a traffic accident and end up in the hospital.

And besides, I was cold. There were goose bumps breaking out all over my body. All the little hairs on my arms and the back of my neck were standing at attention.

My skirt was still on the living room floor, and I scooped it up and slipped it on, pulling the zipper up as slowly as I could to buy time. The blouse had ended up on the floor of the bedroom, and Maybelle kept a narrow eye on me while I walked over to it and grabbed it.

"Sit." She gestured—with the gun—to the sofa.

I walked back into the living room, still buttoning the blouse, and sat. "So now what? Are you going to tell me what's going on?"

"You know what's going on," Maybelle said.

I tried to keep my own voice calm. "Actually, I don't. I've always thought we've gotten along well."

Maybelle snarled wordlessly, and it looked like her fingers tightened on the gun. I made a mental note not to mention what a good relationship we had again.

It was true, though. I may not have liked her, but I had never let her know that I didn't. I was brought up a Southern Belle, and we're nothing if not circumspect. I'd been friendly to Maybelle. I'd been courteous. I hadn't let my true feelings show when I'd heard that she'd gotten herself engaged to Steven Puckett before the earth had settled on Brenda's grave. I had never let on that I'd suspected her of murder.

I'd done the right thing, and once again it had exploded in my face. It was the last time I tried that. For real this time.

"You're interfering in my life," Maybelle said.

"I can't imagine what you're talking about," I retorted.

I'd been doing some research into her past, yes. But it wasn't like she could have known about that. Carolyn Driscoll wouldn't have contacted her, and Bradley certainly wouldn't, and I doubted the second Lenny Wilkins would have had time. So how had she found out?

"I've always endeavored to have a close, strong relationship with my neighbors," Maybelle said demurely.

No kidding, I thought. I mean, Steven Puckett lived right across the street, and her relationship with him had certainly been close. Both before and after his wife died.

And then it hit me. The next-door neighbor who had called the cops on me the other day must have told Maybelle that I'd been there. A blonde in a blue Volvo. He or she might even have listened to my conversation with Spicer and Truman in the backyard, and so had heard my name.

Damn. I should have thought of that.

"It's not like I found anything incriminating," I said.

"That's beyond the point, dear. You shouldn't have been in my house in the first place."

There was no arguing with that, so I didn't try. "Holding me at gunpoint because of it seems like overkill, though. Don't you agree? I mean, you could just have filed a formal complaint and had me arrested."

"Bernice called the cops," Maybelle said, her face darkening, "and she said they came out there and then just let you go."

Again, there was nothing I could say. I couldn't tell her it was because I hadn't technically broken in, since that would implicate Alexandra. If she didn't know that this was Alexandra's idea, it was better not to tell her. At this rate, Maybelle may end up marrying Steven after all, and if so, Alexandra would have to deal with her. At least until Maybelle murdered Steven and moved on to her next well-to-do man in his forties.

"Even so, killing me seems like a lot of trouble. I can't prove anything."

Maybelle didn't answer, just stared at me, and I added, "There was nothing suspicious about Harold's death. No red flags. Nothing. And his body is ashes. I don't think it's possible to autopsy ashes. For all I know, you took them and dumped them in the ocean. So even if you killed him, nobody can prove it. And as far as Uncle Joshua goes—"

"Who?" Maybelle said, and the word sounded as if it was surprised out of her.

"I guess I neglected to mention that." I smiled sweetly. "I was Mrs. Bradley Ferguson for a few years. Althea was my mother-in-law. Joshua Rowland was my uncle by marriage. Hello, Auntie Maybelle."

Maybelle didn't answer beyond looking disgusted, and I added, "That was after your time, of course. Uncle Joshua was already dead when I married Bradley. I never met him. I don't know if you remember Bradley?"

"I remember his mother," Maybelle said, her jaw tight.

No surprise there.

Bradley's mother is like my mother, only more so. We'd gotten along reasonably well, Althea and I, everything considered. I was a Martin from Sweetwater, and I could trace my antecedents back to the War Against Northern Aggression and beyond, same as she could, so I could prove that my family had been on the right side in that epic conflict. My Southern heritage and good manners and that stint in finishing school had made me an acceptable mate for Bradley. Althea had liked me, as much as she was able to like anyone, especially someone who'd married her precious baby boy. She and my mother had been like peas in a pod.

I imagined Maybelle may not have fared as well. No finishing school for Maybelle Hicks from the wrong side of the tracks in Florence, Alabama.

"It must have been a disappointment when you didn't inherit any of Uncle Joshua's money. Why did you bother killing him when you knew you wouldn't get anything?"

"Who says I killed him?" Maybelle asked sweetly.

I smiled back, with about as much warmth. "Nobody says you did. If my father-in-law had suspected anything, he would have nailed your hide to the wall. There was nothing suspicious about Uncle Joshua's death, either. And just like Harold, Joshua's dust by now. Nobody can prove anything. Congratulations. You got away with murder."

Maybelle smiled complacently.

I added, "Except now you're racking up a whole bunch of new charges. Charges that someone might be able to prove, even if I'm dead. There were witnesses this morning, on the interstate. When you tried to make me crash into that truck."

"I can't imagine what you're talking about," Maybelle said airily.

"You drove me home once, back in August. I should have remembered that you drive a white Toyota."

"Blizzard Pearl," Maybelle murmured.

I managed to avoid rolling my eyes. "Excuse me. Of course, Blizzard Pearl. I suppose you unhooked my fuel line this afternoon too? And cut Aislynn and Kylie's brake cables last weekend?"

"That was a mistake," Maybelle said.

Well, duh. "You almost killed two women. Women you don't even know, who did nothing to you. Yes, I'd call that a mistake."

I looked at her for any hint of remorse, and found none. I added, "The police are investigating the accident. Sooner or later they'll figure out that you were in that parking lot that night. I'm sure there are security cameras, and someone might remember seeing you."

"Let them," Maybelle said. "They can't prove I did anything. It's a public place. I had no reason to want to do away with your friends. I don't even know them. And I imagine, with their backgrounds, there are lots of other people who would like to get rid of them."

"Their backgrounds?"

"Alternative lifestyles," Maybelle said.

Of course. "I don't suppose you care that you could have killed Rafe this afternoon, either."

"That young man who was just here?" Her nose wrinkled. "Really, Savannah, didn't your mother teach you better than to throw yourself away on riff-raff like that?"

"Keep my mother out of this," I answered. "You don't know her. And you don't know him, either. You have no idea who or what he is."

Or that, if she managed to hurt me, he'd land on her like a ton of bricks.

Not that that thought gave me much solace at the moment. I was having a supremely crappy day. As Grimaldi had once said, it had been just one damned thing after another ever since I woke up this morning.

Ever since last night, really. I'd had a hell of a twenty four hours, if you'll pardon the language.

And unless I could extricate myself from this mess, it would be the last twenty four hours I'd ever get.

"I guess Steven wasn't much a problem for you after taking Harold away from Carolyn." I put my naked feet up on the edge of the coffee table and inspected my toenails. "Harold at least liked his wife. Nobody liked Brenda."

The polish was chipped in places. I would have to give myself a manicure before Christmas Eve. Gone are the days when I could afford to have someone do it for me.

Maybelle permitted herself a tiny smile at my witticism. "I love Steven," she said primly.

"Of course you do. And it doesn't hurt that he's well off. He probably had a pretty sizable life insurance policy on Brenda, didn't he?"

"I wouldn't know," Maybelle said. When I arched my brows, she added, "Life insurance is common. A lot of people have it."

"Of course they do. Harold Driscoll certainly did. It made you quite wealthy when he kicked the bucket."

Rather than lowering my feet to the floor, I kept them on the edge of the table. It was an unladylike position, and mother would have been shocked had she seen me, but it seemed worth it, in case I could leverage the position into an attack on Maybelle. The edge of the table would hit her in the stomach if I pushed it forward. It might be enough to shock her for a moment. Long enough that I could make a grab for the gun.

"I loved Harold," Maybelle said demurely.

All I needed was a distraction. The phone ringing, a car backfiring outside on the street. A sonic boom. The hand of God coming down out of the ceiling...

"Oh, sure. What's not to love? He took good care of you. Expensive vacations, lovely things. Makes me wonder why you found it necessary to kill him in the first place."

Maybelle didn't answer, and I continued, "I don't think you loved him, though. You may have wanted what he and Carolyn had. And of course you wanted the money. And the house. The kitchen with the glass fronted cabinets and the marble counter. Carolyn's life, with a husband who doted on her. But you didn't love him. I saw the pictures. He was always the one touching you. You didn't touch him back."

Her face darkened. "Men are all the same. Only interested in one thing."

I had a flashback to Perry Fortunato, waving his gun and telling me that all women are the same, always flaunting their bodies and then saying no.

"If you didn't want to put out, you shouldn't have offered," I said.

Dammit, my distraction wasn't coming. There was no sonic boom. No car backfiring outside. The phone didn't ring and God didn't personally interfere. I wasn't sure how much longer I could keep this up, while looking into the muzzle of that gun.

And then it happened, almost as if I'd conjured it. There was a knock on the door.

Maybelle's eyes flickered that way for a second, and I channeled Rafe, seizing the moment and straightening my legs, hard, pushing the coffee table forward. It hit Maybelle in the stomach. She said "Ooof!" as all the breath was squeezed out of her. I'm sure tightening her finger on the trigger was automatic.

The same thing had happened just a few weeks ago, in much the same way, minus the table to the stomach but including the jumpy trigger finger. Then I'd tried to duck out of the way, and had taken a bullet in the shoulder. This time I didn't have time to dodge, and the bullet whizzed past, close enough that I felt it tear through the fabric of my sleeve. It embedded itself in the back of the sofa with a meaty sort of thwack.

Maybelle lost her grip on the gun, and it fell and hit the top of the coffee table with enough force to crack the glass. I scooped it up and turned it on her. "Don't even think of moving."

She didn't look like she could move even if she'd wanted to. At the moment she was sort of green and too busy trying to catch her breath. I hoped she wouldn't throw up all over my living room. Maybe I should go get her a bowl.

But first I had something else to deal with. The knock on the door hadn't been divine intervention, or at least not in the supernatural way.

Someone was out there, banging. I headed that way, while making sure to keep Maybelle covered with the gun. If she came at me, I was totally prepared to shoot her. Theoretically, at least.

I half expected it to be Rafe outside. The banging had his trademark: large, angry male. However, when I turned the lock and pulled the door open, it wasn't Rafe. It was someone I'd never seen before. A young man around Truman's age, early twenties, with fair, shaggy hair and blue eyes, dressed in faded jeans and a padded jacket with sheepskin collar, camouflage patterned. I wouldn't have been surprised to see a hunting rifle slung over his shoulder, but it was missing. When he saw the gun in my hand, he took a step back and lifted his hands. "Whoa!"

"Sorry." I lowered the gun.

"You Savannah?"

I nodded.

"What's up with that?" He nodded to the gun.

"I had a little problem," I said.

"Mind if I come in?"

I did, kind of. I didn't even know who he was. But I did have the gun, so if he tried anything I could shoot him. And he didn't seem interested in me anyway. He just slipped past me and headed down the hallway into the combination living room/dining room. Once there, he stopped in the middle of the floor and contemplated Maybelle.

"You two know each other?" I said.

Maybelle lifted her head and looked him over, head to toe and back, before shaking her head. The young man's mouth twisted.

"Been a long time," he said. "Hello, mother."

Twenty-One

"Clean bill of health," Officer Spicer said the next morning when he and Truman dropped off my car. "The shop said it's fine. They checked everything, and there are no little surprises set to go off."

"I appreciate it." I accepted the keys he dropped into my hand. "I think I'd probably be worried about driving again if someone hadn't taken a good look."

"They were thorough," Truman said, one of the few times he'd actually spoken to me. "Your boyfriend put the fear of God in them yesterday." He grinned.

I blushed. "Sorry."

"No need to apologize, Miz Martin," Spicer said, scratching the top of his head. "He was just making sure the car was safe for you." He put the uniform cap back on. "With Miz Driscoll behind bars, you're welcome to go pick up your friend Miz Mitchell from the hospital yourself. The detective said we could do it, but to give you the choice. Ain't nobody else out there who'll bother you no more."

I nodded. I guess that was true. Maybelle was locked up, along with Hector and Heather. After Lenny Wilkins Jr. showed up at my apartment and introduced himself, I called Detective Grimaldi. And while I waited for her to arrive, I kept the gun pointed at Maybelle while she and Lenny got reacquainted.

By the time the detective got there, I had the whole story pretty straight in my head. Maybelle and Lenny Sr. had gotten married pretty much straight out of high school. Maybelle had gotten pregnant shortly after that, and given birth to Little Lenny. A couple of years into motherhood and being the wife of an auto mechanic in a small town in Alabama, she'd had enough. I was a little unclear on exactly what happened after that, but Little Lenny was pretty adamant that Maybelle had waited until Big Lenny went on a drinking binge, which he did with some regularity—Little Lenny was totally upfront about it—and then they'd gotten into an argument. Maybelle had told Little Lenny to run down the road to his grandma's house, which Little Lenny had done. He'd gone to sleep there, just like all the other times his parents had been fighting. I got the impression it had happened a lot. Everyone knew about it and no one lifted a finger. So it had been business as usual... until a few hours later, in the middle of the night, when the Wilkins trailer had gone up in flames.

Maybelle had had an alibi—she'd been down at the local bar sporting a black eye and a fat lip, garnering sympathy—and everyone figured the fire had been an accident. Big Lenny had been a smoker, and according to Maybelle he'd been dead drunk; the consensus was that he'd been smoking in bed, and had lit himself and the trailer on fire. It burned to the ground with him inside.

Maybelle left town the next week, and nobody missed here. Little Lenny ended up living with his grandma. However, it didn't take long for the manure to hit the fan, especially after it got out that Lenny had had a lot of money in the trailer. He was running a lucrative and illegal sideline the IRS didn't know about, dealing in luxury cars that happened to fall of trailers. Organized car theft, something along the lines of what Hector Gonzales had been involved in, only on a smaller scale twenty years ago. And although all the money he'd had could have gone up in flames, and probably should have, there was speculation that Maybelle had put it somewhere else before the fire. Like, her handbag or the glove compartment of her car.

And now Lenny Jr. was standing in my living room accusing his estranged mother of having had a hand in the fire. That perhaps there was a reason Big Lenny hadn't made it out of the trailer alive. Like, he hadn't just been drunk, he'd been suffering from something else too.

"Lots of antifreeze sitting around the shop," Lenny Jr. told his mother, bitterly. "And you knew what it was. I was just a couple years old, and I remember you showing me the bottle and the skull and crossbones on it."

Maybelle didn't admit anything, had just sat on my sofa with her hands primly folded in her lap, scowling. On the other hand, she didn't deny it either, which went a long way towards making me think young Lenny might have a point.

When Detective Grimaldi took her away, Lenny went along, to make sure Grimaldi contacted the sheriff in Florence. By then it was getting late, and the detective agreed that I could give her my statement tomorrow instead. She said she'd call me in the morning to work out a time and place. I'd asked about Rafe, and she had told me he was on his way to Atlanta.

"The hospital called. Hector's going to be just fine, and by the time he has to go to trial, his voice should be back to normal, too. Your boyfriend did a number on his larynx."

"He fights dirty," I said, with a touch of pride in my voice.

"And then some," the detective agreed. "Anyway, Hector's on his way to Atlanta, and Mr. Collier is riding shotgun."

"He's OK, isn't he?"

"He's armed," Grimaldi said, "and Hector's handcuffed. He's also not alone. Wendell Craig is with him, and so is a representative for the FBI."

"None of your people?"

"Our jurisdiction ends in Nashville," Grimaldi said. "The TBI's jurisdiction ends at the state line, technically, but since this is a joint investigation involving both the TBI and the FBI, and since your boyfriend's spent the past few months undercover in Atlanta, it made sense for him to go back there. He wanted to. Said it was personal."

"Any idea when he'll be back?"

"A few days," Grimaldi said. "Maybe a week."

She waited a second to see if I had anything more to say. When I didn't, she added, "I'll call you tomorrow. And expect a visit from Spicer and Truman in the AM. The auto shop is done with your car. There are no more little surprises."

"Thank you," I'd smiled at Maybelle, who had growled back at me. Young Lenny had given me a nod when they walked out, and that was it. I'd finally made it to bed and had slept like—pardon the pun—the dead until this morning, when Spicer and Truman showed up with my car.

And now here I was, with my keys in my hand, my Volvo parked at the curb, and good news for Kylie.

She and Aislynn had called me after the whole debacle had ended last night, and had dictated a verbal counter for me to pass on to Tim. He'd called his clients, and this morning he'd called back and said they'd accepted the offer. All I had to do was get everyone's signature on all the paperwork, and then it'd be a done deal. I hoped Aislynn and Kylie would be as thrilled as I was.

"Call if you run into any problems," Spicer said with a tip of his cap, and then he and Truman got into their squad car and drove off. I headed back upstairs to the apartment to get ready, after directing a fond glance at the Volvo. It was nice to have wheels again.

By the time I got to the hospital, Kylie was ready to go. She was also alone. "Aislynn went to work," she explained when I looked around at the empty room. "She's been here pretty much 24/7, and we didn't think it made any sense for her to miss another day of work and income to take a cab here just to drive back home with me. She'll be home by three o'clock this afternoon."

I nodded. "Makes sense. I'll help you get settled."

"You don't have to do that," Kylie said.

"I don't mind. It seems the least I can do, seeing as—" I stopped, flushing.

"As what?" Kylie prompted.

"Seeing as it's my fault you were hurt."

"How can it be your fault?"

I opened my mouth to explain, but the rattle of a wheelchair in the hallway stopped me. A second later, a cheerful nurse had pushed herself and the chair through the door into the room. "Ready to go?"

Kylie nodded. "More than ready."

The nurse turned to me. "You must be the sister. Dr. Simon said you looked alike."

"Right," I said. I'd forgotten all about the little white lie I'd told to gain access to Kylie's room the night of the accident. Kylie looked surprised but she didn't set the nurse straight.

"Are you driving your sister home?"

I nodded.

"We'll just get loaded up, and you can be on your way." She maneuvered Kylie from the bed into the chair, and dropped Kylie's bag into Kylie's lap.

"I can take that," I offered as we set ourselves in motion through the door and down the hall.

Kylie shook her head. "I've got it. It isn't heavy. So what's this about it being your fault?"

"Oh." I might have wished she wouldn't have brought it up again while the nurse could hear, but I supposed it was no more than I deserved. I told her the whole story about Maybelle and the Volvos and how the fact that we looked alike and drove similar cars had been to blame for the accident that hurt her.

"So it was someone trying to get you?" There was a wrinkle between her brows.

I nodded.

"Dear me!" the nurse said.

"Does that happen often?" Kylie wanted to know.

More often than I like. I shook my head and smiled. "Hardly ever. And the police arrested her last night. She's in prison. The auto shop went over the car in detail, and there's nothing wrong with it. You'll be perfectly safe."

Kylie nodded, reassured. The nurse didn't look so happy. However, she helped Kylie into the passenger seat without a word, while I put the overnight bag into the trunk and wandered around the car to the driver's side.

I must admit I held my breath when I turned the key in the ignition. Spicer and Truman had assured me the car was safe, and if Rafe had threatened the auto shop owner, I had no doubt he'd done a thorough job, but even so, there was a tiny part of me that expected the engine to blow when the car started. I stopped breathing, my body tense and ready to jump if anything threatened to go wrong. It didn't; the car just settled into its usual sort of growly purr. I pulled on the gear shift and rolled on out of the hospital area and onto Hillsboro Road South.

"Were you worried?" Kylie wanted to know.

I glanced at her. "Excuse me?"

"As soon as we left the hospital, you relaxed. Were you worried?"

Oops.

I bit my lip. It was probably better not to admit that I'd been afraid the car would explode; that wouldn't be reassuring. So I did the next best thing and confessed to something else instead. "I don't like hospitals. I've spent a lot of time in them lately."

Kylie wrinkled her brows. "Something wrong?"

"Not anymore." And since it probably also wouldn't sound reassuring that I got shot recently, I skipped over that part and forced a smile. "I had a miscarriage a couple of weeks ago."

Her face sort of crumpled. "I'm so sorry."

"I am, too. It was really hard." I concentrated on maneuvering the car through the intersection at Hillsboro Road and Wedgewood Avenue, blinking back the tears that still threatened every time I thought too hard about what I'd lost. "It was my second. One with my ex-husband and one with..."

I hesitated, not sure what to call Rafe. I'd gotten to the point of not objecting when someone else called him my boyfriend, but I couldn't quite bring myself to use that terminology.

"Your partner?" Kylie suggested.

There were times I felt very much like we had a partnership, sure. In a way I'd never felt with Bradley or Todd. They loved me—in Bradley's case, I'm sure it had been to the best of his ability, even if that didn't amount to much in the end—and they wanted to protect and cherish me, but they'd never made me feel like an equal. Rafe did.

Yes, partner sounded good.

I smiled. "Something like that. I love him. He likes me. He might even love me, even if he's never said it. He saved my life yesterday. Twice. And when he comes back from Atlanta, we're going to try again."

I'd told him I wanted another shot at a baby, and he'd told me he had plans for me when he came back... in my mind, that translated to lots of lovely time spent between the sheets, and Rafe not being averse to knocking me up one more time.

"Aislynn and I want to adopt," Kylie said.

"That's wonderful. Rafe has a twelve year old son who's adopted."

"Rafe's your boyfriend?"

I nodded.

"Sounds like a romance novel hero," Kylie said with a grin. I grinned back, and didn't tell her how right she was. "So you'll be a stepmother?"

"Oh, no. He got adopted by someone else. Rafe didn't even know David existed until a couple of months ago."

She looked confused, and I added, "It's complicated. But David is Rafe's son, and he got adopted at birth by two lovely people, and everything is great. Adoption can be a wonderful thing." And hopefully, if Rafe got out of his association with the TBI and the undercover ops, and got that normal life he'd told me about, Sam and Ginny Flannery would let him get to know David.

"Sounds like you have an interesting life," Kylie said.

I smiled. "I guess I do. More interesting than I like at times. But at least it's never dull."

"I think I'd like mine to be dull for a while," Kylie said, shifting in her seat. "This has been more than enough excitement for me. I just want to go home and rest."

I imagined she did. I stepped on the gas to get her there faster, and the car responded just as it should. It was nice. I focused on driving and let Kylie snuggle into the seat and get comfortable.

I GOT HER HOME AND SITUATED, and got her signature on the paperwork I needed for the house in East Nashville before leaving. From Kylie's I scooted over to Sara Beth's Café and got Aislynn's signature, creating a binding agreement. It was the middle of the lunch rush, so Aislynn didn't have time to talk, and all the tables at Sara Beth's were occupied, so I couldn't even sit down and eat. Instead, I got back into the car and headed for the office, to drop off the completed paperwork and earnest money check to Tim.

I was halfway there when the phone rang. "Morning, Ms. Martin," Tamara Grimaldi said.

"Good morning. How are you?" She sounded a little better today, as if she'd actually gotten a good night's sleep for once.

"Fine. I thought you might want to grab a bite while we do the report. It's been a while since I've had a chance to sit down and eat."

"Sure," I said. We'd had lunch together a few times before, actually. "I'm on my way back to East Nashville. Where do you want to meet?"

We settled on a sports bar just down the street from the real estate office, and a time that would allow me to park and go inside to drop my paperwork off to Tim before wandering down the street to the FinBar.

Tim was gone when I got to the office, so I gave the paperwork to Brittany instead, and asked her to make sure I got a copy of everything in my mailbox. She flipped her ponytail and asked why I couldn't just make my own copies.

I bit back my original retort, which was to tell her that as receptionist and office support, it was her job. "I'm having lunch with Detective Grimaldi in a few minutes. I don't have the time."

"I saw you on TV the other night," Brittany said.

You and the rest of Nashville. "Good for you. Will you get me copies of that paperwork?"

"Sure," Brittany said, shuffling the pages, clearly not focused on what she was saying. "Who was that guy you were with?"

"Nobody you know. A South American hitman named Jorge Pena."

"Tim said he's your boyfriend," Brittany said.

"Tim's crazy. I'd never date a hitman. My mother would disinherit me. And anyway, Jorge's dead."

"Oh," Brittany said. "Is that why you're meeting the police? Because you killed him?"

"Of course not," I said. "I'd never kill anyone." Although if it had been me instead of Elspeth, standing between Rafe and Jorge with a loaded gun in my hand two months ago, I'd have shot Jorge without hesitation before giving him a chance to shoot me. So I guess it would depend on the circumstances.

"What are you meeting the police for, then?"

"Lunch." I smiled sweetly and headed for the back door. "Tell Tim to call me if he has any questions. About the contract, I mean. And make sure I get a copy of the paperwork in my mailbox."

"What?" Brittany said, just as I closed the door behind me and set off down the sidewalk toward the FinBar.

The detective was already waiting when I got there, at a table for two over in the corner. As is Rafe's habit, she had positioned herself with her back to the wall, in a location where she could see the whole room as well as the front door. As soon as I walked in, she lifted a hand. I drifted over there and sat down, and ordered a Diet Coke from the waitress who appeared. Once she'd taken herself off again, I smiled at the detective.

"Nice to see you. Under circumstances where I haven't been in mortal danger immediately preceding."

"I couldn't agree more," Tamara Grimaldi said, with a thorough look at me. "How do you feel?"

"I'm fine." I shrugged out of my coat and hung it over the back of the chair. "The headache's gone. My wrists feel better. And Maybelle didn't hurt me. Everything's good."

Grimaldi nodded. "I'm going to record your statement. Once I get it typed up, I'll email you a copy for your signature."

"That's fine." She set her phone to record and nodded to me. I launched into my story of what had happened after she and Rafe drove off yesterday, beginning with my stupidity in answering the door without checking the peephole first, because I thought it was Rafe coming back. The detective pursed her lips disapprovingly, but her eyes were laughing.

"That's it?" she said two minutes later when I'd gotten to the end.

I nodded. "It was pretty simple. The knocking on the door distracted her for a second. I pushed the table at her, she dropped the gun, and I went and opened the door. Then I called you, and sat and listened to Lenny and Maybelle talk while I waited. Do you want me to go over what Lenny said?"

She shook her head. "No, thank you. It's hearsay. And I got his statement last night. Thanks." She turned the recorder off, after rattling off the salient details about where, when, who and why.

"So what will happen now?"

"Mr. Wilkins drove back to Alabama yesterday," Grimaldi said. "Maybelle spent the night in jail. We got her on attempted murder and a few other, minor charges. Tampering with your car, trying to force you off the road, causing Ms. Mitchell's and Ms. Turner's accident."

"That's all?" She'd killed three people, and all the police could do was arrest her for tampering with my car?

"It's the best I can do right now. The Davidson County DA will determine whether there's cause for reopening the investigation into Harold Driscoll's death. I've notified authorities in Florence, Alabama, as well as in Natchez, where they are waiting to see what we decide to do before making a decision about Joshua Rowland."

I nodded. Harold was ashes, and so was Lenny Sr. There might be enough left of Joshua Rowland to prove murder, but that would involve my ex-in-laws having the body exhumed, and I couldn't see Althea agreeing to digging him up. At this point, there may be no way to prove that Maybelle killed anyone. "So she might get away with it."

"She'll probably get away with some of it," Grimaldi nodded. "But she won't get away with what she tried to do to you. And she won't be marrying Steven Puckett. That's what you wanted, wasn't it?"

I shrugged. I guess. "Have you called him? How did he take it?"

"Not well," Grimaldi said, and glanced up as the waitress appeared beside the table. "I'll have a cheeseburger and fries."

She waited for me to order—"Cobb salad, please,"—and for the waitress to remove herself (and the menus), before she continued. "At first he didn't believe me when I said I'd arrested her. He seemed to think it was a joke. Then he refused to believe she'd done anything wrong. I don't think he believes she did anything to her husbands. But it's pretty tough to explain away what she did to you."

I made a face. "I feel bad for him. He's been through a lot these past few months. First Brenda's murder and now this. Although I guess it could have been worse. He could have married her."

"Definitely," Grimaldi nodded. "I'm pretty sure you're right, you know. She probably did kill all three of her husbands. There has to be a reason why she came after you, and that's the only one I can think of. Mr. Wilkins made a good point when he brought up the ethylene glycol."

"I meant to ask you about that," I said. "What is it?"

It was antifreeze, according to the detective. Or maybe hydraulic brake fluid. "Sweet-tasting and highly toxic, not to mention readily available. Mr. Wilkins's auto shop would definitely have had it, and it isn't hard to come by for a civilian, either. Any auto-parts store or gas station carries antifreeze."

"What does it do, when you drink it?"

"Bad stuff," Grimaldi said. When I stared at her, unblinking, she added, "Ethylene glycol poisoning mimics drunkenness and results in a total systemic shutdown and maybe a coma."

"That would explain what Lenny said about his father being drunk."

She nodded. "I wouldn't be surprised if, the nights before Harold's and Joshua's deaths, Maybelle poured a little antifreeze cocktail, too. If they survived the night, they'd just put any discomfort down to too much wine and excitement the night before."

I had to agree. "But you can't prove it?"

"Sadly, no. They were treated as natural deaths at the time. Heart failure in both cases. Which is what it was. Heart failure. So there were no autopsies and no tissue samples taken, and by now, there'd be nothing left to exhume. If the bodies weren't cremated in the first place."

"So she gets away with it."

"We do the best we can," Tamara Grimaldi said. "We'll certainly bring it up at trial as a possible explanation for why she tried to kill you. Unless she pleads out and gets out of going to trial."

"What happens then?"

"The judge will sentence her to an appropriate prison term. Don't worry, she'll be going away for a good long time either way."

I nodded, more or less satisfied. Sometimes you just have to take what you can get and be happy.

"So what will you be doing now?" Grimaldi wanted to know. There was something a little bit off about her tone, and I glanced across the table at her. She wasn't looking at me, just focused on making rings on the table with the bottom of her water glass. I'd once sat in this very bar watching Alexandra Puckett do the same thing. She'd been looking for a certain piece of information pertaining to her mother's murder and her boyfriend's possible involvement in it, but she hadn't just come right out and asked me. I wondered what the detective wanted to know, that she wasn't asking.

"I'm waiting for Rafe to come back from Atlanta," I said. "I just got a house under contract that I have to shepherd to closing. And Christmas is coming up. I'll be going to Sweetwater for a few days."

The detective nodded. "Everything OK at home?"

"As far as I know," I said, watching her narrowly. "Any particular reason you ask?"

She shook her head, and because the waitress appeared with our food just then, I let her off the hook. But only until the waitress had deposited our plates—Grimaldi's burger and fries, my salad—and departed. Lifting my fork, I added innocently, "By the way, I meant to ask. Just how well have you gotten to know my brother?"

"What do you mean?" Grimaldi asked.

"You had dinner together, didn't you? That night I called you to talk about Maybelle? He said you did."

"It was business," Grimaldi muttered, without meeting my eyes. Something about those French fries seemed to be very compelling.

"That's what he said. You needed a date who didn't look like a cop, so you called my brother. And he drove an hour from Sweetwater to help you keep an eye on Rafe and Carmen."

"He did it for you," Grimaldi said, looking up.

"No, he didn't."

"Yes, he did. I told him Mr. Collier was having dinner with someone else, someone who wasn't you, and he wouldn't believe me. So I told him to come look for himself."

There was a certain logic to this, even if Dix hadn't mentioned anything about it. "Really?"

"Yes," Grimaldi said and looked me straight in the eye. Since I suspected she could look me straight in the eye and lie through her teeth, I wasn't sure what to think.

"He slept with her," I said.

For a second, Grimaldi didn't answer. Then she put her burger down and leaned forward, her voice low. "There's something you need to understand."

I leaned forward too, unable to resist. "What's that?"

"I've seen the two of you together. And I've talked to both of you. I'm pretty sure I know how you feel about him."

"I love him," I said.

She nodded. "He's spent ten years deep undercover. He's been dealing with the scum of the earth. You know what they say: you lie down with dogs, you wake up with fleas? He's done a lot of things that'd probably scare the pants off you if he told you about them."

I opened my mouth, and she added, "I'm sure he's done things that would scare me too. Sleeping with Carmen Arroyo is minor compared to some of the other things he must have seen and done over the past ten years."

I nodded. No doubt she was right about that.

"He cares about you. He protects you and looks out for you and takes risks to make sure you're safe. If he slept with Carmen—and he probably did—it had nothing to do with how he feels about you. And if you hold it over his head, all you'll do is prove to him that you don't understand. And he has enough strikes against him without that."

"You must have been talking to my brother," I murmured.

Grimaldi shrugged. "Bottom line, Savannah—" I looked up; she so rarely calls me that, especially not in that very serious tone of voice, "if you want him, you'll have to take him the way he is. With the parts of him you don't understand and the parts you wish he didn't have."

"There are no parts I wish he didn't have," I said. "And I'll take him any way I can get him, for however long he'll stick around. And if you talk to him, you can tell him that."

Grimaldi smiled. "I'll do that."

"Do you think it might make him come back sooner?"

"No," Grimaldi said, "he'll have to be there until the job is done. But it'll give him incentive to work fast."

I nodded. I just hoped it wouldn't make him decide to stay where he was instead of venturing back into Tennessee again.

Twenty-Two

spoke to the detective once more in the next few days, on Christmas Eve morning. I was getting ready to get in the car to drive to Sweetwater for mother's Christmas party, and I wanted to touch base with Tamara Grimaldi before I went.

"Any news from Atlanta?"

"No," the detective said. "Why?"

"He said he'd be back for Christmas." Probably.

"Last I heard, they were still working things out."

Bummer. I tried not to let it show in my voice. "I'm on my way to Sweetwater. Or I will be in a few minutes. My mother always has a party on Christmas Eve."

"Your brother told me," Grimaldi said.

My ears pricked up. "Are you coming?"

The detective snorted. "Hardly. I'm working."

"On Christmas?"

"Crime doesn't take a vacation, Ms. Martin," Tamara Grimaldi said. "In fact, it gets worse around the holidays. More money problems, more alcohol, more domestic violence. More desperate people doing whatever they can to provide Christmas for their families, including committing crimes to get what they need. Robberies go up. So do burglaries—lots of houses are empty—and muggings are at an all-time high. Beware the mall parking lot."

"I've already done my Christmas shopping. I bought you a scarf. Turquoise. My brother's favorite color." And a good choice for her coloring.

There was a pause.

"Thank you," Grimaldi said.

"My pleasure. I'll drop it off in downtown on my way. Will you be there?"

"Not until tonight," Grimaldi said. "I'm off this morning."

"I'll leave it at the front desk for you."

"Thank you."

There was another pause.

"I guess I should go. Have a merry Christmas, detective."

"And you have a good trip to Sweetwater. When will you be back?"

I told her I'd be a couple of days. "Catherine and Jonathan are hosting family dinner tomorrow. I'll probably spend the night again and come back the next day."

"Don't be a stranger," Grimaldi said. "And wish your brother a merry Christmas for me."

She hung up before I had the chance to respond.

Thirty minutes later I was on my way. I'd loaded up the car, driven downtown, dropped off my present for the detective at police headquarters, stopped by the office to tell everyone I would be gone the next couple of days, and hit the road. I was passing Brentwood when my cell phone rang.

"Hi, Savannah," Alexandra Puckett said.

"Hi, Alex. Everything OK?"

"Everything's great!" I could imagine the smile flooding her face. "We're in Florida."

"You are?"

"Uh-huh." I heard her earring clicking against the phone and pictured her nodding vigorously. "Spur of the moment trip. It's our first Christmas without mom, and now my dad doesn't even have Maybelle to take his mind off things. So he got us all tickets to Florida. We left yesterday."

"Good for you," I said.

Alexandra lowered her voice. "Thanks for getting rid of her."

"My pleasure. Turns out you were right. She did kill her husbands. All three of them. Or so we think, anyway."

"That's what my dad said," Alexandra said. "I'm not sure he believes it, though."

"Maybe he'll start to believe it once he's had some time to process." It couldn't be easy to realize that the woman you wanted to marry wasn't who you thought she were.

Alexandra didn't sound like she cared too much one way or the other, actually. "The wedding's off, anyway. So do you think she'd have killed my dad, too?"

"Eventually? Maybe. She killed everyone else. I think he's much safer without her."

"Uh-huh," Alexandra agreed. "Thank you, Savannah."

"My pleasure. Have a good time in Florida."

Alexandra giggled and said she would, and we hung up. I focused on driving the Volvo through Christmas Eve traffic, on roads that were slick with sleet, toward Sweetwater.

The Martin mansion sits on a little knoll outside Sweetwater proper, on the road to Columbia. Back in the old days, the plantation had lots of land surrounding it, but now there's just a couple acres left, and a few buildings. An old smoke house and one of the old slave cabins, in addition to the mansion itself.

The mansion is antebellum, 1839, and looks like a Southern plantation. In the movies, plantation houses are big and white and square with tall pillars. In real life, a lot are red or yellow brick, and only the pillars are white. Some aren't made of brick at all, and don't have any pillars. Throughout the deep south, especially Louisiana, you get the French Creole architecture instead: the low spreading roofline and wraparound galleries, all starting well above ground level.

The Martin plantation is pretty typical of its age and location. It's two stories tall, built from red brick, with symmetrical windows and tall, white pillars in the front. Rafe once called it a mausoleum, and although I was a little offended at the time, I can see his point.

It belonged to my father's family, and after his death, my mother turned it into a special events venue. People rent it for weddings and other parties, and at least once or twice a year, a photographer brings several rail thin models down for a photo shoot, while a handful of music videos have been filmed on the grounds. And then there are the school groups, who come to gawk at the slave cabin and the artifacts of the old days laid out in the smoke house.

Growing up, the mansion was just home, where I lived. I didn't think much of it, beyond that. Now that I've been gone for almost ten years, I can see how impressive it is, and also how it's an embodiment of history, a past that means different things to different people. It looked self-satisfied sitting there on its knoll, unapproachable, gazing down on the road below along its metaphorical nose. And it was bedecked with greenery and lights for Christmas, like a picture on the cover of Southern Living magazine. My mother has excellent taste.

Of course, it also looked warm and inviting, with light spilling out of its tall windows. Home. I pulled the car up to the entrance in the front and jumped out, hurrying up the stairs. "Mother?"

"In here," my mother's voice came back, from the parlor on the right. "Is that you, Savannah?"

I said it was. "What are you doing?"

"Just getting ready for tonight," my mother said. I heard a melodic tinkling, which made me think she was pouring M&Ms into a bowl. This hypothesis was born out a moment later when she appeared in the doorway with an empty candy bag in her hand. "Hello, darling."

She leaned in. I air-kissed first one cheek and then the other.

My mother is lovely. She's in her mid fifties, and looks at least ten years younger. Some of it is nature, plus a lot of hard work, but some is artifice too. She spends a good bit of money on looking like this. Then again, it's her money, and I guess she can use it however she wants.

"Have you had lunch, darling?"

I said I hadn't, and she whisked me off to the kitchen to feed me. Some things never change.

We don't have servants. Mother employs a service that comes in and cleans once a week. Other than that, she's on her own. She does her own day-to-day cooking and cleaning, and her own laundry. Granted, most of her wardrobe is dry-clean only, but she does wash her own socks and underwear. I didn't grow up spoiled; I had to clean my own room and help with the rest of the house, and I also know how to do my own laundry and cooking.

The Christmas party tonight would be catered, but buffet-style, so we wouldn't have to be bothered with serving staff and could enjoy being 'just the family,' as mother put it.

"Todd told me he's coming," I said, lowering my roast beef sandwich.

Mother looked a touch guilty, but only for a second. "Bob's coming, dear. He has no other family. Nor does Todd."

"I know that," I said. "With the way you and Bob Satterfield are carrying on, I'm not surprised you want him here. And I guess you couldn't very well leave Todd out. I just don't want it to be awkward."

"Just don't say anything embarrassing," mother said.

And there, in a nutshell, you have my mother. Concerned that

I would say something to embarrass Todd. In *my* childhood home during *my* family's Christmas party.

"I'm not worried about his feelings," I said. "I'm worried about mine."

"Nonsense," my mother answered. "Todd loves you."

"That's the problem. He won't take no for an answer."

My mother's face puckered. Not in a sour way, but as if she were trying not to cry. "Are you sure you couldn't..."

"I'm sure," I said. "I'd make him just as miserable as Jolynn did once he got used to me. There's no way I'd be able to live up to his expectations. And I'd be miserable, too. You don't want me to be miserable, do you?"

"Of course not, darling," mother said, since it was the only thing she could say, "but are you sure..."

"I'm positive. Rafe's in Atlanta, but when he comes back, I will figure out a way to keep him around. If I can get him to propose, I will marry him. If I can't, I'll live in sin. And I don't care what anyone thinks of it. I hope you can find it in your heart to wish me the best, but if you can't, I'm still going to try."

"Of course, dear," mother said, choking slightly on the words.

I took pity on her. "I love you, mom. I know he isn't what you envisioned for me. But he makes me happy. And if you give him a chance, I think you'll like him."

Who was I kidding? He'd terrify her. But that was her problem, not mine. I had enough on my plate just making sure he stuck around. My mother's feelings were of secondary importance. And it wouldn't hurt her any to be dragged, kicking and screaming, into the new century. So I just devoted myself to my sandwich and didn't say anything else about it.

She kept me hopping for the rest of the afternoon. I'm not saying there was any correlation between that and our conversation—for instance, that she wanted to make sure we had no more time for a heart to heart—but the truth is, we didn't exchange any meaningful comments after that. I spent my time filling candy dishes and replacing candles and hanging mistletoe. Just after four o'clock mother sent me upstairs to get ready, since every Southern Belle with self-respect needs at least two hours to get herself dressed for an occasion.

I took a bath, slathered myself with lotion, dried my hair in loose waves I piled on top of my head, dunked perfume behind my ears, and painted my face. And got dressed in that emerald green velvet dress I'd been admiring at the mall that afternoon I'd seen Carmen walk by. After everything that happened—and after inking the binding contract with Kylie and Aislynn—I'd convinced myself I needed (and could afford) a new dress for Christmas. My red satin wasn't back from the cleaners yet, and between you and me, I had grave concerns that they'd never be able to turn it back into what it had been before I'd been manhandled and kidnapped in it. But the green velvet was an acceptable substitute. Heavy velvet, fitted bodice, low-cut and elegant, with a full skirt that made my waist look smaller. I looked good, and when I walked into the parlor later that evening, Todd took one look at me and forgot to breathe.

My heart sank. I should have worn an old sack or something.

"Savannah, darling!" mother trilled. "You look lovely!"

She looked pretty good herself, in a tight black skirt and a sequined top that matched her champagne-colored hair. She was sitting on great-aunt Marie's peach velvet loveseat, and I think she was holding hands with Todd's dad, the sheriff.

"Can I get you a drink, Savannah?" Todd asked.

I smiled at him. "Chardonnay, please."

He clicked his heels together and gave me a little bow. Todd's on his very best behavior whenever mother is around. It's as if he thinks that if he just keeps impressing her, she'll talk me into marrying him one of these days.

"Y'all right, darlin'?" the sheriff wanted to know. Todd's father is an older version of Todd; still tall and lean, but with gray hair that's thinning now that he's pushing sixty.

"I'm fine, thank you. Everything's great." I gave him a brilliant smile.

"They got that whole mess up there in Nashville figured out?"

I assumed the 'mess' he was referring to was the situation with Hector and *La Havana* and all the rest of it, so I said I believed they had. "I spoke to Detective Grimaldi before I left this morning. She sends her regards." I glanced at Dix when I said it, since she'd really only told me to give her regards to him. I'm pretty sure the tops of Dix's ears colored, but he didn't comment. I didn't, either.

Todd came back with a glass of white wine he presented to me with a flourish, and I thanked him and drifted off, into the corner where Catherine and Aunt Regina sat. "Mind if I join you?"

Catherine smiled while Aunt Regina moved over. "Sit, sit. Tell me everything!"

"Everything what?" I took a seat next to my aunt.

She lowered her voice. "About your new boyfriend, dear. Catherine's been filling me in."

I glared at my sister, who shrugged unrepentantly, grinning. I turned back to Aunt Regina. "This isn't for the paper, is it?"

My aunt writes the society column for the Sweetwater Recorder, and if there was one thing I could do without, it was news of my new relationship—which I didn't even know if existed yet—being trumpeted all over town.

Then again, if everyone knew, would there be less chance of Rafe being able to wiggle out of anything?

Aunt Regina made a sort of halfhearted cross in the vicinity of her bosom. "Of course not. Would I do that to you?"

"I sure hope not," I said, and tried to make it sound like a threat.

"Is Catherine telling me the truth? You're involved with LaDonna Collier's boy?"

"He's not a boy anymore. And yes. I am." If I sounded a little defensive, I think it's understandable.

Aunt Regina giggled and glanced across the room at mother and Bob Satterfield. "I imagine that doesn't make your mother very happy."

"She'd like me to marry Todd," I said.

My aunt nodded. "Todd's a nice boy. He'd do right by you."

"Rafe will do right by me, too." Even if I wouldn't call him a nice boy.

Aunt Regina giggled. "You're like your great-great-great-grandma all over again!"

"Excuse me?"

"Your great-great-great-grandmother. Caroline."

"William's mother?" Great-great-grandpa William had been married to great-great-grandma Agnes, whose dressing table was upstairs, in what used to be Catherine's room.

Aunt Regina nodded. "Quite the firecracker, Caroline was."

"Did you know her?"

She shook her head. "She died before I was born. Long before. She grew up during the War Between the States. A hundred and fifty years ago."

"How do you know what she was like?" And that I was like her?

"Haven't you ever wondered where William got that dark hair and complexion?" She winked at me.

"Great-great-great-grandma Carrie had an affair?" Catherine said, looking down at her hands. They were, it had to be admitted, a shade or two darker than mine. Dix and I take after mother's family, the Georgia Calverts. Blonde and pale. Catherine, like Aunt Regina, looks like a Martin: short and curvy, with coarse dark curls and sallow skin.

I grinned. "What did she do, sleep with the stable boy?"

"He was a groom," Aunt Regina said primly, "from what I understand. After the war—" She pronounced it wo-ah, like any self-respecting Southerner, "when all the slaves were emancipated, he stuck around to help run the place. He was born here, it was the only home he'd ever had. And the Martins weren't one of *those* slave-holding families."

'Those' as in the slave-holding families who mistreated their slaves, I assumed. Not everyone did, you know. Obviously the Martins didn't, if great-great-great-grandma Caroline had shared her bed with this guy.

"One thing led to another," Aunt Regina said, "and Carrie found herself in the family way. She gave birth to your great-great-grandpa William. He was brought up with Carrie's other children. William looked a little different, perhaps, but it wasn't as if anyone would question the lady of the manor, was it?"

"So how do you know?" Catherine wanted to know.

Aunt Regina turned to her. "She told him the truth. And he told his son, who told his son, who eventually told me and your dad."

"Dad knew?"

Aunt Regina smiled. "He did. But I don't think he ever bothered to tell your mother."

We all turned to look at mother, who was smiling at something Bob Satterfield said.

"She'd have a conniption," Catherine said.

I nodded. "Better to just keep it between us." At least until she gave my boyfriend the cold shoulder, and maybe then I could trot it out and put her in her place. Or just share it with Rafe and make him feel better.

The front doorbell rang, not for the first time. People kept coming and going, dropping off presents and staying for a glass of eggnog before heading out again. It was the way these parties always went. Todd had admitted most of the visitors, but this time Dix was already on his feet. "I'll get it."

He headed for the door.

"Is he expecting company?" Aunt Regina asked, a tiny wrinkle appearing between her brows. "Surely that's a little soon after Sheila's death?"

"I'm sure he isn't," Catherine said. "Maybe he knows someone's coming to drop off a gift for the girls."

I nodded. I had my suspicions about my brother and Tamara Grimaldi, but Aunt Regina was right: it was much too soon for Dix to consider getting involved with anyone again. And he wouldn't be getting a visit from Grimaldi anyway. She was on duty tonight. She'd said so.

Our hypothesis—the one about the presents—was borne out a couple of minutes later when Dix came back inside the parlor with two brightly colored gift bags he distributed to his daughters, five-year-old Abigail and three-year-old Hannah. "There's one for you too, Savannah," he said, glancing at me across the tops of their curly, blonde heads. I'd helped him pick out the girls' Christmas dresses a few weeks ago—Abby's in satin and pink tulle with tiny white pearl embroidery and Hannah's in red velvet with a black, white and red tartan skirt— since Sheila hadn't been around to do it. Both girls had matching bows in their hair, and all in all, I thought Dix had done a fine job trying to make Christmas seem normal in spite of Sheila being gone. Hannah, who had taken to sucking her thumb after Sheila's death, had gone back to her normal happy self again, and both she and Abigail were digging eagerly into their gift bags.

"One what?" I asked, watched them burrow.

"Gift. Out there." He gestured over his shoulder with his thumb, his eyes on the girls.

I got to my feet. "Why didn't you just bring it with you?"

"She said the last one needs to be delivered in person," Dix said, as Abigail triumphantly held up her prize. "What is that, sweetie?"

"Police Barbie!" Abigail said.

I smothered a grin. That couldn't be from anyone but Tamara Grimaldi. Wonder what she had for me, that she didn't want Dix to pass along? Why hadn't she just come inside the parlor to give it to me herself, if she had to make the handoff personally?

And then that old fear raised its head again. *Rafe's dead. She's come to tell you the news.*

She'd told me she'd be on duty tonight. Something must have happened to bring her down here, and that one was always close to the surface where I was concerned.

But no, I told myself, if something bad had happened, Dix would have tipped me off. He wouldn't send me out to the hallway without warning. Maybe Grimaldi had a message for me, something she didn't want to pass along within hearing of mother and Todd.

I put my wineglass on the table inside the door and ducked out. The coolness of the air felt good against my cheeks after the heat inside.

The parlor leads into the central hallway that runs from the front of the mansion to the back. In the old days before indoor air conditioning, during the always hot Tennessee summers, the Martins would open the front and back doors and get a breeze going. For Southern Belles like Caroline, decked out in hoop skirts and multiple petticoats and bloomers, those throughways were lifesavers.

In the front of the house, the hallway opens into a huge two-story foyer, one with a sweeping staircase on either side and an enormous chandelier, circa 1842, hanging from the second story ceiling. At the moment, there was greenery strung all the way up the railings to the second floor, and a huge Christmas tree stood in the middle of the floor, the star at the top almost brushing the drippy prisms of the chandelier. Even the weather was cooperating. The double doors to the outside hung open—even as the glass storm doors were closed—and the sleet outside had turned to soft flakes of drifting snow while I'd been inside the parlor. The whole picture was stunning, worthy of a magazine spread, in a way that bespoke excellent taste and plenty of money to indulge it. Mother spares no expense on these occasions, and it shows.

I didn't notice any of it. I knew it was there, because I'd seen it earlier, but it all paled in comparison to the man standing just inside the door, the shoulders of his leather jacket wet from the snow, and his hands in his pockets.

My chest hurt. Actually, physically hurt. And for a second, all I could do was stare.

He was back to looking like himself again. Smooth-shaven, his hair in its usual barely-there crop, and he was dressed in jeans and a black leather jacket, with what looked like a corduroy shirt underneath; I guess in deference to it being December. He looked cool and calm, just standing, looking around.

Until he turned his head and saw me, and the instant our eyes met, I knew he was just as rattled as I was. He just hid it better. With a grin and a slow appraisal, top to bottom and back. "Nice dress."

I stepped from the hallway into the foyer, putting a little swing in my hips. "I thought you'd like it."

He stayed where he was and let me come to him. When I stopped in front of him, he reached out and put his hands on my waist. "Gonna let me take it off you sometime?"

I curled my fingers in his shirt, feeling the heat of his body and the pull of hard muscles through the fabric. "Right now if you want."

He grinned down at me. "You ain't gonna play hard to get?"

"Would you believe me if I did?"

Stupid question. Of course he wouldn't.

"You're back," I said, stating the obvious.

He nodded. "It's Christmas. Every good girl gets what she wants for Christmas."

"So you brought Police Barbies for Dix's girls. From Tamara Grimaldi, I expect? What do I get?"

There was a pause. Then— "You get me. If you want me."

"Really?"

He nodded. "The job's done. Hector's in jail. The gang's broken up. Clean sweep."

"You're finished? A civilian? Pipe and slippers at five o'clock?"

He shook his head. "No pipe and slippers. But you can meet me at the door in your skivvies. I wouldn't mind."

I smiled. I wouldn't mind either. "Now?"

He laughed softly. "You should prob'ly go back to your family now."

I lifted my head to look at him. Incredulously. "You're not staying?"

He looked incredulous, too. "With your family? On Christmas Eve? I don't think that'd go over too well, darlin'. Ain't that Satterfield's car parked outside?"

It was. And he had a point. Bringing him into the parlor to join the rest of the family without warning would be awful for everyone. This transition would take more time and thought than that.

On the other hand, there was no way I'd let him leave again either.

"You can't come here and tell me that I can have you, and then leave before I can actually have you!"

A sound from behind saved me from saying more and embarrassing all three of us. I turned to face my mother, outlined in the door to the hallway. "Oh. Hi, mom. You remember Rafe."

My voice was perfectly steady, and the challenge was clear. *Be nice, or else.*

Mother nodded, her nostrils flared, as if she'd smelled something unpleasant. I held tight to Rafe's hand. The last time mother had seen us together, in the hospital after my miscarriage, she had caught me touching his hand, and I had snatched mine away, hoping she wouldn't notice. That wouldn't happen again.

"Won't you come inside, Rafe?" mother said. "Join us?" She sounded as if the words were pulled from her with pliers, but she got them out. His name sounded strange in my mother's voice. I didn't think I'd ever heard her use it before. Although I appreciated the effort.

"Maybe later," I said. "We're going upstairs. I need some privacy to unwrap my present."

"Miz Martin." Rafe nodded politely, although I could see his lips quiver as I pulled him behind me toward the stairs.

Mother didn't say a word. She stood in the doorway and watched us, every step of the way up to the second floor. I stopped on the upstairs landing and looked down. "Merry Christmas, mother."

"Merry Christmas," my mother said. She disappeared down the hallway in the direction of the parlor again. I turned to Rafe.

"She'll get used to you."

"I hope so. I ain't planning on going nowhere."

"You'd better not. My room's down here." I tugged on his hand.

"Almost like being in high school again, ain't it? Sneaking off during the party?"

He looked left and right as I led him down the hallway. Family portraits, Martins of old, looked down at us from the walls. One of them was great-great-grandpa William, and I thought about stopping and telling Rafe the story Aunt Regina had told me. But then I thought better of it. I'd rather just get him into my room with the door closed as soon as possible. Great-great-grandpa William had waited a hundred and fifty years; he could wait a little longer.

"I never did anything like this in high school," I confessed, and opened the door to my room and pulled him inside. "I was a good girl."

"We can pretend." He looked around, at Grandmama Louise's four poster bed with the hanging canopies and virginal white sheets and blankets, and the dressing table with my pots and tubes and pencils still scattered across the surface. It hasn't changed much since I lived in it as a teenager, and it didn't change much in the fifty or a hundred years before that either. The disparity between this and the room Rafe grew up in, in the trailer in the Bog, was mind-blowing.

"I'd rather not." I closed the door, locked it, and maneuvered him up against it. "I was afraid of you in high school." I pushed the leather jacket off his shoulders and went to work on the buttons in his shirt. He didn't move, just stood there and looked down at me.

"You had reason to be."

"Really?" I pulled the shirt out of his jeans and pushed it, too, off his shoulders and onto the floor. There really was a new scar: a three inch long slice across his stomach, still pink and puffy. I put my lips to it, murmuring in distress, and felt his muscles tighten.

"Hell, yeah." His voice was hoarse, and he had to clear his throat. "Wasn't like I didn't notice you, you know?"

"You never told me." I looked up, into eyes that had turned darker than before.

He smiled down at me. "Dix Martin's little sister? Perfect Savannah?"

"I'm not perfect." God knew I'd missed perfect by a wide margin, especially lately.

"Sure you are. And way out of my league." He closed his eyes as I reached for the button that held his jeans closed, his whole body tensing. I smiled. He added, his voice tightly controlled, "You were fourteen. Maybe fifteen. Jailbait. And I figured your brother and Satterfield woulda ganged up on me if I looked at you sideways."

"You could have taken them. Both of them." I curled my hands over the waistband of his jeans and pulled them down, and the underwear with them.

He didn't deny it. "That woulda gone over well, wouldn't it? No, darlin', I knew to stick to my own kind. And just as well, since..." He had to stop to catch his breath. "...since... God... you were afraid of me."

"I'm not afraid of you anymore." When I leaned forward, I think he lost his breath for a moment. Then his lips curved, and his hand slid down to caress my hair.

"You sure you wanna do this, darlin'?"

"Positive."

"You do it for Bradley?"

"God, no." He would have enjoyed it, no doubt, male chauvinist that he was. But I'd never wanted to.

"Just me?"

"There's a whole lot I'd do for you—and with you—that I'd never do for Bradley."

And wasn't that the truth? It shut him up, too. When he suddenly laughed, I looked up at him. "What?"

Was I doing something wrong? It seemed like he was enjoying himself, but maybe I had no idea what I was doing.

Correction: I knew I had no idea what I was doing, but it had seemed like he was enjoying himself anyway. But maybe I was wrong.

Or not. His eyes were warm when he looked down. Not just filled with sexual heat, although there was plenty of that, but warm with amusement and pleasure. "I guess I'm having a hard time believing it. That I've got Savannah Martin on her knees in front of me. Here. During a family Christmas party, no less. And doing... that."

I smiled. "Believe it. You've got me. Any way and anywhere you want."

"Ah, darlin'." He grinned and lifted me to my feet. "You don't wanna be saying that. I can think of a whole lot of ways I want you, and some of'em may not be to your liking."

"If it involves you and me, I think I'll probably like it just fine." I smiled back, recklessly. "I love you, you know."

It took a long time. Seconds while I waited, holding my breath. Then— "I love you too."

"Really?"

He chuckled. "Yeah. Really."

"It took you long enough to admit it."

"Yeah," Rafe said, "well."

"Well, what"

He shook his head. "Guess I just wanted to be sure you meant it."

I blinked. How could he doubt that I meant it? "I told you. On the phone, with Hector." When I thought I might die and I'd never get another chance to tell him. "Didn't you believe me?"

"You didn't say it again. Later."

"You didn't say it back to me." And it hadn't crossed my mind that he needed me to say it more than once before he'd believe me. "Did you think I lied?"

He reached up to brush my cheek with his knuckles. The skin was still rough from the fighting he'd done. "Remember that time with Perry Fortunato?"

"Hard to forget," I said, leaning into the touch.

He smiled in appreciation of my throwing his own words back at him. "You told me you'd do anything I wanted if I got you outta there without letting him touch you."

I nodded. I remembered it vividly. I'd been scared out of my mind and I would have promised him anything if he'd help me. Anything at all. I was lucky he'd been too decent to collect. "You thought I told you I loved you so you'd come and help me get away from Hector?"

He shrugged.

"That wasn't why. I thought he might kill me, and I just didn't want to die without telling you."

And since it was obviously confession-time, I might as well get it all out there. "I fell in love with you a long time ago. Before you went to Memphis the last time. Before the thing with Perry. I was in love with you almost from the beginning. That's why I couldn't say yes when Todd proposed. That's why I drove all the way back to Nashville that night and showed up at your door."

"And here I thought you just wanted an orgasm," Rafe said with a grin.

I blushed, but shook my head. "It wasn't about that. I mean, I enjoyed that part of it..."

The grin widened, and my blush deepened. I pushed on. "A couple of days later I saw you kiss Yvonne McCoy, and I wanted to kill her. And then a couple days after that, I thought you'd died, and I lost my mind. And then I realized I was pregnant, and you weren't there, and I had to deal with whether to have your baby when I didn't have you..."

I looked up at him. "I would have told you that night in the hospital. Everything. About the baby and that I loved you, all of it. But my mother showed up and you walked out—my sister said to tell you she's sorry, by the way. She didn't know any better."

He shrugged.

"But I love you. It took me a while to tell you, you weren't here, but I told everyone else. Dix and Catherine and Tamara Grimaldi and my mother..."

"You told your mother?"

I nodded. "I want everyone to know. That way, if you ever think of leaving me again, I'll have a whole support network of people dragging you back."

He smiled. "I won't leave you again."

"Promise?"

He nodded. "I promise. I'll never leave you."

His voice was solemn, and so were his eyes looking into mine. It had the weight of a vow, and I held on to it—and to him—as he pulled me close and kissed me and we tumbled onto the bed together.

ABOUT THE AUTHOR

Jenna Bennett writes the *USA Today* bestselling Savannah Martin mystery series for her own gratification, as well as the *New York Times* bestselling Do-It-Yourself home renovation mysteries from Berkley Prime Crime under the pseudonym Jennie Bentley. For a change of pace, she writes a variety of romance, from contemporary to futuristic, and from paranormal to suspense.

FOR MORE INFORMATION, PLEASE VISIT HER WEBSITE:
WWW.JENNABENNETT.COM